GO EASY ON ME

BRADLEY JAMES

ISBN:

E-Book: 979-8-9992899-0-2

Paperback: 979-8-9992899-1-9

Book Cover Design by ebooklaunch.com

Edited by: Mountains Wanted Publishing

Formatted by: Tati B. Alvarez

To Heather Christine – I talk to you every day and I hope you hear it. This book wouldn't be anything without you.

AUTHOR'S NOTE

You're only given one life.

Raise your hand if you've ever been told this by someone. Now, put your hand down, especially if you're in public, because I don't want anyone looking at you like you're the weirdo raising your hand for nothing.

In life, we all experience ups and downs. We experience calm and chaos. And we experience love and pain. If you don't experience these things, then I think you're not just lying to this book, but I think you're lying to yourself.

There are so many tough subjects out there that are covered in books such as mine, and sometimes we, as readers, don't have the privilege of knowing exactly what topics are going to be touched on unless there is a friendly author's note like this. I could say *back in my day we didn't have trigger warnings.* But that would make me come off as a patronizing white man, and I'm not about that life. As a mental health therapist, I know the importance of preparation regarding mental health first aid, and as a writer, I know the importance of a preface.

My hope is that you don't see this page and run away. Run from the mentions of death, drug addiction, domestic violence, motor vehicle accidents, hate-crimes, war, traumatic brain injuries, and trauma related to caregiving.

In fact, my hope is that you see these topics throughout this book and you empathize with the characters experiencing them—that you see how chaotic, painful, and larger-than-life downs have impacted their lives and forced them to make (or not make) difficult decisions that they believed was best for them. Yes, we're all only given one life, but that doesn't mean we are able to dictate how someone else's life should be lived.

Reading is all about building empathy and understanding others' feelings and experiences. It perturbs me to know that in 2025, the act of reading is being challenged with book bans by our leaders, our fellow-parents, our schools, and people who don't even read the first page of a book they swear is inappropriate. These people are taking away your right to understand human-kind.

Don't let them.

Keep reading. Whether it's a romantic comedy, a literary classic, a horror, mysteries/thrillers, or even a children's book about a boy who carries a purse. Keep learning. Keep empathizing. Keep believing. Keep reading.

Without further ado, I hope you feel something while reading this deeply personal story of mine and if you enjoy it, please consider leaving a review wherever you may find yourself rambling about books. If you don't enjoy it, that's okay too—just *Go Easy on Me.*

RESOURCES

National Domestic Violence Hotline: 1-800-799-SAFE (7233); Text START to 88788; www.thehotline.org

Trevor Project: 1-866-488-7386; Text START to 678678; www.thetrevorproject.org

Caregiver Action Network: 855-227-3640; www.caregiver-action.org

988 Lifeline Crisis: Call/Text 988; www.988lifeline.org

The sirens and lights die down as all the emergency vehicles drive away, leaving behind a cold and empty scene. The neighbors close their blinds or find their way back inside their homes. The show is over, but little did they know, it is just beginning for my family and me.

An hour later, in a cold, spiritless hospital waiting room, I stand behind my mother and next to my sister, listening to the doctor tell us that my father is unresponsive, a three on the Glasgow Coma Scale. From his explanation, I piece together that the trauma to his brain caused so much damage, they don't know whether Dad will wake up on his own. Even if he were to become responsive, there is still a seventy-five percent chance he'll lack the ability to engage or function independently. Now, life support is the only thing keeping him alive.

"Do you understand what this means?" My mother turns to face my older sister and me, her empty expression doleful at best. Where her eyes are usually wide with hope, now they're red-rimmed and defeated. Her usually constant smile has been replaced with downturned lips. "It means, if we choose to keep him alive, we can't predict what he's going to be like when or if he leaves this hospital. If we want him to keep fighting, I will tell them to keep him on life support. If not, then we'll need to say goodbye to your dad forever."

She can't know what she's asking of us, can she? If I say no, then I'm not only killing my father, but I'm taking away the love of her life. If I say yes, then I'm giving our family the chance to keep going as just that—a family—no matter what that looks like in the future. And if I refuse to answer, I'm letting her down because she needs me at this moment. Me, her fourteen-year-old son, the new *man of the house*. A role I was unfairly designated just an hour ago.

I know what she wants to do, what she wants us to say. She needs to know she's not alone in this decision. She wants him to live. She wants her husband back. She doesn't want her children to grow up without a father. She needs me to say that I'm okay with the doctors doing everything they can to keep my father alive.

"He should stay on life support," Haley answers. The decision was so *easy* for her. "He wouldn't want us to give up on him." She wraps her arms around our mother's neck for a short embrace.

Fear smacks me in the face because I realize the answer I want to give is not the same as my sister's. My dry eyes moisten, and my puffy peach-colored cheeks are blotched with wetness.

"Theo? What do you think, honey?"

It's my turn to be held. I fall into my mother's arms. My snot and tears soak her shoulders as I give the feedback the two most important women in my life are waiting to hear. Despite my doubts about making the right choice, I find myself saying, "I just want Dad back. We have to do whatever it takes."

The rest of the night is full of dread, doubt, and uneasiness. A constant panic has somehow found property within my soul, leaving my mind and body a complete mess. My life has permanently changed in this moment, and I've never been so scared to face the unknown. I have no idea what my dad is going to be like when he wakes up and comes home.

If he comes home.

All I know is that I'm not ready for whatever is going to change. None of this is fair. The future as we know it will not be *easy*. Whether we made the right decision or the wrong one...we've chosen to save Thomas Branson.

There's no going back now.

ONE

"Come on, Theo. You have to give these guys a chance! Some of them look like Greek gods, dude," Lianna says, quickly swiping right on the dating profiles through the app she downloaded on my phone.

Sitting at the edge of my bed, she brushes her fingers through her ginger hair, laying her curly waves across the top of her shoulder. She shoves the device toward my face.

"This guy? He's climbing a rock shirtless, looking like Edward-fucking-Cullen, glistening and shit." She pulls the phone back. "I'm messaging him."

"You know romantic relationships don't come easy for me, Li. It's incredibly difficult to balance dating with the responsibilities I have here at home."

"You say *relationship*; I say *first date*. You don't have to marry the next guy you go out with, boo."

"It's like you get it, but then again, you don't. When would I fit in dating someone? I have to be home at a certain time each night so I can wash my dad's testicles, Li."

"Theo," her eyes widen, "please tell me you don't use

that as a conversation starter on dates, because that might be the exact reason you're not getting any."

"I've gotten plenty!" I protest. "It's been a while, but it was good while it lasted."

"How long *has* it been since...what's his name?" Lianna asks. "I feel like it's been a lifetime since Little Theo had a friend." Her fingers conspicuously tap the screen on my phone.

"First, don't call my penis *Little Theo*. That's rude. Secondly, his name is Damien, and it's been ten months since we broke up, thank you." I roll my eyes, knowing her attention is focused strictly on doing something I've specifically asked her not to do.

"Ten months too long!" She reaches across my bed and nudges my shoulder hard, forcing me to plant my right foot off the bed and onto the carpet to catch myself before I fall over.

Damien and I started dating when I was a junior in college and he was a junior manager at Harris Teeter Supermarket. He ended things because *apparently* I didn't meet his expectation of being sufficiently *spontaneous*. He wanted to see me every day and do adventurous activities, which I always ended up paying for. Or we'd stay at his mom's house, and I'd watch him play video games until three o'clock in the morning.

"He didn't treat you right, Theo. I heard how he talked about your dad," Lianna says.

"It did bother me when he would make jokes about my dad's head shunt."

"Oh, yes, when he called your dad *The Tom-inator* and said, in the worst Arnold Schwarzenegger accent, 'I'll be back,' when he left the room? Asshole."

"At the time, I thought he was good for me, Li. I thought we had something special. He fit into my caregiving schedule perfectly."

"Is that how you saw that going?" she asks, her voice high-pitched.

"Yeah?" But now I'm contemplating her obvious sarcasm. "When I was in my morning classes, he was at work. After classes, I came home and switched places with Mom to start my responsibilities with Dad. Damien came over and chilled for a bit until Haley came home from the hospital around eight o'clock. Then I'd go over to Damien's until midnight, come home and crash in my bed, and do it all over again the next morning."

"I'm saying this as your best friend," she prefaces, "it sounds like you were trying to fit him into *your* schedule. Love him or hate him—which, by the way, I *hate* him—it wasn't really fair to him."

Her honesty surprises me. I shake my head, clearing away the deadpan stare I locked onto her. "In the end, it doesn't matter. Damien didn't understand that taking care of my dad is more than a choice for me. It's a job." I run my fingers through my hair before saying, "Damien breaking up with me not only shattered my heart, but it also ruined every hope I have for a normal relationship. It was the wake-up call I needed."

Being a caregiver became my identity. Sometimes, I think it's the only special thing about me. While my mom waited tables and my sister began her nursing career, I was at home after high school and undergrad tending to and taking care of the man who raised me until he couldn't anymore.

"As someone who is starting a mental health counseling graduate program in a couple weeks, let's hope you learn quickly that it's not healthy to generalize one failed relationship with all relationships. I really hope you get a *second* wake-up call and learn the importance of putting time and energy into yourself over other people."

"There are only twenty-four hours in a day, Li. You're asking for too much."

"I'm serious! You do so much for everyone else, T. Don't tell me you don't see that you've given up a lot of your happiness for your family's needs."

Lianna is right, and I know she is. Looking back at the past eight years, I'm not sure how my family would have survived without me. Now, I don't deserve all the credit. I only can claim 33.3% of it, as my mom and sister have also been in the trenches with me, but I have given up a lot to make sure Thomas Branson comes first.

I bite down hard on my lip before shrugging. "Sacrifice is a part of caregiving, and freedom, whether it's a small or large amount, is the first thing given up."

Ignoring me, Lianna refocuses her attention onto my phone, her fingers tapping ferociously on the screen once again. "Oh!" she exclaims. "This guy says he's into water sports." She looks up and connects her eyes with mine. "Does that mean he likes kayaking?"

"I hope to God you are not messaging anyone on that thing, Li," I say sternly, staring into her beguiling hazel eyes. "Dating is not in the plan right now. With school starting next month and working out a new nighttime routine with Dad to incorporate the homework I'll get, there is too much change to focus on. Grad school is going to be way more intense."

I throw a dirty sock at her from my bedroom floor. "And no! That doesn't mean he likes kayaking!"

For fifteen years, Lianna Michaels has been my ride-or-die, though she drives me insane sometimes by always trying to set me up with someone. Downloading this dating app on my phone isn't even the craziest thing she's done. One time, I went with her on an errand to cash out some of her rolled coins at a bank. She trapped me by "accidentally" unrolling her dimes and pennies, then leaving me to stand there counting them alongside the attractive bank teller named Evan. He wasn't too pleased and didn't find the obvious hour-long *Parent Trap* situation endearing.

Aside from interjecting herself into my dating life, Lianna has been there for me during other less pleasurable parts too. For instance, when I needed someone to show me how to apply cover-up the first time my dad threw his fist at my face in a fit of brain injury rage. Lianna gave me some great pointers on how to mask the finger-length bruise under my eye with concealer that perfectly matched my blond hair and swarthy skin tone.

Unlike my dating life, Lianna doesn't have to work as hard at hers. She's highly admired. With her perfectly prominent cheekbones and her four freckles equidistantly placed under each eye, she always turns heads no matter where she goes: the grocery store, the back row of a darkened movie theater, even driving on the other side of the highway.

I don't have that luxury. Or at least I don't think I do.

The phone rests between us on my bed, glowing with the light streaming in through my bedroom window. Lianna picks it up and begins scrolling through the dating app, her nails clicking softly against the screen. I've mostly been ignoring her commentary—some bullshit about how I need to "kiss a bunch of toads until I find a prince"—until her sharp intake of breath grabs my attention.

"Oh. My. God," she says, her voice a mix of shock and delight.

I lean forward, the bed springing under my weight, and glance at the profile she's frozen on. My stomach does a little flip. The photo I'm staring at is of a guy whose body is toned —not over-the-top, like I'd be intimidated to go over and talk to him, but just toned enough to where I'd lose only *some* social skill when I approached him, stumbling over my introduction and then blurting out the first question that comes to mind: *What kind of cheese do you like?*

She continues, "It's Javi. Shirtless Javi."

"Javi? You know this guy?"

"Yes, this is Javier. He's my brother's music teacher. He comes over to my house twice a week after my brother gets home from school. Since when did he get so hot?"

The next photo slides into view: Javi with a guitar, eyes crinkling as he smiles at the camera. Another one: Javi sitting at a piano, fully clothed this time, but it doesn't help. He's still... breathtaking.

"Uh, why is this the first time I'm hearing about this man?" I mutter. My eyes catch on the streak of gray in his short hair. It's striking. He's like something straight out of a movie. "Why does he even need a dating app?" I'm only half joking.

Lianna laughs and shakes her head. "I'm not even mad about it. Look at him! He's, like, stupidly attractive." She turns to me, wide-eyed. "I need to show my mom."

"Why? Would she be weirded out?"

"Hell no, she would be mad at me if I didn't show her photos of a shirtless Javi." Li laughs again. "Speaking of being weirded out, what if you dated my brother's teacher?"

"With a body like that?" I shoot back. "It sounds like you and your mom would date your brother's teacher."

Lianna smirks, not denying it. "Fair."

I lean back into my stack of pillows, exhaling like I've been holding in bad breath Javier's photo could smell. "He's so out of my league, though. I mean, come on. Look at him."

Lianna sets my phone down, studying me with that mix of annoyance and affection only a best friend can manage. "T, the fact that you think *anyone* is out of your league is a crime against humanity. You are the most beautiful person I know. Any one of these schlonged dingbats would be lucky to score a date with you."

"You're just saying that because you have to."

"I said what I said," Lianna replies, rolling her eyes in that over-the-top way she does when she wants to end the conversation. It's become her signature move with undertones of lacking credence, giving positive praise, and still somehow being entirely too smug for her own good.

The door creaks open, and Hamilton waddles in, his bat-like ears perked, and his squishy face full of snotty purpose. He snorts, pauses, then launches onto the bed with a grunt.

"Hammy!" Lianna scoops him up mid-bounce, grinning. "Come here, you little rascal."

Lianna scratches behind his ears, then plants a noisy kiss on his snout. Hamilton snorts again, his tail wiggling furiously, soaking up every second of attention like the little prince he is.

Lianna may be my best human friend, but even she knows she comes second place to Hamilton. There is no one or thing that means more to me than my four-legged baby.

I toss a Garrison University sweatshirt into the hamper stationed across my room, a sweatshirt that once belonged to Damien and has the name of the graduate university I initially applied to but got rejected from. "Once I start school and get settled in, maybe fate will bless me with an attractive classmate who understands what it's like to have responsibilities and who cares about the same four F's that I care about. Hopefully, I won't need your app."

I've caught her attention. She stares at me. "Friends, French bulldogs, fucking, and...food?" her voice expels sarcasm, high-pitched for the dramatics, of course.

"Biiitch." I purse my lips. "I. Can't. With. You." I laugh. "Family, finances, and future planning."

Lianna lifts her hand toward her face and begins to mouth numbers, slowly pointing up one finger at a time until she reaches three. "What's the fourth F again?"

"Oh! You were right about one of them." I smirk. "Fucking."

A cacophony of hilarity bursts through the room as we both fall back side by side on my bed. "Well, in the meantime," she raises my phone above our heads, "before you meet your perfect grad school man, and since you won't swipe right on my brother's teacher, let's stalk this wannabe Channing Tatum's profile. It looks like he has a thing for feet."

After going through a couple more dating profiles and explaining several more kinks to her, Lianna stands at the front of my bed and throws my phone down on the covers. "Listen, twerp. I'm meeting my mom tonight for dinner. Did you want to come?"

"You know I'd love to, but, alas, I've got Dad duty tonight." I slide off the mattress and onto the heels of my feet.

"I know, I know." She sucks her teeth. "Figured I'd ask because you know my mother is obsessed with you."

"I can't help it. I have that effect on women." I smirk.

"Oh, let's put *that* in your profile," she says with a laugh. "You *should* be focusing your effects on these men." She points to my phone lying on top of my comforter. "I'm going to text you tonight, and you better report back with how many dates you've got lined up, sir."

My eyes widen in what feels like a crazed expression, and I notice myself blinking erratically. All I can hear is the sound of my heart beating in my ears. I ask in a slow, nettled tone, "How many people did you fucking message?"

"One," she bites back quickly before haltingly emphasizing her next statement: "Maybe four."

"*Jesus H*, Lianna." I shake my head. "If I say 'fine,' will you go easy on me and stop harassing me about this?"

She opens my bedroom door and turns to face me. "I'm not the one who needs to *go easy* on you. You have to go easy on *yourself*. I'll stop harassing you once you start taking care of *your* needs first."

Again, I roll my eyes. Yet, a little part of me hopes one of the guys she messaged on my behalf was Javier.

"I saw that!" she shouts halfway down the hallway, out of my line of sight.

Within a minute, a gentle vibration from my phone quavers in my hand. I glance at the screen, and a notification from the dating app pops up. William, age thirty-four, from Bluehaven, Maryland, wants to connect. There are two options to press: OPEN or CLEAR.

I press the one that closes the notification and hold down the app's icon on the main screen. Another box with options pops up: EXIT or DELETE. Contemplating the best decision for myself, I hesitate before not choosing an option and then eventually closing the screen. I know I don't actually want to meet anyone from the app, but it doesn't hurt to look every now and then, right?

I check the time and realize I have about one hour before my mom leaves for work. Once she leaves, I have some chores I'll need to get done before I start the typical night-time routine for dad.

Snack.

Occupational therapy checklist.

Medicine.

Physical therapy checklist.

Dinner.

Wash his dishes.

Shower.

Dress occasional body wounds.

Medicine.

Tuck him into bed.

With all that on my agenda, how in the world does anyone expect me to find time to date, let alone get close to someone else just to have my heart broken again?

But who knows?

Tomorrow, when I go to campus for orientation, I could meet someone. Someone willing to hold my hand through this crazy life I lead and actually understand my needs.

"Theo," my mom calls up from downstairs.

"Yes?" I shout back, but I know she can't hear me. "Coming, Mom."

TWO

"**A**re you ready for your first day, sweetheart?" my mom asks as she pulls the peel back from my father's morning banana. His breakfast starts exactly ten minutes after his 8:00 a.m. medicines.

"It's not my first day," I remind her. "It's just orientation. I'm meeting with the advisor I was assigned to. Her name is Dr. Ambrose. Apparently, she likes to get to know her students before she recommends class schedules." I place a stack of papers in a single folder and pack it in my bag before throwing it over my shoulder.

"Oh, that's right. You did tell me about that." Her attention is solely on watching my father eat. "I hope you like this *Dr. Ambers*." She pats my dad's chin dry with a paper towel. He missed his mouth when he shoved a large spoonful of cereal toward it. Flakes of Raisin Bran and droplets of milk ran down the corners of his mouth before she was able to catch the spill.

"*Dr. Ambrose,*" I say more loudly and clearly, hoping she realizes her tendency to half-listen irritates me.

She ignores the correction and continues the conversation, "I'm just glad we had a good morning today. Isn't that right, Thomas?" She tilts her head toward my father before patting his chin dry for a second time. "Usually when one of us has a big day, your father likes to cause a commotion."

"Like the day of my admissions interview last spring?"

Her eyes lower for a moment, a shadow of something unspoken passing over her face. She shifts slightly, almost imperceptibly, as if the weight of my question settled somewhere she wasn't ready to acknowledge or even recall.

But I remember the day very vividly.

A loud crash from my parents' bedroom woke me early the morning of my admissions interview, and I stumbled down the hallway to find Dad sitting on the floor, his heavy oak dresser toppled over, drawers scattered, and socks tied in knots. Mom was outside, savoring a rare moment of peace with her tea. When she returned, chaos ensued as it normally does if Dad's left alone for more than five minutes.

My father, unwilling to accept his brain injury, blamed me for the mess, a habit that frustrates me even though I know it is never intentional. Mom, exasperated and overwhelmed, scolded him, insisting I wasn't to blame, taking my side as she always does.

Before she resigned herself to cleaning up the wreckage left by Hurricane Thomas, she said something that etched itself into my memory. A statement I wish I could erase from my own vernacular when I get upset but can't: *"God, I don't know what I did to deserve this."*

The clanging of the silverware in the bowl as Mom puts Dad's breakfast dishes in the sink pulls me out of my memory. "You're right, Mom. Let's just be glad he decided not to pull any stunts this morning."

"You know he can't help it, sweetie." No matter how much resentment she builds for the man, she always reframes our conversations about our frustrations with him in a positive light. Thomas Branson could be responsible for an actual murder, and my mother would be the first person to negate any intentional wrongdoings on his part.

Speaking of resentment... "Mom, we're going to need to talk about schedule changes and me potentially getting a job to help pay for school. I don't know what that's going to look like for Dad's care..."

"Honey," she interrupts. "We'll talk about that when the time comes. We'll figure something out. We always do. Now, have a good time with your teacher and make sure you ask her questions so there are no problems on your actual first day, okay? Worry about that."

"As we all know, asking for help is my favorite activity." I turn my body away from my mom so she doesn't see me roll my eyes.

I've never been one to speak about my problems to anyone else, let alone ask for help. Friends. Teachers. My aunt Kay. Everyone always checks in on me, but my response to them is always a smile or a nod. The occasional *"everything's going great, thanks for asking."*

It feels like it's been a long time since I was truly honest with someone about how I feel on a day-to-day basis. It's quite isolating, in fact, but it keeps everyone at a healthy distance. I've gotten used to isolation being *my* protector, and I've gotten really comfortable with self-isolation being the way I protect others. The last thing I want to do is burden someone with all the tragic shit crammed in my mind.

After Haley became a registered nurse, it got easier to understand what parts of my dad's brain was injured and why he would act the way he did sometimes. We learned how to separate Thomas Branson, the person, from Thomas Branson, the brain injury. His injury consisted of damage to his frontal cortex (decision-making skills and judgment), his hippocampus (learning and memory), his occipital lobe (vision), and his amygdala (the part that controls his emotions).

I'm able to wrap my head around all the medical stuff and be totally okay with all the horrible things my father has said and done to me over the years. The thing I have trouble with is having to continually remind myself to see the difference—difference between the person and the brain injury.

AN HOUR after leaving my house, I drive over a yellow-and-blue-painted bridge to access northern Baltimore, where Colesville University is located. The bridge is decorated with vibrant graffiti, the majority of which seems cordial and hospitable. Although Colesville was my second choice when it comes to graduate programs, it's hard to deny its campus is a well-kept secret in such an artistic and stunning city.

I navigate under the entrance gate after typing in the four-digit passcode I was given in my acceptance letter. I find a parking spot fairly easily, which checks off one of the main anxious thoughts I have running through my mind.

The campus welcomes me with large, wide concrete steps and barrels sitting at the ends of every other level. The barrels are full of an overlay of flowers and greenery, giving the illusion the plants grew from within and blossomed to the top.

I place my feet on the top of the steps and look around.

Not seeing anyone near me, I breathe in a large gulp of air. "Good job, Theo. You made it!" I say out loud before exhaling a giant breath of relief.

The landscaping around the steps is pretty, I guess, but next time, I'm taking the ramp. My big ass can't risk losing all this oxygen.

"Holy smokes! I reckon I lost three pounds coming up these concrete blocks."

I turn my head and see a vision of perfection. He's standing there with pectoral muscles bulging from a tight green shirt and baggy camouflage cargo pants. Immediately, his features garner my attention, begging for further inspection. His mahogany hair is shaved on the sides, leading up to a tight fade. Shiny silver dog-tags hang across his chest, the sun's reflection bouncing off them. His boots, thick and heavy, look as if they individually weigh more than my messenger bag full of textbooks and organized binders.

"Well, I should hope so, with those twenty-pound weights on your feet." I run my hand nervously across my button-up to try and straighten any wrinkles that might have popped up.

"These old things?" He looks down and laughs. "I've had these steel-toes forever. I don't even feel them on me anymore."

"You serve?" I ask, hoping to sound nonchalant even though the insides of my stomach flutter like something out of a Hitchcock movie.

"I feel like it's been a hundred years, but I'm finally out." He readjusts his backpack on his shoulder. "I'm excited to give this whole school thing a try."

"You're dressed like you just got off the plane from a

foreign country." I suck in my gut, noticing his abs are protruding from his shirt above the waistline of his pants.

He answers without missing a beat, "I had a meeting at the VA this morning before I came here. I figured I'd get all dolled up for that, you know?"

"Listen, I didn't mean to judge," I start to apologize.

"Nah, I get it. It's a good question," he says. "I did actually just get back home. I promised myself during my last deployment I'd enroll in school when I returned because I didn't want to miss out on this college life thing I keep hearing about. I was surprised to find out I had enough credits from the military to get my bachelor's degree."

"Oh? You're admitted into a grad program, then?" I don't know if it's his story that is piquing my interest, or if it's his handsome cheekbones that are so sharp, they could cut a Christmas ham. *Through the bone.*

"Sure did," his southern twang slips out, "I got accepted into the counseling program here."

"Nice! That's the program I'm in too!" Excitement jumps through my throat like a deep sea diver gasping for air.

He's quiet but nods and smiles as he looks around in awe at the four brick buildings surrounding us. I can't help but stare at his strong jawline when he moves his neck from side to side. I've never seen anyone so beautiful. He reminds me of one of those unobtainable guys on the app Lianna downloaded for me. I wonder if he hikes ice mountains or swims in exotic waterfalls, wearing sexy speedos that show off his thigh muscles.

"My name's Theo, by the way." I quickly avoid eye contact when he catches me gawking at his face.

"I know," he replies.

I tilt my head, confused as to how he knows my name.

Lianna.

Fuck.

"Oh, I see what's happening here." I shake my head. "Did someone with my face message you on a dating app and ask if we could meet here?"

"No?" The corner of his mouth travels further up his cheek. My question leaves him lost for words, but he manages to follow up with, "I've never used one of those, but I did hear you say your name out loud when you reached the top of the steps."

Damnit, Theo.

"Oh? Then...forget what I said." I wave my hands in front of me, pretending to erase my embarrassment. "I thought you were someone else for a second there. Forgive me."

"I see," he says. "The name is Stevens." He pauses, seeming to forget that, outside the military, people more commonly use first names. "Randall Stevens."

He reaches out for my hand, and I meet him with mine. We shake. His grip is strong but polite. He's not one of those men who try to intimidate you by squeezing your hand as hard as they can. I can't stand those types of guys. What are they trying to prove? I don't get it.

"Nice to meet you, Randall." I smile, softly blink, and lower my head in hopes it comes off as flirting. "School doesn't start for another three weeks. Do you have your meeting today with your advisor?"

"Yeah, I forgot his name though. I think it's Dr. Armarose? Amarose? Somethin' like that." He slides his hand through his hair and begins walking, leaving me standing still in the same place on top of the steps.

I didn't realize my fists were closed until I unraveled my

fingers, letting cool air dry out my sweaty palms. It was one thing to stare at him from his side profile, but it's a whole other miraculous sight staring at him from behind as he makes his way toward the humanities building, the same building I'm headed to.

"It's Dr. Ambrose," the volume of my voice ticks up. I take a giant leap, being mindful not to trip over my feet. I follow behind him and call out, "And *he's* actually a *she*."

THREE

As soon as Randall walked through the glass doors to the humanities building, I lost him. I didn't feel like I was that far behind. I guess when you have buns of steel and calves as firm as a kickboxing kangaroo, you get places more quickly.

I see the elevator in use, next to the set of the helical staircases leading to the second floor. I have a total of zero fucks to give as I press the up arrow and wait for the elevator car to meet me on the first floor.

When I reach the second level, I take one step off the elevator and begin my trek toward the office number listed in the email invite Dr. Ambrose sent. I pass empty classrooms and offices, eventually coming to a stop at the last office door. Affixed to the door is a bronzed nameplate with my advisor's name engraved on it. The door is closed, so I assume Dr. Ambrose is still meeting with another student. I take a seat in one of the empty cushioned chairs right outside her office.

Fiddling around in my messenger bag to find my weekly planner, I notice someone take the other cushioned chair right beside me. A giant duffel bag plops down beside my feet.

"I hope this seat isn't taken," Randall says as he sits down. He shifts his body from one armrest to the other to try and find comfort. If his chair is anything like mine, I can attest that the seating arrangement here isn't too pleasant.

"No, no, of course you can sit here." I slide my body slightly to the left of him to make sure he has some room since the chairs are super close to one another.

The same nervousness that tormented my stomach when we first spoke comes rushing back. I put my right hand over my left and bend at the knuckles, sending a loud crack out into the void of silence. When the bottom of my fingers touches the palm of my hand, the damp feeling comes back like a nosy neighbor waiting to see why the ambulance was outside of your house.

This guy makes me feel like a schoolboy with a secret crush. I dry my hand on the sleeve of my shirt to make it look like there is some lint I'm brushing off. Hopefully, he doesn't notice.

"Nervous to meet Dr. Ambrose?"

He noticed.

A cough comes out as I clear my throat. "Urhm, yeah. Yes. I hope she likes me."

I hope she likes me? Why did I just say that? I'm not going on a date with this woman. *Snap out of it, Theo.*

The sole of my foot presses to the ground, and I bounce my heel up and down, making my knee jump. My anxiety is really showing itself today. I don't know what's making me more anxious: talking about the next two years of my life with a stranger, or sitting next to a heartthrob who is going to be a therapist someday as well. Man, what I would do to be one of his clients...

Actually, I take that back. It is highly unethical to sleep with your clients. I know this. I would never want to impose that on him. Right? *Ugh.* Theo, meet Boundaries. Boundaries, meet Theo.

My cell phone vibrates against my leg, pulling me out of a brief fantasy of me fucking this man in a chaise chair in some therapy office somewhere. I lift my shoulder and reach in my jean pocket.

Let's hope the act of me retrieving my phone shows Randall I have friends in the world who have made the cognizant choice to text me—that I'm not some awkward loser around hot people.

Not only does the pocket of my Wranglers hold my phone, but I also have some loose change and my scrunched-up headphones in there too. Given how tight these jeans are, I'm only able to wrap four fingers around my phone and toggle it out slowly.

This pants pocket will be the death of me. It's like a Venus flytrap made of leg and fabric. My hand begins to succumb to the vacuum that is this pair of skinny jeans. I think I read on Buzzfeed somewhere that I'm too old to be wearing any article of clothing this tight.

I stand up, allowing more room for my hand to resurface. However, the loose change and wired headphones have a mind of their own and make their way out of my pocket before my hand and my phone. My face reddens once the light, sharp clink of coins hitting the ground fills the air. I immediately crouch to collect the nickels and dimes when Randall jumps off his chair at the same time and meets me at eye level.

"Has anyone ever told you it might be a good idea to relax?" He smirks.

"Has anyone ever told you that, in the history of telling someone to relax, it has never helped them relax?" A smile comes to the corner of my mouth no matter how much I fight it.

"You're right; you're right," he says as we both make it to our feet.

As he wraps my headphones around his fingers before handing them to me, he breathes in and lets out, "I just have a feeling you have nothing to worry about in there. Colesville accepted you into the program because they saw something in you. Remember that."

I ball the headphones in my hand and shove them in my messenger bag. I straighten my back. "Well, I appreciate that. I sometimes forget that about myself."

"Forget what?"

"That I might be good enough." I pause, tightening my lips and widening my eyes. *Did that really just come out of my mouth?*

Dr. Ambrose's office door opens, and a girl with deep blue hair walks out. She thanks the advisor and looks in my direction. "All yours!" Her fierce and confident stride down the hallway tells me her meeting was everything she wanted it to be.

A tall woman with straight black hair and lovely brown skin enters the door frame. She's wearing red high heels, a black pantsuit, and a beautiful silver necklace that holds ruby gemstones throughout it. Her crimson-colored lipstick is flawless when she opens her mouth. "Theo Branson? Hi, my name is Dr. Lovey Ambrose." She reaches for my hand

and shakes it. "I'm the advisor and the internship coordinator for this year's cohort. Let's chat for a bit."

The soft tone of her voice and the way she invites me into her office without actually asking if I wanted to come in gives me a sense of overwhelming comfort. Like I belong here. Just by this one interaction with her, I can already tell I'm going to like her.

I pick up my bag and turn toward Randall. He's smiling as he holds up both of his thumbs.

"It was really nice to meet you, Randall."

"The pleasure is all mine, cutie."

As soon as my heart stops racing, it drops.

Did he just...?

Dr. Ambrose's office is bright, organized, and extremely clean. A full, vibrant green pothos plant sits in the windowsill, surrounded by small succulents that would die if under my care. For some reason, plants are harder to take care of than people. It's something I've learned to accept.

Before sitting down on the small gray couch against the wall in her office, I trail my finger on the bookshelf to the right of it, just to see if I can catch any dust. Spotless. Her perfectionistic personality is everything I aspire to be and more.

She takes a seat in the matching gray armchair catty-corner to me. "I like to sit here because I feel like the desk puts a power differential between us, and that makes me feel uncomfortable." She smiles. "My job is to be a support to you during your time here at Colesville, and I want you to feel comfortable reaching out to me about anything you want, whenever you want." She points her elegantly manicured nail at the closed door. "My door is always open, except when it's not. That usually means I have a student in my office, obviously." She laughs.

I let out a nervous chuckle. "Thank you, Dr. Ambrose." I reach in my bag and pull out my planner and a notebook. "So let's talk about my schedule. From what I've read, classes are Monday, Wednesday, and Friday, with one weekend a month dedicated to a one-credit elective. That's going to put me on track to graduate..."

Dr. Ambrose places her hand in the air before my words trail off. "Before we get into the logistics, I want to get to know you better, Mr. Branson."

"Theo, ma'am. Please call me Theo." Mr. Branson is at home sitting in his wheelchair, probably playing with large building blocks made for two- to four-year-olds.

"Alright then," she nods, "I want to get to know you better, Theo. What makes you want to be a therapist?"

I bite down on my bottom lip with slight frustration because I thought I was coming here to discuss my class schedule and maybe an internship or two. I've already been through the interview process and answered the *What makes you want to become a therapist?* question about a hundred times, it seems.

"I, um..." At a loss for words, I panic and say the most cliché thing I can think of: "I just want to help people who feel alone in the world."

"What makes you think every person you treat will be lonely?"

"Well, that's easy..." I'm stalling. Anxiety and self-doubt fight their way back into my head. "They wouldn't be coming to a therapist if they had someone to talk to."

"I see." She takes a moment. "You know, Theo, I got into this profession because I wanted to help people too."

Her statement seems obvious, but I want to hear where this goes.

"I came from a really bad neighborhood. It didn't help that I also had an abusive father who cared more about vodka than me. He left me at a convenience store by myself when I was four years old."

My jaw slowly drops as I try to imagine her as a young child standing in a dirty corner store, waiting for her father to come back.

Cold.

Confused.

Alone.

"What happened?" I ask hesitantly. "How long were you alone in the store?"

"Alone?" she highlights. "I didn't feel *alone*. I felt relieved. Leaving me that day was the best thing my father ever did for me. When the police came to the store, I told them I was afraid to go home because Daddy was drinking. They linked me with social services, and I found a new home. A better home. A loving home."

I run my fingers through my hair and let out a breath I was holding in. "I appreciate your candor, but what's this have to do with why I want to become a counselor?"

A light but animated smile widens on her face. "My story is every reason why you *should* want to become a counselor, Theo. Therapists become therapists because they want to provide relief to individuals who might be struggling, or might just want to embrace positive change. Clients aren't always lonely. Yes, some are, but a majority of them just want a sounding board to help them decide which paths they want to take in life. It's not up to us to decide how people should feel when they walk into our offices. We're a part of their journey; we're not their solution."

Calm suddenly drapes over me as her words begin to make sense. I refocus my attention on her sandy brown eyes. "It won't be my job to *make* people feel something, but it will be my job to help them figure out *how* to feel anything."

"Exactly," Dr. Ambrose's praise soothes me again. "Now, what makes you want to become a therapist, Theo?"

The question rings in my head but doesn't linger as it has before.

"When I was fourteen years old, my dad got into a motorcycle accident. My sister and I have been helping our mom take care of him since then. I'm twenty-two now, and sometimes I don't know what it's like to feel free. I have friends, and I love my family, but there is a part of me that feels trapped. Like I'm never going to be able to chase the real dreams I have in my life."

She sighs. "Would chasing your dreams make you feel less lonely?"

"Maybe? Maybe not." I pause. "Now that I think about it, I don't know if it's loneliness. Maybe it's grief? Grief for not being able to live the life I always thought I would."

"That's quite the insight you have, an important skill for a therapist. Grief comes in many forms, and I'm sure loneliness can be one of them." She pauses. "I appreciate your candor, Theo." A lighthearted smile peeks through the seriousness of it all. "Which brings me back to my question, how does what you've shared with me relate to you wanting to become a therapist?"

Her question echoes a previous thought of mine, but the answer comes out with no restriction, "I want to be able to give people their voice back, to help them understand what they are feeling and not let those feelings control them. Dealing with mental health is hard enough, so I want the people I help to know they can be free, make choices for themselves, and be whatever they want to be."

"Okay, then. That's a wonderful answer." She reaches over and grabs her laptop, a sheet of paper, and a pen. "Now, let's talk about your schedule."

Thirty minutes later, feeling refreshed and motivated for the next step of my journey, I open the office door. I breathe in the sense of success, knowledge, and a little bit of dust from the fake plant outside of Dr. Ambrose's office, which was surprising since inside was spotless.

I look down at the empty chair that once had an attractive veteran sitting in it calming me down before my big meeting. I wonder where he could have gone and if he's going to miss his meeting with our advisor.

Behind me, Dr. Ambrose gathers her name-brand bag, throws a flashy red coat over her shoulders, and grabs her keys from her desk drawer, appearing as if she's leaving for the day.

"Do you have anyone else scheduled, Dr. Ambrose?" I ask, doing a slight investigation to find out if Randall still has his appointment today.

"You were the last one!" She tries to hide her excitement, but I can tell she's ready to get out of here early.

I bite the corner of my lip and wish her a safe drive home. Maybe Randall is scheduled for another day? All I know is that, after the conversation with Dr. Ambrose, I'm going to make this counseling program everything I wanted, and in the process, maybe even keep running into the cute army boy with a beautiful smile.

FOUR

Once I leave the city limits, the drive back home is scenic and full of beautiful nature. Around this time, the trees are a bright lime green with subtle hints of yellow and orange throughout their leaves. It's not hard for me to glance up ahead at the picturesque view as I'm driving on the straight and narrow for about ten miles.

It's not until I stop at the intersection right before my neighborhood that I pull out my phone, just to see if I've missed any messages. I hate driving with my phone anywhere near my line of sight, but I know at this particular stoplight, I always seem to be waiting for several minutes before I can press the gas.

I glance at my screen and see a text from Lianna. She's asking if she could come over this evening to make her mother's famous mac-and-cheese casserole while we binge a television show. It's most likely a show she's watched twice already and plans to use as research for her next book.

After college, Lianna stumbled upon a career in publishing after she wrote a book about the philosophy of laugh tracks in sitcoms. She majored in film studies with a minor in creative writing. She decided to submit her manuscript to an agent, who then got her a contract with one of the biggest nonfiction publishers on the East Coast, Real Books. Even though it took me about four months, I read it and actually loved it. I could be biased though.

Her book is titled *Who's Laughing Now: The Theory of America's Laugh Track*. It became wildly popular, especially among students and professors of film studies at college campuses. Within six months, she sold 13,000 copies nationwide. Ever since then, she's been working on this new book about successful sitcoms that originated on low-budgeted networks. My pride in her keeps growing.

When planning to get together, Lianna knows it's best to come over to my house if she wants to see me, rather than asking me to meet her somewhere else. Usually, when people ask me to hang out, I'm too busy taking care of my father. However, with Lianna, she's accepted that I come with baggage and doesn't mind inviting herself over so we can spend time together. It's the give-and-take of our friendship that make it strong.

Celine Dion's "I Drove All Night" comes to an end when I pull into my driveway. Lianna is sitting on my front porch step with her ankles touching, her elbows sitting on her spread knees, and her head resting in her palms. She looks like one of those city stoop kids waiting for someone to play with them.

"About time you showed up," Lianna calls as I'm stepping out of my car.

"Why didn't you just go inside?" I close the door and press the lock button on my key fob. "My mom's home today; she could have let you in."

She blinks nervously, looking back and forth between me and the window above the front porch. As I get closer, the volume of the shouting from inside increases. The voice belongs to my dad. Lianna's reaction makes more sense as it becomes clearer that a spectacle is occurring inside my home, waiting for me to come and end it.

I step past her and open the storm door, trying to locate my house key on a keychain filled with keys I don't even use anymore. My dad's yelling is getting louder, and a huge bang rocks the doorframe. My guess is he's thrown something down the stairs. I'm wondering what my mom said *no* to today that is making him lash out.

"Do you want to go somewhere else?" I look at Lianna and try not to show my embarrassment. "When I get everything calm in there, we can go pick up a box of noodles and some cheddar cheese. We probably don't have those here anyway."

"It's okay, Theo," she says kindly. "We can do it another time."

I finally find my key and insert it into the lock. I throw my hand up toward Lianna and gesture that it'll take five minutes, and then I'll come and get her.

The concern on her face will never go away. She's been at my house before while Dad was having a tantrum. She gets it, but I don't think she'll ever get used to it.

Not like I have.

I don't think anyone should get used to coming home to this.

The front door creaks open, and I step in. The first thing I see are the kitchen stools that are usually set up at the breakfast bar. The stools are lying at the bottom of the steps, surrounded by a variety of trash that most likely originated from the kitchen trash can, which is now located on the floor in the living room.

I walk up the steps of our split foyer. My blood is boiling because the thought hits me: my mom has probably been dealing with *him* all day, and it's devolved into this mess I will most likely have to clean up.

In the dining room, I see my dad throwing his arms and fists at something trapped in the corner of the room.

That *something* is my mom.

I run over to him and, from behind, grab his arms and force them to cross each other in front of his chest. This is a safety restraint I learned in one of my undergrad field placements where I performed therapeutic crisis intervention with youth on the autism spectrum or who had major behavioral issues. Ironically, with an aggressive and unpredictable father with a brain injury, the holds and restraints I've learned have come in handy.

"Get off me!" my dad yells, throwing his head back in an attempt to headbutt me.

"Dad, it's okay. Calm down. I don't want to hurt you, but we have to calm down, please."

I hate having to coddle him this way, begging for him to relax and knowing my mom is the true victim here. My mom, smaller and shorter than him, gets the brunt of his aggression. He doesn't dare pull this punching shit with me or Haley anymore, now that we know how to conduct a proper restraint and put his ass on the ground.

After several deep-breath exercises, most of which I'm doing myself and trying to get him to complete with no luck, he finally deescalates. He may have been able to recover his strength in the past four years and is capable of pushing his wife to the ground, but he's no match for his six-foot-tall, 240-pound son.

I gently guide him away from the dining room and request he sits on the couch. With reluctance, he finally agrees, and I let him go from my hold. He mumbles a few derogatory names but finds his seat.

I walk back over to my mom and help her to her feet. The bruises on her forearms quickly start to show the purple and blue shades we've come to know well. Her t-shirt is loose at the neck, and a large, see-through rip shows a few bloody scratches on her shoulder. "I'm okay, baby. I'm sorry. He just wanted the TV remote, and I told him he wouldn't be able to see the buttons. I didn't want you..."

"Mom, it's okay," I interrupt her unnecessary apology, "I should have come home sooner." The guilt had already started to suffocate me.

This is my typical response. I hate seeing my mom in pain—and worse, heartbroken. No one deserves this, especially when that person has given everything up just to take care of their abuser. The thing is, it's not okay. This whole situation is *not okay*. My mom shouldn't have to be dodging fists when she tries to tell her husband he doesn't have good enough vision to operate a fucking television remote.

Lianna.

Shit. The five minutes I told her to wait for me to come get her is definitely up by now.

"Mom, one second, I'll be right back." I lead her to a chair and check across the room to make sure my dad is still sitting. I quickly make my way down the steps and open the front door. Lianna's still sitting on the porch step. *God bless her.*

"Hey," I pause and catch my breath, "look, I don't know if today is going to be a good day to hang out."

"Oh? Okay. Yeah," she stands to her feet and wipes down the back of her shorts, "I think I have some writing to do anyway. You know deadlines. You chase them; they don't chase you."

I throw my arms around her waist and lay my head on her shoulder. She returns my embrace, telling me I don't need to keep explaining.

"Thank you for understanding, Li."

"Don't worry about it, boo." She pulls back but continues holding on to my arms. "Go help your mom. We'll eat carbs and quote Moira Rose another day."

"Who's Moira Rose?"

"Oh, don't you worry, you disgruntled pelican. You'll see." She smiles.

"Should I be offended?"

She lets out a laugh and shakes her head while she treads backwards to her car. "I also want to hear about your day, so give me a call later?"

"Yes," I call out, "I also need to tell you about Randall."

She halts and throws her body against her car in dramatic Lianna fashion. "My dear sweet boy! Who is Randall?"

I smirk. "Be safe driving home, Li. I know how you like to follow way too close behind people."

"I live life on the edge, baby!" She throws her proud fist in the air. I sigh as I watch her drive away.

"Honey, who was outside?" my mom asks as I turn the deadbolt.

My plan is to ignore her question and act like my best friend wasn't just at the front door and that I had to turn her away. Yet, Mom always knows when something is wrong and never lets anything go. She repeats her question.

"It was just some guy trying to sell us power washing for the house, Mom. Don't worry about it." Agitation tickles my throat. "I sent them away."

"I know my son is not sassing me right now." Her warning comes as no surprise. I do my best not to back-talk her, but sometimes it happens. She knows it's not intentional, but it's still her place to put me in mine.

During my time in the driveway with Lianna, my mom seemed to have cleaned up the bar stools and changed out of her bloody shirt. She holds her hair curlers in her arms and announces she has to finish getting ready for work. "Do you think you could..."

I interject, knowing what she's going to say, "Yes, I'll clean up the trash."

"I gave your father two Seroquel pills while you were outside with Lianna," she deadpans. "I hope that will keep him calm for you tonight."

She caught me.

She must have looked outside the window and saw Lianna. "I'm sorry for..." I start.

"It's bad enough, Theo, that you can't be a normal twenty-two-year-old," she cuts me off. "I ask you and your sister to do way too much. I know this, and I'm sorry for it. I really am. But you don't need to lie to me about who is at the door, just so I won't feel guilty that you had to send them away. Nothing is going to stop me from the guilt I feel every single day, okay?"

"You're right. I'm sorry, Mom," I step closer to her and press my pursed lips to her cheek. I look over and see Thomas in deep sleep, slobbering on his sweatshirt and snoring so loud, it rumbles the loose bolts on the armrest of his wheelchair. We always feel guilty when we have to resort to drugging him up, but he doesn't sleep at night, which worsens his irritability during the day. At least I'll have a solid two-three hours of peace so I can finish cleaning up.

As a reward to myself, I'll call Lianna tonight. Who knows? Maybe I'll allow myself to scroll social media for one Randall Stevens and see what I can find.

FIVE

"He's nowhere to be found," Lianna shouts into the phone.

After picking up the last bit of trash from Thomas's meltdown, I sat myself down on the couch and called Lianna. I spent the last ten minutes of our conversation describing in full detail about the mahogany-haired military beauty I met this morning who helped soothe my rising anxiety before my big meeting.

"What are you talking about? I hope you're not social media stalking him before I can," I say, unsurprised.

"I'm talking about Randall Stevens. Keep up, boo." A maniacal laugh echoes from the other end of the receiver. "Theo, if I were to wait for you to make a move, Christmas would come and go twice."

"Fine. Have you found anything yet? What's he look like out of uniform? Does he have any pets? Oh my gosh, what if he has a small dog like Hamilton, and we can set up park playdates for them?" I sigh dreamily, letting out a soft moan.

I fostered Hamilton three years ago from an animal sanctuary that investigates and saves animals from hoarding situations. For a French Bulldog, he's a runt, with a tan coat and three quarter-sized dark brown dots on his belly. His little running wet nose makes these cute snorts when he's excited. When I met him, it took me less than ten minutes of holding him in my arms to know I wanted to keep him forever.

At first, I was worried about having a small dog around the house. With my dad being blind, we have to be extra careful to make sure he doesn't squish Hamilton when he takes a seat on the couch.

The day I adopted him, he fell asleep on my lap on the drive home. I promised little Hammy I'd take care of him, even if it was to teach him how to avoid being squished by my stumbling father. All of my fears washed away, and I knew I needed him in my life.

The saying *Who Rescued Whom?* fits perfectly when I think about Hamilton. Those soft ears, his adorable pointy teeth, and those gentle looks he gives comfort me like nothing else. When I'm cuddled up next to him in my bed, the world becomes a better place. Finding someone who loves me means they will need to fall head-over-heels for Hamilton in the same way I have.

"I feel like I'm always going to come second to Hamilton," Lianna says. "I want Randall to have a best friend I can go on playdates with too."

"Something is wrong with you, girl." I laugh. "You are completely fine with finding playdates for yourself."

"I actually have a date tonight. I think his name is Kane? Maybe Zane? I don't know. He's picking me up around midnight."

"Why are you going out so late with a man whose name you don't even know?" I shake my head.

"I know him!" Her voice is stern. "I met him at the gym."

"You don't have a membership."

"Is that tone full of judgment, bestie?

"Yes. Yes, it is," I say, smiling.

"Well, you're right. I saw him driving into the gym's parking lot, and he was cute, so I followed him. I had to sign up to take a tour of the facilities because the old lady at the front desk wouldn't let me in, but at least Wayne thinks I'm into fitness now."

"Have I ever told you that you're my favorite?"

"All the time, poodle. All the time," she pauses, "but seriously, this Randall guy is not coming up anywhere. I've checked Instagram, Facebook, Twitter, and TikTok. Hell, I even tried boring-ass LinkedIn. Nothing!"

"Maybe he doesn't do social media. He's been enlisted, and I'm sure he's had more important things to worry about than keeping up with his family's political rants and disturbing photos of his friend's babies with spaghetti sauce on their mouths."

"That's oddly specific, but I appreciate it," she says. "This just means you'll have to ask him out in person, get his digits, and send a couple nudes back and forth. But make sure he sends one first!"

"What have I already told you about my dating life, Lianna?"

"That you need to get laid, and who better to fuck than a sexy, buff army man who uses effective communication skills?"

"You've either been watching a new kind of porn or reading my textbooks. But, no, I told you I don't have time to date."

Lianna lets out a grunt from the other end of the

receiver. She's easily annoyed when I shut her down about these things. It's frustrating for me too, but in order for me to stay focused on my priorities, I need to sound like a broken record to her sometimes. I know she wants to help me experience things other people our age are experiencing.

Especially with dating.

Not even taking school into account, it's hard enough just to juggle everything with family. When I look around my house, I try to imagine candlelight dinner dates at the kitchen table or movie night dates in the living room. Then, when I hear my dad's loud-ass snoring from across the room, I'm reminded he'll always be there in the background. He'll ask for his own plate during those dinner dates or ask to go to the bathroom three to four times during those movies. No man wants to date someone who has their disabled father in the same room with them.

I'll get there one day, but today is not the day.

"Let's talk about *your* dating life. So you'll probably get it in with Kane/Zane/Wayne tonight, but when's the last time you got laid, Miss Thang?"

Lianna chuckles. "First off, I haven't been watching porn. Only Fans? Maybe. Secondly, I had a gentleman friend over last weekend."

"Since you have a date with someone else tonight, I'm assuming last weekend didn't go well?"

"Actually, it went splendidly. He's Taiwanese, and he showed me a few things from his home country." She pauses.

"For example?"

"Oh no, dear boy," a bashful giggle erupts, "I can't go into detail, but let's just say what we did to each other is only legal in Taiwan."

"Gross!" I laugh. "Listen, I have to go. I need to make dinner for my dad."

"Wait!" Lianna regains my attention. "Would you want to go away this weekend? I'm thinking of getting a couple friends together and heading down to Smokehole Caverns in West Virginia. I'm thinking we can leave Friday morning to avoid the weekend traffic and head to the caverns really early on Saturday morning so we can see as much as we can. We'll be tired Saturday night and leave early on Sunday morning, so I think it'll be much more enjoyable for you if you came down with us on Friday. I know Fridays are rough because Momma Branson works, but I think it would be really good for you to hang out with some friends before everyone gets too busy in the next couple weeks. What do you say?"

Initially, the thought of leaving for the weekend excites me. One more hurrah before classes start would put me in a positive mind frame to start the school year. Yet, Lianna is right about my mom having to work. I also don't want to ask Haley if she is able to watch Dad, because I don't even really understand my older sister's schedule these days. It's just a known fact that I'm stationed with him on Fridays.

Let's say I do leave for the weekend. Even though I'll tell her I don't have to, Mom will force me to go because she'd know how much I want to. She will either call out of work, which doesn't bode well for her paycheck, or she'll scramble to find someone to watch Thomas, someone who doesn't understand his nightly routine as well as me.

I'll ruminate and feel guilty, which will then ruin the trip before it even starts. Lianna and the rest of our friends will get annoyed with me, and I'll regret going when it's all said and done.

I hate the way my mind works sometimes.

Going on weekend trips is something all of my friends do with no second thought. Making a split-decision to travel and jumping in the car to go is a privilege I have never been able to experience.

My face reddens as warmth circulates throughout my body. The longer Lianna waits on the phone for a response, the more she expects me to decline her invite. I hear long-winded inhales and exhales breaking the barriers of silence. She knows me. She knows this request has caused me to overthink and back out of the plan without even problem-solving what I could do with my dad on Friday night. In our friendship, it's a known fact that Saturdays are my only free day to spend with friends, but the small desperation in her voice tells me it would mean a lot if I went on this trip with her.

I hate myself for turning her down. I remain quiet on my end.

She takes a deep breath. "It's okay. Maybe next time." I didn't even get to tell her no, but like I said, she knows me well. "Go feed your dad. Have a good night, Theo."

The word *sorry* almost escapes my mouth before I realize Lianna has already hung up the phone.

In moments like these, I pick one thing in the room to focus on to avoid bursting into tears. This time, my concentration lands on a string fringe dangling from the couch pillow resting on my lap, about an inch long. I twist it back and forth between my thumb and index finger.

Unfairness is a trigger for my negative emotions. I'm tired of always being the odd one out in my group of friends and having no one understand why.

My dad's accident happened so long ago, and people have forgotten about it. But I can't. I live with it every single day, and I'm reminded just how unfortunate life will always be.

My pity retreat is cut short when I hear the floor creak from footsteps coming up the stairs. It's Haley. With all the chaos and trash pick-up, it slipped my mind she was home. I could have used her help cleaning up Dad's mess.

"I totally forgot you work the night shift tonight," I say. "You were quiet down there."

She points to the hanging headphones around her shoulder. "I was sleeping. The music helps."

I nod. She knows exactly why I made the comment about her being quiet. Lately, she avoids all of Thomas's outbursts. I can't remember the last time she comforted me or my mom after them.

"Has Dad eaten and gotten his meds yet?" Her dry, indifferent tone mirrors the way I feel, so I understand.

I let out a deep, heavy sigh. "Not yet, but I'm on it."

"Just wait. I need to do something first." Exhaustion seeps into her voice, and she shuffles toward the pill case that holds Dad's evening medications. Haley's hospital shift starts at seven o'clock, so she'll need to leave within the next twenty minutes if she wants to be on time. Her schedule is intense with three consecutive twelve-hour overnight shifts followed by two days off. I have no idea how she does it, but somehow she manages.

"I can get his meds, Haley. How about you finish getting ready? You don't want to be late." Every day before my mom leaves for work, she organizes my dad's medicines into two pill containers, one for seven o'clock and one for ten o'clock. I have no clue what medicines he takes, but I also don't care enough to ask. The task of managing the medication belongs to Mom and Haley. I trust they know what they're doing.

I walk across the living room, into the kitchen. Hamilton follows along beside me. Grabbing the back of his wheel-chair, I push my dad toward the counter where he usually eats before heating up a Tupperware container of chicken drumsticks and broccoli. Wrapping an adult bib around his neck marks my effort to keep Dad's clothes clean and food off the floor. But a Thomas Branson mess is inevitable.

"Get ready to catch the scraps, Hammy." I blow a kiss at my snotty, wrinkled-nosed sidekick.

In my peripheral vision, I see Haley picking through my dad's pill container.

"What are you doing?" I ask.

"I'm checking to see if Mom did what I asked her to do. I suggested she switch Dad's gabapentin to his morning pill regimen to help with his neuropathy." She dumps the medication into her palm and pinches out a yellow and white capsule. "And, once again, she didn't listen to me."

She rolls her eyes and puffs out a breath. "I don't know why she spent all that money on me to go to nursing school if she wouldn't trust my medical advice. If she wants him to stop complaining about the numbness in his feet throughout the day, she needs to give him his gabapentin in the morning."

She puts the rest of his pills into a small plastic cup and then hands it to me. I place it beside my dad's water bottle so he can take them himself. We allow him to do as many things independently as possible, so giving him that small plastic cup makes him feel empowered. We used to just ask him to open up his mouth and pour the pills in. He still does that himself, but it's the little things that make him feel good.

"Alright, I'm out of here." Haley slips on her black floral Danskos and throws her Shock Trauma-branded jacket over her shoulders. "I'll see you tomorrow morning," her voice slurs, weak with dread.

"Be safe." It's a normal warning I give to each family member when one leaves the house. "I love you, Haley."

Her mumbled response is incoherent, but what I do hear as she leaves the house is the little voice inside my head telling me something with Haley isn't right.

Now that Dad has his meal, and I seemingly have the house to myself, the thought of having some alone time lures me down the hallway. I close the door to my room behind me, leaning against it for a moment as I let out a long breath. Our nighttime routine, day in and day out, always leaves me drained. I drop my forehead against the doorframe, trying to shake it off, but the reminder I only have a couple minutes to spare lingers.

I collapse onto my bed, the mattress creaking under me. My mind drifts, uninvited, to the image of my mysterious new crush. His face came into focus like it's been vying for my attention all night.

Randall Stevens.

Randall and his sharp jawline and the steady, confident way he carries himself. I can't get him out of my head. His military haircut—a little too perfect, his uniform neat and pressed—even though it was probably the last thing on his mind. When he looked at me, before we said goodbye, there was something in his eyes. Was it curiosity? Was it attraction? Or was I imagining that?

I run my hand over my face, trying to push the thought away, but it only makes it worse. I can still hear his low

Southern twang when he introduced himself. I can still feel the slight brush of his hand when he handed me my headphones, a casual gesture that felt like so much more.

My chest tightens as I lie back against the pillows, staring at the ceiling. I close my eyes and let the memory unfold, filling in the gaps with what I wish happened between us. His hands reaching for my hips, pulling me in closer. His mouth softly pressing against mine as his tongue penetrates my wet lips. The warmth of his touch making me feel wanted.

Needed, even.

Without thinking, my hand slides to the hem of my shirt and then underneath the edge of my waistband. I trace the lining of my underwear and feel myself harden.

It's not just Randall getting me excited. Well, not entirely. But it's the way he made me feel. He made me feel noticed, like I was someone worth seeing. I haven't believed that about myself in such a long time.

I breathe deeply, caught between the reality of my life and the fantasy in my head. My hand resurfaces, knowing I don't have the time, nor the freedom to finish what I've started. I decide to give myself two more minutes before going back out there. But for now, I let myself be. I stay in this quiet, imagined space, where there's nothing but the steady beat of my heart and the thought of him.

SIX

I t's been five days since Lianna and I last spoke, and my classes start on Monday. Judging by her Instagram photos, she had a nice time in Smokehole with our friends Tristan, Shelby, and Kelly. They pre-gamed before going to the caverns with spiked espresso vanilla lattes, told juicy stories about their love lives near a foggy pond, and played a game of Frogger on a desolate backwoods road before lying down in the middle of it to gaze at the stars. It's fascinating how social media can tell the story of an event you weren't a part of. I would give anything to be able to go back and change my response when she asked me to go.

But I can't.

I need to move forward, get out of my head, and wait for her to respond to my text I sent two days ago. I asked her if she wanted to go with me to Colesville's school store to buy my textbooks. Her read receipts are turned off, so I have no idea if she's just been super busy or ignoring me. My guess is the latter.

It sucks, but I get it.

My eyes hurt from staring at my phone screen. I throw my comforter off my body and roll out of bed, shuffling my way to the hallway bathroom. My mom comes up from downstairs holding a laundry basket full of lavender-scented bed sheets, my dad's pajamas, and two pink and white sleeping pads we took from the hospital years ago. Her hair is pulled back in a ponytail, with several estranged hairs poking up from the top. Her affect is sullen, with circles of the darkest purple around her eyes.

The start of the day tends to dampen her mood. She hardly sleeps because Thomas needs her periodically throughout the night. He'll wake her up because he's hungry, because he has to go to the bathroom, or even because he's bored and wants to take a walk outside.

He never sleeps.

The aroma of urine wafts heavily through the house, piercing through my hazy veil of sleep with the harsh scent of ammonia and apprehension. I step out of the bathroom and push my nostrils together in an attempt to block the smell from bothering me.

"I was too late waking him up," her voice is weak, cracked even. "It's my fault; I shouldn't have hit snooze on my 2:30 a.m. alarm."

My mom and dad used to share a bed until his nighttime enuresis started about a year ago. Now, Thomas sleeps on the couch in the living room. Recently, he's been pulling his pants down and peeing on the carpeted floor, thinking he's on a toilet. Mom's been trying to set alarms on her phone every two hours to keep him from doing that. She's tried everything: cutting off liquids after a certain time, condom catheters, even adult diapers. Nothing works. To top it off, the doctors don't even have any good suggestions on what we can do.

Last Christmas, I asked my mom if we could consider putting Thomas in a group home or a treatment facility. I hated asking because it felt like I was taking back the promise I made the day we decided to keep him on life support and do whatever we could to bring him home. Mom wasn't too happy with my request, but she agreed to find out more information on what we could do. His behaviors are getting worse by the year, and it's been difficult to keep up with it all. Sometimes, I feel like our family is drowning with no rescue in sight.

She called the insurance company to see what our options were, and because he gets social security and my mom makes pretty decent money being a server, there are no resources available for us. My parents' insurance won't cover any residential or treatment placements. The only option is for him to get so medically ill that my mom would need to give up rights as his wife and essentially abandon him.

For her, that is not an option.

"What are your plans today, sweetie?"

"I'm headed to the bookstore to get my textbooks." I wipe the crusties out of my eyes, hoping to wake up a bit more. "Let me go pull the carpet cleaner out of the closet so we can shampoo where he peed."

"No, honey," she says, "I'll handle this. You have somewhere to be. Plus, you know it's best to blot it up with a towel first, then use carpet cleaner a day or two after. If we do it now, the carpet will just get stained brown until it officially dries."

"If you say so."

"Let me get my credit card to help you buy the books.

Don't they have cheaper electronic versions of those things these days?"

Coming from the one person who still calls text messages *emails*, it's hilarious that she's asking me why I don't use electronic versions of textbooks. "Sarah Branson, I am twenty-two years old, and I am the one who made the decision to continue with my master's. I can afford my own textbooks, thank you." I try to hide my agitation. "Plus, I'm old-school and need a physical book to grasp on to when I'm highlighting every single line as I read."

"Is there another Sarah Branson in this house?" Her brow rises. "Because I know you did not just call me by my legal name, boy," her tone shakes me out of my irritability.

"I'm sorry, Mom. I just don't need you to buy everything for me," I plead.

She shakes her head at me. "Is it so bad you have a mother who likes to take care of her child? Now go on. Have fun at the bookstore. Buy me something with the mascot on it. Be safe, okay?"

I smile. "Yes, ma'am."

AN HOUR LATER, I'm walking into the school bookstore. I don't know what I was expecting, but I can tell you I wasn't prepared for the store to be so small. There are more books than there are shelves, display cases are filled to the top with boxes of antivirus computer software, and clothing bins are erupting with merchandise printed with the school's logo and mascot on them.

I make my way down the first aisle and pull out a wrinkled piece of paper from my pocket. It's a printout of all the expensive textbooks I need to purchase for each of my classes. *Introduction to Helping* by Clara Hill is the first book on my list; next is *Counseling Theories* by Gerald Corey. I bite my lip as I calculate how many books I need for just one semester. The taste of blood makes me want to vomit dollar signs.

"I'm walkin' here!" a deep New York accent from behind me causes me to halt. I stare down at my list of books, choosing not to look up. I hope the shout isn't directed at me because I really didn't want to have to beat someone's ass today.

All my life, people have doubted I can throw down, but I always seem to surprise them when they least expect it. The last altercation I got into was with an old lady on Black Friday circa 2011. I told her to *fuck off* as I preceded to push her cart down a neighboring aisle just so I could grab that last DVD copy of *Supernatural* season twelve—the one she hid behind the pickle jars. She was lucky she was wearing her Life Alert bracelet.

Come to think of it, I'm still on season four, and I've been watching the episodes on Netflix. I probably didn't need to take out my one stud earring and intimidate that poor woman for a DVD. I don't even know if my DVD player works anymore, but the point is I can hold my own in any type of fight.

It's been a minute, and I'm sure my new school bully from New York has forgotten about me by now and has walked away. Or at least I hope. I slowly lift my head to see if the coast is clear. I drop my jaw when I realize the guy I thought was shouting at me to move was really the one person I've been dying to see since our last encounter three weeks ago.

"Randall! Oh my god," I laugh, "I didn't recognize your voice. I thought I was going to get pulverized by some big city meathead." He's wearing the same tight green shirt and baggy camouflage cargo pants I saw him wearing the first time I met him. I assume this is the kind of outfit he feels most comfortable in. He wore it for several years serving our country, after all. He still looks just as delicious as he did the last time I saw him, so who am I to judge his fashion sense?

"No meathead here, sir. Just a fake, horrible accent." He reaches for my booklist, which also shows the times and sections of each class. The paper is saturated with my palm sweat, so let's hope he doesn't notice. "I'll be damned. You're in all of my classes."

My heart flutters as if a shot of espresso is just kicking in. "I hope that's a good thing?"

"It's fixin' to be a great thing. I'll have someone to sit next to." A smile peaks at the corner of his mouth. "Although, that might not be such a good idea, now that I say it out loud."

His thought takes me back, and I can't help but raise my eyebrows in confusion. *Shit, do I stink?*

"I'm just thinkin' it'd be too distracting lookin' at you. I might not be able to concentrate." His perfect, flirtatious smirk gives my heart third-degree burns.

So hot.

My face reddens, and I try to hide it by bending my neck slightly downward. I'm starting to understand what Bashful, one of Snow White's dwarf friends, felt like when Snow gave him a little tickle under his chin. I need to change the subject because, if there's one thing I know I'm good at, it's bombing any attempt to return a flirt. I usually end in stroking out or accidentally spitting on the other person.

"Anyway...have you, um, got all the books you need?"

"Yes, I just put them all in my car." His gentle tone reduces my blood pressure just a bit. "I came back in to buy myself a Colesville Miners sweatshirt."

"You gotta rock Miners memorabilia!" I awkwardly throw my fist in the air like I'm rooting for my home team. I immediately pull my hand back down to my side and force out a cough. "I need to get one too, but I'm worried about the cost of these books. How much did yours end up being altogether?"

He reaches for his pockets. With his hands, he pats the front of his cargo pants. I can't help but look down and see his fingers graze against the bulge in between his legs as he searches for something in his pockets. "I must have left the receipt in the car." He touches his chest, smirking because he forgot he doesn't have a pocket there. "I think the total came out to be four fifty-something. I even got all *used* textbooks too."

"Dude, I need to get a job to pay for these damn books." The corners of my mouth tick up in the fakest of ways. I knew grad school was going to be expensive, but I didn't think about the smaller financial responsibilities.

For undergrad, I got a large portion of my tuition paid for by the state. I worked on the weekends at the fast-food joint down the street from my house, which helped me save a lot of money. I planned to use that money and go sixty-forty with my mom for tuition this time around. Maybe I do need to revisit the idea of electronic books?

"Your prayers have been answered." Randall bends down. "Look here." He picks up a flyer from the ground. It has pin holes around its corners, indicating it must have flown off an activities board somewhere. He wipes off the dusted footprints and hands it to me. "It's a list of professors looking for graduate assistants, and it looks like Dr. Ambrose is in need of one."

I scan the flyer, and my eyes immediately go to the bottom where it says the yearly salary of a graduate assistant —$27,566 plus partial tuition remission. "Holy shit! What does a graduate assistant even do?"

"I don't know, maybe assist the graduates?" His wide, sarcastic smile is contagious. "Do you want to stop by Dr. Ambrose's office to get more information? I can go with you."

"Oh, thanks, but I'll need to talk to my mom first to see if I can even do this. I wouldn't want to waste Dr. Ambrose's time."

"Talk to your mom first?" he asks, his eyes widening.

"Yeah, it's complicated." I pause, trying to come up with a logical reason that doesn't make me sound like a child. "I have another job where I work with my mom. I'll need to run it by her first to see if a new schedule can be arranged. You know how it is, adulting and all." I shrug.

"What kind of job?"

I sigh. "I'm a caretaker for my father. He was injured a long time ago and needs twenty-four-seven care."

Let's hope that's all he needs, or wants, to know.

He nods. "I see. That sucks. I'm sorry about that. But you'll need to decide fast before someone snags the position."

He walks past me and makes his way through the aisles of the nearby bookshelves. He collects a pile of books and stacks them in the pit of his elbow. With every book, his protrusive veins throb in his arms. I try to keep from staring, but I fail at every attempt. It's like my eyeballs are ferromagnetic materials with no sense of control, and his arms are sucking them in.

"Here you go." He places about eight books on the

counter behind us. "These are all the books you need. I should know, because we have the same classes and all. I also grabbed all used copies. I hope you don't mind."

"No!" His kindness surprises me. "Thank you, you didn't need to do that."

"I know I didn't." He looks at me, and I swear he teases my innards to explode. "I wanted to."

It's confirmed. He could absolutely take me right here, right now, on this dirty-ass countertop full of pens and stickers with little Miners on them. The Corey Matthews look-alike cashier who's stocking books in the next aisle over can stay and watch too. I don't even care at this point.

"I have some money from my leftover BAH funds. I'm not going to use it. Would you want me to help pay for some of these?"

"BAH funds?"

"Basic Allowance for Housing. It's a military benefit. You're supposed to use it for housing, technically, but, really, we can use it for whatever we want."

"Whoa, no. No," I stutter. "You d..d..don't have to. No, I don't want you to do that. That's far too much. Ah, plus, isn't giving someone else your BAH money highly illegal?"

"I won't tell if you don't." The right-side corner of his mouth curls upward.

"That's very generous of you, but I'm going to have to officially say no. But thank you." Our coquettish gaze lingers for an extra couple of seconds.

The cashier takes his place behind the register and removes the headphones he was wearing. The music he's listening to remains at the highest volume, blaring from the earbuds. He begins ringing up the books without greeting me or Randall. The only goal he seems to have is to finish this transaction so he can get back to rocking out to Aerosmith.

I unzip my wallet attached to my cell phone case. So many people have made fun of me for this phone purse I have, but I don't care. It's convenient. It doesn't seem like Randall is judging me for it, as he watches me struggle with the zipper.

I slide out my Target charge card, thinking it's my regular credit card. I stick it in the credit card reader and hear Randall laughing as the cashier tells me they only accept MasterCard and VISA. I scurry through my wallet again and find the correct card, showing it to the cashier to prove I have the right form of payment now. He nods and slowly picks up his headphones and places them back on his head.

"I need to run, but I'm glad I got to see you today," Randall says as the word *Initializing* blinks repeatedly on the credit card reader.

He walks behind me, and I pivot my body toward him. "Do you think I could get your number or something? Maybe a social media account?"

"Social media?" His eyebrow quirks.

"Yeah, like, your Instagram account?"

"Oh? Um, I don't have one of those. You know...military and all. We don't really keep track of those things. Why don't I just take your number, and I'll give you a call?"

"Right." I manage a smile, accepting the fact this man clearly does not keep up with the social norms of the twenty-first century. "I guess that'll work."

He doesn't say anything, but neither does the cashier as he makes a drum roll movement with his hands after handing me my receipt. I glance at it and see the cashier's name typed on top. "Thanks, Angelo."

Still jamming, he doesn't give a response.

I reach across the counter, spotting a pen near the register. I try to write on the back of the receipt, with no luck. The texture of the paper makes it hard to write on without the ink smudging.

Discarding the receipt, I let out a short sigh, then look at Randall's hand before meeting his eyes. He returns my gaze, his eyebrow lifting just a bit.

I clear my throat. "Uh...is it okay if I...?"

His mouth curls into a tiny smile, and he gives me his hand. "Go ahead."

I take his hand in mine, my heart beating a little faster than I'd like to admit. His skin is cool against my palm. My grip is light but steady enough to keep his hand still. Slowly, I start writing my number across the smooth stretch of his hand, making sure each number is clear. When I finish, I let my thumb graze his skin for a moment longer before looking up.

"Just in case you...uh...want to get in touch when we're not on campus," I say, trying to sound casual.

Randall looks closely at his hand, his thumb brushing over the numbers. "Good to know," he murmurs, a faint smile spreading across his face. With that, he shuffles his way toward the exit of the store.

The fact that he doesn't give me his number stings a little.

As he walks away, a rush of heat creeps up my neck, embarrassment washing over me like a cold wave. I shift my weight from one foot to the other, glancing around the store, suddenly aware of how empty it feels.

To avoid seeming like a total loser in front of Angelo, I throw a pack of Colesville Miners mints on the counter. Forcing a smile, I hand Angelo my credit card again. "I promised my mom I'd buy her something with the mascot on it."

"The mints are on me, dude." Angelo combs his fingers through his long, curly brown hair. "The credit card reader is slow, not to mention it was super hard for me to watch that. I hope everything works out for you, bro."

"Um, thanks?" I blink, caught off guard by Angelo's unexpected kindness and impressed with his ability to multi-task. "You caught all that with the headphones on?" Heat steals across my cheeks as I grab the mints and toss them into my bag of books.

Angelo chuckles, clearly enjoying my embarrassment. "Don't worry about it. And if it helps, I think he was nervous too. He forgot to buy the Miners sweatshirt he said he came back in to purchase."

"How long were you listening to our conversation?"

"Long enough." Angelo shoots two hand pistols my way, nods and blinks one eye as he slowly backs away. "Have a good day!"

I watch Angelo slink into a back room, shaking my head with a mix of amusement and mortification. It's nice to know I wasn't the only one looking awkward. With a sigh, I turn to leave the store, the weight of the moment lifting just a bit, but not too much.

As I step outside, the cool air hits my face, but it does nothing to soothe the ounce of rejection I feel as the thought settles in—I offered my number, and he didn't give his in return.

Maybe my lack of assertiveness is a sign I'm not ready to

put myself out there. The whole interaction was like me stumbling through a door that wasn't even slightly ajar. If this is what dating feels like, I don't want anything to do with it at this point in my life. I'll just stay home, binge-watch some television with my best friend, and take care of my family.

Sounds just fine to me...

Now, if only my best friend would answer my texts so she can tell me how neurotic I'm being. That would be ideal.

<h1 style="text-align:center">SEVEN</h1>

The phone rings and rings until I reach Lianna's voicemail yet again. *You've reached Lianna. I'm sorry I missed you. Please hang up and try again. Texts are preferred!*

The last bit of her outgoing message bothers me. I try to be mindful of how I come across when leaving my message. "That's the thing, Lianna. I've tried texting, and you're not answering me back. I get it. I messed up. It's just, you know I have baggage. I'm not excusing myself. I should have coordinated care for my dad and just left with you. I should have asked Aunt Kay to watch him. I just feel guilty when I do that, okay? Please call me back. I want to hear about the trip. Call. Me. Back... Please."

Within seconds of hanging up the phone, I hear mumbles from across the room. I ask Thomas to repeat himself. He mumbles again with no rise in the volume of his voice. My neck stiffens, and my fists clench and unclench rhythmically on my lap. My request to him is louder, "What did you just say, Dad?"

He mumbles again.

"Dad, I cannot hear when you do not speak up. This is my third time asking, and I'm not going to ask again. Tell me what you just said, damnit!"

"I fucking want something hot to drink," he screams.

"Why couldn't you just speak up!" Sharpness bites the end of my tongue.

"Because you always say no." The veins on the side of his head pulsate. He's definitely not getting what he wants from me now.

"That's bullshit, and you know it, Dad. I make you a cup of tea every night. And guess what? Tonight, you're not getting one. I'm not going to be spoken to like that."

"See, you always say no."

My feet pound the carpet as I step into the bathroom. I've learned when he pushes my buttons like this, it's best to just step away. I splash sink water on my face, pat dry with the towel hanging on the wall, and stare into my reflection. I place my elbows next to the faucet and lean my body closer to the mirror, with my cell phone squished between my hips and the edge of the sink. My vision lines the features of my face, pointing out all of the defects I hate about myself. The plump cheeks, the sharp jaw, and the crevices in my neck rolls. Unattractiveness is all I see.

My cell phone vibrates, making a noise against the sink and gently rattling my hip bone. I retrieve it from the pocket of my hoodie. My mood changes swiftly when I see it's Lianna calling me back.

I answer the phone, barely above a whisper, "Hello."

"Did you leave one of those long voicemails that take up storage on my phone again?" Her reply has a light tone but is nonetheless dry as a Little Debbie's donut.

"Yes. You can listen to it and delete it later. I want to know why you haven't called me back. I ran into Randall today and had the worst experience ever, and all I wanted to do was tell you about it. Are you that upset with me?" I ask, getting to the point.

"No, I've just been busy. Yes, I was annoyed you didn't even bother to ask your mom if someone else could watch your dad for one night. I mean, you do have an extended family that always offers to help. I'm sad you couldn't come, but it's over, and you're going to come next time."

"I promise I'll plan to involve Aunt Kay to sit with my dad next time, okay?"

"You better," she says. "I miss you, punk."

"Miss you too, Li."

"Oh! By the way, I've been making a really good headway on my book. I've been in the zone since I got back from the trip."

"That's awesome!" My lips smack together. "Am I going to get a chance to read an early copy?"

"Of course, nerd. Now, tell me about what happened with Randall today?"

I summarize what occurred at the bookstore. As I tell the story about my awkward encounter with Randall and how he barely knew what to do with my phone number, let alone knowing what social media was, Lianna gasps, exclaims, and, at one moment, she even yelps. She also asks if Angelo, the cashier, is hot and if he is single. To her dismay, I ignore that part of the conversation.

"Maybe he's similar to you in that way? Awkward, number one. Number two, he might not be interested in dating right now. He's been in the service for a while, and he's probably making education his main priority."

I'm unsure if it's because she's an author, but Lianna knows exactly what to say and what words to use in order to make sense of a situation. I appreciate that she brings back my words against me, that I'm not ready to date. It helps me see I'm in my head about Randall not wanting to be more public with me. Being in my head is exactly why I don't want to spend any more time thinking about guys. Moving forward, it's school, my family, and this potential graduate assistant job I need to secure.

"Tell me more about this job. Do you think your mom will go for it?" Lianna asks.

"I'm going to talk to her about it tonight, but I hope so. I was doing some more reading about it online through the school's website. It seems legit, and they'd pay for half my tuition, plus the salary. It's pretty hard to pass up. Plus, it'll be good for my resume."

"What are the hours?" Lianna knows this will be my mom's first question.

"It says I need to work twenty hours a week at minimum to be eligible for the assistantship. I'd proctor exams if Dr. Ambrose can't attend a class. I'd help with grading papers. And after class hours, I'd assist Dr. Ambrose with researching past literature, entering data, and getting IRBs approved."

"You're going to be the teacher's pet, my boy!" Lianna bubbles with enthusiasm.

"You could say that." I smile. "When can I see you next? I miss your face."

"Let's hang out next Saturday. We can have a bonfire at my house."

"A bonfire would be delightful, as long as your mom

joins in on the fun. I'll see you then, Li." I press the red circle on the screen, ending the call.

To say Lianna's bonfire parties are iconic is an understatement. With autumn being her favorite season, she goes all out with decorations, music, games, snacks, and desserts that fit the mood of the weather. She's most known for her peanut butter and Oreo chocolate s'mores, smashing together marshmallow and Reese's peanut butter cups in between Oreo cookies. Her family's townhouse is perfect for small gatherings, and since they have the end unit, their yard is slightly bigger, leaving enough room for the firepit without their neighbors complaining.

Now that we're over the legal drinking age, it doesn't matter to us anymore, but Lianna's mom used to buy us alcohol when we would go to her house. Currently, Lianna lives with her mom, Ms. Gloria, and her little brother, Trevor. Lianna's dad left when she was eleven years old, which is why I think Lianna understands my need to take care of my mother now that she doesn't get the support she used to from Thomas.

In my opinion, Ms. Gloria's marriage is the reason why Lianna chooses to love herself first when it comes to relationships. When questions came up about the divorce, Ms. Gloria used to tell Lianna that Mr. Charles couldn't figure out how to love her and the kids the way they deserved to be loved. I think that's a healthy way of rationalizing what Mr. Charles did to her and the family.

It took years for Lianna to come to terms with her father cheating on her mom with our middle school history teacher, Mrs. Henderson—who was also married at the time.

Back then, I would have loved a scandal like that, but

when it involved your best friend's family, the excitement blew away as fast as Mr. Charles moved out.

I FLIP THROUGH THE CHANNELS, hoping to find something satisfying for Hamilton and me to watch. The front door's lock clicks, and Haley makes her way into the foyer. She doesn't greet me, so I call out, "Welcome home," before she makes her way up the steps.

She mumbles, "Good to be home," and saunters into the kitchen. I don't know what is up with this family and mumbling, but it boils my blood.

She grabs a jar of pickled beets, a can of soda, and a stick of string cheese from the refrigerator. I wait for her to come sit down and talk to me about her day like she used to, but that loving sibling behavior stopped a long time ago. Now, she collects a bunch of odd food choices and hides herself in her basement room until her next work shift.

For months now, I've been worried about my sister. She keeps to herself, doesn't really help with Dad anymore, refuses to eat anything but canned foods, lashes out with irritability, shifts blame onto everyone else, and hasn't asked me how my day was since my last birthday in February.

It's September.

She doesn't seem happy. I know she's lonely and depressed, but she never speaks to me about any of it. When it comes down to the both of us, our dad's accident affected her the most. She and my dad were extremely close. She was the epitome of a Daddy's Girl. Haley and our father did everything together from shopping for running shoes to taking midnight walks when one or both of them couldn't sleep. Dad never missed a day of softball. He attended so many practices and games, the team asked him to be one of the pitching coaches because he was always around. Supporting Haley.

If there was an argument, Haley would always take Dad's side no matter who he was up against: me; our mom, the neighbor, or even the priest he got snippy with after he was reprimanded for holding up the drop-off lane at our Catholic elementary school.

He was her rock, just as much as she was his.

Growing up, my dad and I didn't have much in common, nor did we have many deep conversations. He was an energetic man with strong, laddish interests, and I'm more reserved, trying to figure out what I'm passionate about.

I always felt like my dad wanted me to be someone I wasn't. He wanted me to work for him during the summer with his roofing company, join the community wrestling team, or play high school football. He wanted me to be this perfect, younger version of his uber masculine self —something I knew I just didn't want to be.

The day I quit football, a week into my freshman year of high school, my dad's disappointment took over any resemblance of a relationship we had and spread it as thin as a thread. I knew his fatherly love for me was unconditional, but I wasn't the son he imagined having.

It wasn't all strained. There was one moment in my life I felt he was proud to be my father. When I was about twelve, my parents took my sister, some of her friends, and myself out to a neighborhood bar and grill for Haley's birthday.

The event of the night was karaoke, and I desperately wanted to sing my favorite song. My sister begged me not to, telling me it would be an embarrassment. My dad, however, gave me the go-ahead and told me I could sing anything I wanted. I ended up singing Reba McEntire's "Fancy" in front of a bar full of neighborhood drunks and my sister's friends. Even though I was singing lyrics about a poor, broken-down girl whose mother encourages her to be a high-class sex worker just to dig herself out of poverty, I felt free.

I felt like myself.

With every high note and with every country run, my sister's jaw dropped lower and lower to the ground. Yet, my dad's smiles, his claps, and his standing ovation lit up the room, leaving me feeling seen and unstoppable.

Today, if my dad were better, and if there wasn't a brain injury putting a wall between me and him, I honestly think he would have accepted my queerness as truth when I came out. He wasn't a man of judgment or fear. He was a great man. Yes, we didn't have the strongest relationship, but he was my dad. I think that's why I've chosen to help my mom take care of him. He would have done the same for me.

"What are you watching?" Haley asks, her demeanor cold.

"I haven't found anything yet. Want me to turn something you like on?" I ask, desperately trying to use television programming as leverage for her to stay upstairs.

"No, I should get to sleep." Her arms are full of snack food as she slowly steps down the stairs.

"Wait, Haley!" my tone stops her. "Is there anything you want to talk about?" I ask, deciding which bomb wire to cut before she explodes on me.

"No, why? Is there something you want to talk about?" Her answer is quick. Curt.

"It's just...I feel like you haven't been doing well. Every single night, you grab the unhealthiest dinner and take it downstairs. The plates and the trash never come back up. I see trash building by the side of your bed. Not to mention the overflowing ashtray full of smoked buds and cigarette ash staining the carpet. Mom has asked you not to smoke in your bed several times, and you don't listen. You—"

"I don't need a third parent, Theo," she snaps. "Please don't tell me what to do. You're my younger brother, and you have no idea what I eat during the day. I'm not hungry when I come home from my stressful-ass job, so I grab a couple snacks. Sue me. Why don't you try working an actual job and see what you feel like when you come home from it? Oh, that's right. School is your job. Mom doesn't make you work and go to school at the same time. I forgot."

"Mom didn't make you work and go to school at the same time either. That was your choice. As for my *real job*, I spend my nights taking care of our father, Haley. Did you forget about that too? Because you're never upstairs to help me," I bark back.

"How dare you," Haley bites down hard, so loud I hear her teeth click from behind her closed lips. Her stare shoots daggers through me, her pupils dilated, glossy, filled with rage.

She's becoming someone I don't even recognize anymore. "We're supposed to be doing this together, Hales. I feel like it's just me and Mom sometimes."

She leaps up from the second step and charges toward me, dropping her food items on the carpet. Hamilton jumps off the couch and skitters away in fear. The room gets smaller, and the distance between us is arm's length.

She bends down and comes centimeters away from the tip of my nose. Her breath is warm and smells like a mixture of hot coffee and nicotine. "Who the fuck do you think you are, Theo? A fucking savior? Bow down to Theo. He's the golden child. He does everything right. What about that fucking gazebo I built Mom with my first six months of checks after getting my job at Shock Trauma, huh? Or what about the time I had to take an entire weekend to fix the hot water heater when it was the fucking well that was messed up the whole time? Do you have any idea what I've had to give up for you and Mom?" Her face is shaking, veins pulsating in her neck, and spit spewing from her mouth. "The next time you ever come at me again with this bullshit, I will end you. Do you understand me?"

"Hale..Haley..." Her name is the only thing I choke out.

"That's what I thought." She turns her back, walks toward the stairs, and picks up her food. Before she stomps away, she looks over at our father sitting in the dark area of the dining room in his wheelchair, with his head rolled back and his eyes shut tight. Sleeping. Oblivious to what all just went down. She scoffs and shakes her head. Her door slams when she makes it down to her bedroom.

I know why she looked at him with such disappointment. It breaks my heart to even think about it. Not only did Dad miss the entire argument, but he also wasn't there to take her side.

EIGHT

I push the coffee shop door open, the bell above jingling softly. Before entering completely, I hear the ending of a music note, followed by soft clapping and bodies rearranging some chairs and tables. The warmth of roasted coffee beans and spiced chai greets me, perking me up as if there is an excited endorphin bouncing around somewhere in my head. I've never been one to make a routine out of coming to a coffee shop first thing every morning, but when I have extra time before classes, I make it a point to treat myself.

Speaking of a treat, I get to see Randall today in class, and the thought alone makes my stomach flip. I debate whether I should buy him a coffee—something simple but thoughtful, like an iced vanilla latte. Would he think it's sweet, or would I come off as trying too hard? I can already picture his surprised smile, the way his eyes light up when he thanks me, and just the idea makes me want to sprint to the counter and order it right now.

But then again, I don't want to seem too eager, like I'm trying to buy his attention. A second thought of buying him a surprise coffee makes my stomach flip again, but this time, in a mortified way.

My feet carry me toward the line almost on autopilot. I'm close to being fully awake, but there's something in my mind still processing what it's like to be functional. All I can think about is the sweet, spicy perfection of my favorite "treat myself" order: a large caramel vanilla chai. It's one of those *hugs in a cup* sort of drinks, and I need that kind of hug this morning, especially after my fight last night with Haley.

I step into the line, shoving my hands into my jacket pockets. The place is busy, but that's nothing new. Every time I come in here, it's always bustling, especially in the mornings before most people's work days start.

My eyes wander absently over the tables, the clusters of people chatting and sipping their lattes. The individuals in a rush to get to work, shoving their croissants in their mouths and chugging their espressos.

And that's when I see him.

Javier.

Or at least, I think that's him. The guy Lianna knew from the app she forced me to download.

At first, I think I'm imagining him. My brain isn't exactly firing on all cylinders yet, and maybe this is just some kind of caffeine-deprived hallucination. But then I notice the sleek guitar slung across his back, the singular gray streak in his short, dark hair, and the unmistakable chiseled jawline.

It's him. Lianna's brother's music teacher. The guy whose profile I studied a little too long, trying to figure out how someone could look that good in a 1:1 aspect ratio pixelated square photo. The guy whose profile I lingered on long after Lianna left my house that day, and I was left triple-dog-double-daring myself to double tap or swipe right, or whatever you do on those stupid apps.

Clearly, I'm not one to fall for peer-pressure—even if it's myself daring me to do something.

But now he's here. Real, impossibly gorgeous, and just a few feet away from me.

I swallow hard, feeling an embarrassing warmth creep up my neck. My palms go clammy in my jacket pockets, and I quickly wipe at the corner of my mouth, just in case there's actual drool involved. With my luck, I wouldn't put it past me.

The two women in front of me are chatting loudly, their voices cutting through the general hum of the coffee shop. "I'm telling you, I'd wait in line for hours if it meant I could keep listening to him sing and strum that guitar."

"Right? His voice is so dreamy. Who knew waiting in a long line for coffee could make my lady parts feel that good?"

I follow their gaze, and sure enough, they're talking about him. Javier. Of course they are. I don't blame them; he looks like he walked out of some indie musician fantasy. The guitar, the casual yet perfectly put-together outfit, the way his fingers tap rhythmically against his leg as he makes small talk with the coffee shop employees.

My brain starts spinning in a hundred directions at once. Should I say hi? I mean, it's not like he'd know who I am. I'm sure Lianna has never talked about me to him. But what if she has? I could say something natural, like, "Hey, you know my friend Lianna." Or would that come off weird? Too stalkerish? Maybe I should just introduce myself. Play it cool.

As if I have any idea of what playing it cool really means.

I glance at him again, and my heart stumbles. There's something about him that makes him seem...untouchable.

Like he's from a different world, one I don't quite belong to. I want to say something, anything, but the words get stuck somewhere between my brain and my mouth.

It's the same feeling I get when I speak to Randall. What is with me pining over these guys I clearly do not have any chance with whatsoever?

"Next!"

The cashier's voice pulls me halfway back to reality, but I'm still too lost in my own thoughts to register that she's talking to me. My eyes are glued to the menu board, even though I already know exactly what I'm going to order. My brain is screaming at me to focus, but it's hard when Javier is right there.

"Next!" the cashier says again, sharper this time.

Before I can snap out of it, a low, smooth voice cuts through the air. "I've volunteered for the chill vibe music session in the morning for the past couple of months now, and I've learned one thing: don't make the people behind you wait even longer for their coffee unless you want to get stepped on."

My head jerks up, and there he is. Javier. Even closer. Standing nearer than I expected, one eyebrow raised and a small, knowing smile on his lips.

"Oh," I stammer, my heart racing. "Uh, sorry."

Behind me, I can feel the annoyed stares of the other customers in line. I want to shrink into my jacket and disappear. Instead, I manage to mumble a sheepish "thanks" in Javier's direction.

"No problem." A smirk tugs at the corner of his mouth at the same time my insides do a back-and-forth somersault. "I'm Javier."

Before I respond with *I know*, I quickly remember he has

no clue who I am, and that would obviously not be the best response to what he believes is his first introduction. Plus, I never swiped right on him, so how could he know who I am? I clear my throat. "My name's Theo."

"Hi, Theo." He smiles again. And then, as if that wasn't enough, he winks.

He actually *winks*.

And I'm dead.

I have died.

I have gone to Deadland, where all brain circuits are cut short.

I have literally no more words, and once he realizes I have nothing else to add to the conversation, he steps back into the line, and I finally shuffle up to the counter, trying to pretend like my entire face isn't on fire.

"What can I get you?" the cashier asks, her tone suggesting she's already moved on from being annoyed to just wanting to get through the morning rush.

"Large caramel vanilla chai," I blurt out, louder than I intended. "Hold the foam. Please?"

The cashier nods, rings me up, and I swipe my card with a shaking hand. I step to the side, clutching my receipt like it's a lifeline, and glance back toward Javier. He's watching me, his eyes warm with amusement. He mouths something that looks like, "Solid choice," and I feel like I might actually combust on the spot.

I try to act nonchalant, though I'm pretty sure the red tint in my face is a dead giveaway that I am, in fact, not very nonchalant. My thoughts are a jumbled mess as I wait for my drink, replaying the past few minutes over and over again.

Did he really just wink at me? Was that just a friendly thing, or did it mean something more? Was he flirting? What would Randall think about this guy possibly flirting with me? And why do I care what Randall thinks? I'm not dating Randall. I'm single. Do guys like this not realize the power a wink wields? Say that ten times fast, *wink wields, wink wields, wink wields, wink wields, wink wheels...damnit.*

The barista calls my name, snapping me out of my spiral. I grab my drink, mutter a quick thanks, and practically bolt for the door, my heart pounding like I just ran a marathon. This treat-myself coffee stop isn't playing out like I imagined it would.

As I step outside, the cool morning air hits me, and I take a deep breath, trying to calm myself down. I glance back through the window, and there he is, still standing in line, still looking like he belongs on the cover of some indie album. The fact he's waiting in line, after performing and literally bringing in customers with his striking masculinity—I mean, musicality—is so endearing. So much so, he should add *patience* and *humbleness* to his dating profile bio.

I sip my chai, the sweetness spreading across my tongue, but it's not the drink that has my thoughts spinning.

It's him.

Javier. The guy I'll probably never see again beyond my phone screen if I ever open up the app again.

But it's also Randall and how I get to see him soon.

And the small ounce of conflict I feel when I realize the idea of buying him a coffee to impress him now feels like a very distant memory.

NINE

I am the first person to step into Introduction to Counseling Skills, and there is a plethora of seats available for me to choose from. Dr. Ambrose stands by her podium flipping pages and looking back and forth between her notes and the PowerPoint slides she displays on the projector screen.

The ease of her voice brings comfort as she welcomes me to take a seat. "The early bird gets the best seat in the house," she says after I choose the desk right smack-dab in the center of the classroom.

I place my coffee at the corner and reach in my messenger bag to pull out my textbook, a notepad, and a pen, and line them on my desk for easy access.

"Wow!" She's brimming with delight.

"I'm sorry?"

"It's just that I'm used to seeing students with laptops and tablets, so when I see someone whip out a pen and paper, it brings me back to a much simpler time. It's nice to know I don't have to worry about you being on Facebook during class," she says with a simper.

"I'm not sure you'll have to worry about anyone being on Facebook," I reply.

"Oh, and why's that?"

"Because no one uses Facebook anymore." I tap my fingers on my desk in the rhythm of a drum roll.

"Oh man," she laughs, "I really am behind the times." She takes a moment before she collects a stack of papers in her hands and straightens them out on the edge of the podium, "You seem very reliable. You're on time. You're old-fashioned. I don't normally do this, but are you looking for a GA position by any chance?

"Really?" My eyes widen. "I mean, yes! I'm very much interested. I actually saw your flyer and was going to speak to you about it today after class."

"Great! You're hired. I'll give you this first week to get acquainted with your own class schedule, and then we can start the assistantship next week. Does that sound good?"

I nod, accepting the position. "What would the hours be like? I know the flyer says twenty hours per week."

Lianna's question pops into my head. A question we both knew my mom was going to ask me when I broached the subject with her.

"How you spend your hours is up to you. You do have one office hour, but other than that, your schedule is all yours. I just ask that you don't grade any of my papers while you're trying to write your own."

The information she gives me is helpful for when I relay all of this to Mom. My hope is she sees this as me *helping*, rather than adding more on my plate...or hers.

THE ROOM BEGINS to fill as students come in from the hallway. From the chatter and commotion as they find their seats, it's evident some of them already have made new friends among their peers. Isolation breathes deep as I throw my jean jacket over the empty chair next to me in hopes that, when Randall comes in, he'll see it and choose it.

Choose me.

Just like with Javier, my mind keeps circling around the idea that Randall might not be interested in me. Even though he hasn't called since I gave him my number, I still want to be his friend. I want him to understand that I'm not necessarily looking for a relationship, if that's what's holding him back.

With a minute before class starts, Randall strolls in. I jerk my jacket from the chair and lift my hand past my ear, waving at him to get his attention. He smiles and nods before squeezing his way to the now vacant seat. He's wearing the only outfit I've seen him wear, his tight green shirt and camouflage cargo pants. His dog tags are still hanging from his neck, bouncing in between the muscles of his chest. I can't take my eyes off him.

"Do you ever change your clothes?" I smirk.

His flirtatious grin returns. "I'm kinda forced to wear this. It's part of the job."

Before I ask what job he's referring to, Dr. Ambrose gathers everyone's attention. The noise slowly dissipates as she starts to go over the rules of her classroom: no electronics unless it's for notes, no speaking over one another, no judgments. Above all else: be honest.

A male student in the front of the class raises his hand. "What do you mean by 'be honest'? Like no cheating?"

"That's a good question," Dr. Ambrose says. "You all are entering a field where relationship building is the primary focus of your work. If you can't be honest with me or with your peers, then you won't know how to be honest with your clients or yourself.

"Honesty leads into empathy." She clicks the projector remote, and her first slide pops up. "Who here believes you have to separate honesty from empathy when it comes to your clients?"

Everyone raises their hands, with the exception of Randall. Dr. Ambrose calls on the boy who asked the question about her rule of honesty.

"You can't always be honest with your clients because then your feelings will manipulate their ability to gain insight," he says.

"That's a good point. It's important to note that you're talking about self-disclosure. You can share self-disclosures, but you have to be mindful of how you use them. Who else?"

Silence.

"C'mon! You all had your hands up a second ago." Dr. Ambrose smiles, looking around the class.

Randall projects his voice, "I think you need to be honest in order to be empathetic. You have to know your values, your morals, and your ethics in order to fully understand someone else's. I, however, get confused on what I'm feeling sometimes. Is it empathy, or is it sympathy?"

His words move me to echo out loud what he said, "Yeah, when it comes to honesty, how do you draw the line between empathy and sympathy?"

"That's a fabulous point, Theo," Dr. Ambrose praises.

"Let's talk about how empathy and sympathy are two unique, totally different feelings. Sympathy is *what* we feel for someone, whereas empathy is *how* we feel for someone. As therapists, we must always be honest about our own feelings related to our clients. Our sympathy won't help our clients in the long run, but our empathy and understanding them will."

"Now," Dr. Ambrose commands, "if you turn to page thirty-six in your textbook, you'll find a self-inventory about empathy. Feel free to process the questions alone, or if you want to discuss it with a partner sitting next to you, you may."

The questionnaire takes me several minutes to complete. From afar, my shaded bubbles look like a Rorschach test showing me a subjective narrative about my personality. As soon as I finish, I place my pencil down and look over toward Randall. He's sitting, twiddling his thumbs and humming, not seeming to bother anyone around us. He isn't working on the questionnaire, nor does he have a textbook in front of him. He taps his fingernail against the top of his desk in a rhythmic pattern and mouths the words, "I did this test last night."

The others around me begin to make noise, pulling their chairs toward each other to talk about their results. I straighten my body and turn toward Randall, careful not to give any sense of desire to interact with any of my other classmates. "So, what did you get—" I take a whispered cough into my elbow, clearing my throat. "How empathic is Randall Stevens?"

He smiles. "I'm as empathetic as a farmer milkin' a cow. Question thirteen did throw me for a loop though. What did you answer for that one?"

I look down and find the question. It's about how our family perceives our communication patterns. I immediately think about the argument I had with Haley. How she called me the savior and threw in my face how she could pay off mom's gazebo in six months. All I was trying to do was find out what her issue has been lately. Am I that horrible of a brother to be concerned about his sister? I don't think so.

The vertebrae in my neck cracks as I roll it from side to side.

"Judging by that reaction, I'm assuming you had a hard time answering that question too?" Randall gently nudges my shoulder, bringing my attention back to the moment.

"You could say that." I tense my muscles and let out a heavy sigh. I look around to see if anyone else caught my fairly loud exhale, but my peers all seem to still be in deep conversation with their partners.

"Talk to me about it," he says, his voice tender like the wind in the spring months.

I contemplate for a moment and then let it out, "I think my sister is in trouble. I don't know what's wrong with her. I don't know if she's not sleeping enough, if she's working too hard, or if something is medically wrong. I just know in my gut something is not right."

"What does she do to make you think something isn't right?"

"I saw her the other day messing with some of my dad's medication. Then, this past weekend, she lashed out at me for asking her if there was something going on I should know about."

"Do you think she's doing drugs?" he asks bluntly.

"No," I bite back. My tone is so defensive, it even catches

me off guard, "She's a nurse. A smart one, for that matter. She knows better than to abuse drugs."

"Sorry, it's just, you mentioned she was messing with your dad's medicine. So I assumed it was drugs, with how you presented it." He shrugs.

As I reposition myself at my desk, a shooting pain ricochets through my chest. I swing my hands behind the back of my chair to stretch my arms. My fists tense as I try to gain control of the searing pain in my sternum. The thoughts in my mind race. It's like every idea popping up is fighting to get to the finish, begging to be the answer to all my questions. Does Haley have a drug problem? Is she lying to me? Is she in danger?

She's a nurse, Theo. Nurses don't abuse drugs. They help people who abuse drugs. Not only is she a nurse, but she's also my sister. My sister doesn't abuse drugs. Our family has been through too much to do something so stupid.

Right?

"Hey, listen, man," Randall lightly knocks the edge of my desk with his fist, "I didn't mean to offend you. I shouldn't have been so judgmental. I don't know your sister. Hell, I don't even know you. It was just the first thing that came to my mind, and seeing you upset caused something in me to get..." he stopped.

"Empathetic?" I lifted a brow, wondering if the questionnaire prompted this discussion.

"Protective," he remarks before lowering his head.

A brief moment of quiet rattles the air between us. Randall and I sit in silence, a gesture indicating we're both confused about what his comment means.

Protective?

Dr. Ambrose calls out, asking the class to wrap up the

activity. She requests a few members of the class to report on their responses and reactions to the questionnaire if they feel comfortable doing so.

An older woman with chestnut-colored hair introduces herself as Miriam. I remember her from the group interview. She's a second-career student, meaning she's lived a whole other life before starting her new one as a therapist. Miriam admits she's learning empathy changes over generations, and people above a certain age sometimes see being empathetic as being permissive. When she's finished, another female student raises her hand to share her perspective of the activity.

I'm distracted by a soft clicking. I look over at Randall, whose tongue is flicking between his top and bottom teeth. He smiles now that he knows he has my attention. He mouths the words, "I overstepped. Can I make it up to you?"

Trying not to gain the attention of the rest of the class, I mouth back, "You're fine. Promise."

Dr. Ambrose announces a ten-minute break before moving on to the next discussion. Randall stands up and stretches. His scent of floral and citrus wafts its way to me, permeating my senses, leaving me intoxicated and wanting more than the subtleness of it.

He takes a lap around the room as I reach for the water bottle in my messenger bag. Before I finish gulping down half of my drink, Randall surprises me from behind, bending down over my shoulder. His quickness jolts the grip I have on my bottle, leaving a little squirt to drip down my chin, wetting the collar of my shirt.

"Take a walk with me?" He reaches for my hand, and I gladly accept.

He rushes ahead and stands by the door to the classroom,

waiting for me to catch up. I smile and roll my eyes as I walk by him and into the hallway. Voices and noises from the classroom drift away as we stroll down the empty corridor. He circles around and in front of me, forcing me to stop abruptly.

"I'm serious," he whispers, cocking his head toward the side. I can't help but notice his sensitive light-green eyes staring directly at my lips. "I want to make it up to you."

"What do you propose?" I swallow.

"I want to take you out," his smooth voice sends a shiver from my ear down to the side of my neck.

"On a date?" I suck in my gut, hoping Randall, being so close to me, doesn't hear any heavy breathing.

"On a date," he confirms.

In my stomach, nerves jump from side to side. The temperature in the hallway warms, and my hands are clammy as I cross my arms. If Lianna were here, she would have interjected by now to make sure I didn't say anything ridiculous to ruin this moment. She'd encourage me to whip out my phone and tell Randall I'd have to put him on my calendar. I've never tried her techniques, but Lianna's game-play usually ends well for her. She'd tell me to give it a minute before my body is thrown against the wall in a heated passion by Randall's strong arms because he wouldn't take no for an answer.

"I'm not sure." I bite my tongue.

"I'll come to you. Are you free tonight?"

"Tonight? I don't think I can." I pull up the calendar on my phone, but it's not because I'm trying to copy Lianna's moves. I'm looking to see if I'd have wiggle room before Haley leaves for her night shift tonight. Plus, it's way too late to find a sitter now.

"Sure you can. I'll be at your house at six p.m."

"I don't think tonight will be good. How about Saturday?" *Take the bait, take the bait.*

"Life is so short, Theo. Let's live tonight, shall we? I know you're worried about stuff at home, but give yourself a break and come out with me. If you don't, you'll miss the sharks." He tilts his head.

Fuck. Sharks?

"Let me see what I can do, okay? Can you be at my house at six thirty p.m.? I can text you my address."

Randall reaches for a flyer on one of the cork boards hung on the wall in the corridor and rips it down. "Here, write your address on this. It's easier for me this way."

I hesitate and lift a brow in his direction. I pull a pen from my pocket, scribble my address down and hand it back to him. He takes the paper and folds it up, placing it in his pants pocket.

"You are a strange man, Randall Stevens. Do you not have a cellphone?"

"Strange is not the worst thing I've been called." He smiles before playfully surging past me to get back to our classroom. He calls out, "You should get back to class, sir. Break's over."

I follow him, still stunned by the idea of going on a date with him.

Dr. Ambrose welcomes everyone back to their seats. Randall sits back down, sending me one last flirtatious wink before the lecture restarts.

There it is.

Another *wink.*

What is with these hot guys and their winks? It's getting to be a bit ridiculous, but I kind of like it.

My mind is too busy ruminating on whether or not I'm going to be able to make tonight happen. I really want to go, but I hate asking others to do things for me. If not speaking to Lianna for only a couple days taught me anything, it's that I do have people I could ask. Something in me struggles so much with it though.

I pull out my phone and search through my contacts list, landing on my Aunt Kay. I open a new text chat:

> Hey, Auntie Kay. Hope your day is going well!

You never call me Auntie. What do you want? Love you.

> Love you too. I hate to ask so last minute, but I'm wondering if you can watch my dad tonight? For like two hours?

Yes. What time?

Well, that was easy, wasn't it?

TEN

Much like planning, punctuality is just as important to me. Time is a precious thing, especially when you know it's limited. There is nothing that lasts longer than watching a minute on a microwave clock change to the next. When 6:29 p.m. finally turns to 6:30 p.m., I hear a knock at the front door and let out a sigh of relief. It's not that I was worried if he'd show up on time. No. I was more worried if he'd show up at all. But, like he promised, he's right on time.

In the framed photo hanging on the wall of the staircase, I catch a glimpse of myself in the reflection of the glass. My hair is combed and stuck in place from the two to three spritzes I used for hairspray, the collar of my black polo is evenly folded down, and I check my teeth to make sure there isn't anything in between them. Although, the fake Rembrandt doesn't really give me a clear visual of any left-over particles from the early dinner I had just in case Randall took me out somewhere to eat. I didn't want to be *that* first date who ordered the appetizer and the entree.

As I open the door, Randall is leaning against the frame. His shoulder bears the weight of his body, and his biceps are protruding from his tightened sleeves with his arms crossed. If charisma was a language, he'd be fluent in it. The only thing quicker than the adrenaline rushing through my body are my eyes scanning his dapper outfit.

He is dressed in captivating head-to-toe fall attire. The white of his button-down shirt peeks out from underneath his light navy-blue Lacoste sweater. His brown Chelsea boots meet his dark blue jeans that are ever so perfectly rolled just above his ankle. His beige blazer is the finishing touch to his outfit which illuminates his hazel eyes.

"Hi," I whisper softly, "you look really great. New outfit?"

His smile lights up the darkening sky. He puts his two fingers to his forehead and sends off a short salute as a thank you for my compliment. He slowly tilts his head, but his eyes remain level with mine. "Hi." He pauses. "Yeah, I called in a favor for this look. I'm glad you like it."

I invite him into the foyer, grab my coat from the banister and slide it around my shoulders. He releases his gaze attached to mine and begins poking his head past me, looking around at what he could see within the corners of my house.

Behind me, my humble abode appears empty. Quiet even.

In order to avoid an awkward first meeting with my family, Randall is unaware I strategically asked Aunt Kay to sit with my dad on the back porch so he could enjoy his daily cup of nighttime sleepy tea. It was an easy sell because what calms Thomas Branson down the quickest is drinking something warm and listening to the birds sing in the trees above the backyard. Sometimes it really is the little things that can make someone happy.

"Are you ready to go?" Reaching for the knob, I step forward, then close the door behind me.

"Oh! I was hoping to meet your mom. Is she home?" Randall inquires, refusing to budge.

"She's actually not home. Next time though. Promise." I cup my hand in front of me like a gentleman leading the way for his date. I scan the driveway, but I don't see a vehicle. "Did you drive here?"

"About that, I actually don't drive."

My heart skips a beat. I stare at him, expecting to hear more of an explanation.

"I got a taxi. Not big on driving."

"Oh? So, you expected me to drive?" I ask, confused.

"It would be ideal. Hope that's okay?"

"Sure..." I convince myself, giving him the benefit of the doubt. "Just let me know the address, and I'll plug it into my GPS."

"GPS?" Randall asks.

"Yes," I laugh, "this is why you should have a cell phone. I have this app called Waze, and I wouldn't know how to get anywhere without it."

Randall makes his way to the driver's side. He opens the door and invites me to take a seat. "In that case, the address is 372 Brickton Drive."

A jitter flutters inside my stomach as I buckle my seatbelt. I smile when I see him do a little hop-skip dance in the front of the car. I stretch over the middle console and open the door. "See, I can be romantic too!"

He thanks me and glides himself into the passenger's seat. He shifts his body and pulls the seatbelt over his chest.

"Before we start driving, I brought you something. It's to keep you safe." He takes a silver clip out of his pocket and attaches it to the visor above my head. The clip is of a winged angel, with the words *Always Watching Over You* engraved across it.

"Thank you, that's so kind." I kiss my thumb and run it against the clip, showing my appreciation for the small gift.

I stick the key into the ignition and turn. The engine revs, and as the sky gets dimmer, the lights on the dashboard shine bright green words and radio station numbers. I put the car in reverse, but before I let off the brake, I glance down toward Randall's lap. My eyes catch the item he's holding on to. Between his fingers and his palm, he squeezes a middling brown elongated furry object.

At first, I think he's holding a mouse. The shock jolts the muscles in my arms and legs because, if there is anything I despise in life, it's small hairy things. I tighten my eyes, hoping not to see whatever rodent he's brought into my car.

"What's wrong?" Randall's look is both confused and worried.

"Nothing, I just..." My eyes are sore with relief as I slowly open them, "I have a phobia of rodents, and I'm hoping that's not what you have in your hand right now."

"Oh, shit! I'm so sorry," he chuckles, "that's my lucky rabbit's foot."

"That's a rabbit's foot? I thought they were smaller, more...colorful, and fake, or something? That looks like a real animal ligament."

"Because it is!" He marvels, "This baby is an authentic rabbit's foot charm. I got it when I was stationed in Turkey. It was a gift from my captain." The excitement in his voice goes cold and his head rolls forward, looking up toward his visor at the guardian angel wing clip he gave me moments ago.

"A gift?"

"It's a long story, and I really don't like reliving it."

"I understand." His choice of words is intriguing. Reliving it feels more intense than remembering it. I have never known someone in the military, let alone someone who's gone through what a soldier has seen, what they've experienced.

"However, I should talk about it. I promised myself I wouldn't run from my grief like I did back then."

"If you don't want to, we don't have to."

"Nah, it's not that. I want to. But I also don't want to be late." He smiles. "Is it cool if we get goin'?" His Southern twang gives me comfort, and I return the smile. I nod, letting him know I'm okay with his decision to keep driving. I back out of my driveway and start moving forward.

About ten seconds into the drive, Randall starts, "You see," he starts, "in my senior year of high school, I went out partying with my boyfriend, Marco. Even though I promised him I wouldn't get too crazy, I did. I got too drunk. So, Marco chose to be the designated driver.

"There was this guy at the bar we were at who kept buying us shots. We were the first gay couple he ever came across, apparently, and he wanted to know everything about our lives. You know those straight guys who want to pretend they are..."

"Woke?" I finish his sentence.

Randall's brow furrows. "No, he was wide awake. He was just really drunk, acting like he was being all supportive of the gays and shit."

Realizing I need to teach Randall what *woke* means at a later time, I wave my hand, gesturing he can keep going.

"When we left the bar, we noticed the guy who was buying us shots was leavin' at the same time. We pulled out and stopped at the next red light. Next thing we knew, instead of stopping at the intersection, the drunk put his foot on the gas and rammed his truck right into the driver's side door. They rushed Marco to Shock Trauma."

"If you don't mind me asking, did he make it?" I keep my eyes on the road, nervous to see his reaction to my question.

He shook his head. "We were goin' together for three years before the accident. We had plans to move in together, get jobs, get married—you know, do the damn thing. After I lost him, it was too hard. I blamed myself. I blamed myself for not being responsible. I still blame myself for not being the one in that goddamn driver's seat. It should have been me."

"Wow." I feel a knot in my throat, not knowing what else to contribute.

"Marco was smarter than me, more athletic, more sociable. He did a lot of things. And me? I don't know what he saw in me, but I wasn't worth it."

"Don't say that..." my voice drifts off. Randall's story wasn't complete.

"So I punished myself. I turned to what took the one person I loved most. Whiskey and I were inseparable. I took it everywhere with me—until one day, I couldn't."

"What happened?" The gentle push came out of honest curiosity, not just me digging for information.

"I crashed my car into a gas pump, and my car instantly set fire. The gas attendant pulled me out of the car window and toward safety. I stayed a couple nights in jail and was let out on bail paid by my family. The judge gave me an ultimatum. He said I had two choices: one, serve two years in jail and join Alcoholics Anonymous; or two, join the military."

The distance between my nose and my upper lip narrows. "That's such an odd ultimatum. Can judges even do that?"

"Judges can do whatever they want. They can order you to go, but the military can decline you. That was something my lawyer told me about before I took the agreement. Instead of going to jail, I chose what option I thought would keep me out of it. The funny thing is, the closer I got to enlisting, the more I realized that servin' our country was what I wanted. I wanted to spend my life servin' other people, instead of servin' myself. When I was drinkin', I was consumed with selfishness. I was self-medicatin', and it wasn't fair to anyone 'round me."

"So where does this rabbit's foot come into play?" I tilt my head toward his lap.

"During my first deployment, my captain could see I wasn't focusin'. He could see I wasn't present. He pulled me in and asked me what was goin' on. So I told him. I told him everything. He was surprisingly accepting of the fact I was gay. I'll never forget that."

He smiles, remembering his captain's kindness. "He told me a story of when he was younger. He was asked to share a memory at his grandpa's funeral. Captain was super close with his grandpa, and when he went to speak, nothin' came out. He ran off and cried himself into a ball under a tree in the cemetery. Later on, a groundskeeper found him, called for his mama, and tried to console him in the meantime. He ended up givin' him this here rabbit's foot."

"Why a foot though? Like, couldn't he have given him

something else? A prayer card? A rosary? A lucky penny? I don't know. Something that didn't have a bone?"

He laughs and places his empty hand on my knee. Our eyes quickly find each other. Putting my hand on top of his, I accept his touch.

"According to the groundskeeper, rabbits are considered lucky creatures in European myth because they have the power to communicate with spirits of the dead. Rabbits often live and travel underground, which allows them to connect with deceased souls. When groundskeepers would find rabbits roaming around cemeteries, it was common to trap the rabbits and keep them until they died of natural causes. They would preserve the part of the rabbit's body that dug deep to find the souls and carry it around with them in hopes that even after the rabbit's death, they would be able to communicate with loved ones who passed away."

I can't help but smile. "That sounds both super sweet and kinda like a creepy taxidermy story."

"Hey! I didn't say I cut off any legs."

We both laugh.

Randall continues, "When I told my captain about Marco, he told me, even though he was gone, it didn't mean I had to stop speaking to him. That night, this rabbit's foot ended up in my duffel, and I've kept it by my side ever since."

"Does Marco ever talk back?" I grip the steering wheel, hoping my question isn't too personal.

Silence engulfs our shared space. My question goes unanswered.

I've never lost anyone in the way Randall has. Even though he's not dead, I have lost my father, but I would never admit that to anyone. It's a raw truth I'm not ready to say out loud. Most days, Thomas Branson's involuntary selfishness and medically explained impulsivity erupts my soul with anger and resentment, and it's hard to feel grief for someone you've been forced to give your whole life to.

About thirty minutes later, my GPS says we arrived at our destination. I pull the car in an empty parking spot, right next to a tall light pole. Looking around, I see a familiar giant neon-blue light in the shape of a dolphin riding a wave. "You brought us to the Annapolis Aquarium? After hours?"

"What gave that away?" He opens his door and steps out. Before closing it, he shouts, "Let's go!"

I unbuckle my seatbelt, open my door, and place one foot outside the car. "I hate to tell you, but it closed at five."

"Nah," he scoffs, "this place is notorious for not having good surveillance, and the back door is always open."

Randall walks behind the car and toward the back entrance. He halts, turns, and reaches out for my hand, gesturing for me to catch up so he can hold it. My feet remain firmly planted.

"I don't think this is a good idea." A panic attack begins to brew. My arms and legs tremble, and breathing becomes impossible.

He waves me over and calls out, "I promise, it's going to be okay. Are you okay?"

Am I okay? He's making me break laws, and he's asking me if I'm okay. *This is rich.*

"I want to...I want to go home, I think." My teeth click together, and my words come stuttering out. I pull fresh air into my nose and swallow, letting out a gust of breath. I repeat my deep breathing four more times.

Randall slowly shuffles over and reaches for my hands. He brings them up over our heads and holds them still. His eyes are closed, and with every new deep breath I take, he joins with me.

"This is what we used to do overseas. After someone saw whatever terrible thing they saw, we would do this when they couldn't calm themselves down. When we lift our arms high, our lungs have more space to work."

"I don't want to go in. We're not allowed." I feel the soreness of my calf muscles locking tight in place.

"Listen, Theo," he lets go of my raised hands and places his finger underneath my chin, "I know you're scared, but I'm not going to let anything happen to you. You deserve this night, just like you deserve to live. This is going to be exciting. It's going to be exhilarating. And it's something we're going to do together."

The knot in my stomach gets smaller, and oxygen surpasses my airwaves with less issue. The fogginess in my head clears.

Randall continues, "We can leave if you want, but I already scanned this place out before. I'm for certain we're not goin' to get caught. It'll be our little secret, okay? I got you."

Whether it was deep breathing or his charismatic voice, my panic diminishes faster than it ever has before. He rubs my shoulder and extends his neck, giving me a peck on the cheek with his soft lips. He steps back, and the reflection of the light pole glimmers in his eyes. His mouth gives me a wide, infectious smile. "What do you say, Theo? Do you wanna live a little?"

I'm not sure what's gotten into me. He's been able to take every single fear of mine away. Where there once was worry, there's thrill and anticipation. My negative thoughts cease to consume me—thoughts of us getting arrested, being kicked out of school, of me not being there for my dad when my mom gets home from work. All of the things that have made me think and rethink every decision in my life—all gone.

"I can't believe I'm saying this…" I take one last breath in my nostrils and out my mouth.

"Are you in?" His voice is full of mischief.

"Lead the way."

ELEVEN

Randall was right. The back door was unlocked, and sneaking into the aquarium was as easy as walking through my front door. As soon as we step in, there is a light switch on the wall behind a couple of hanging ponchos and some standing brooms. Randall rubs his hands against the wall and flicks on the switch.

When he pulls his arm back, one of the mop handles loses its place and falls over, making a loud crack against the concrete floor. My panic returns, and my heart skips a beat, hoping a straggling maintenance worker finishing up their shift didn't hear. He swiftly turns his head and puts his finger to his lips to shush me. I smirk at his playful smile, and my anxiety disperses.

We make our way through a hallway leading to three different destinations—the restrooms, the Reptile Room, and the employee break room. Randall pushes through the swinging doors labeled *Employees Only*. I see a private bathroom, several lockers, a conference table, and a kitchenette. Randall opens up the locker appearing to belong to someone named Charlie and grabs a lanyard connecting a key fob, a couple lock keys, and a photo ID with Charlie's information on it.

Apparently, Charlie O' Toole is the Annapolis Aquarium's very own herpetologist who specializes in crocodilian care. His key fob comes in handy when Randall uses it to open the Reptile Room next door.

"You're not scared of snakes, right?" Randall holds the door as I step past him.

"Absolutely not. Actually, I love them because they eat mice."

"Ah, yes. You don't like the rodents." He gently tickles my back and makes a soft sucking noise using his tongue and his bottom teeth. I jump a few centimeters off the ground, laugh, and swat his arm away.

"Gross." I let out a flirtatious whine and keep walking ahead, subtly checking underneath my arms to make sure my armpits aren't damp.

They are. Dammit.

Randall turns the lights on in the Reptile Room, lighting up the habitats for all the little caged Reptilia. The thought of him knowing where the lights are makes me wonder how many times he's done this before.

"Turtles!" he shouts, his voice echoing in the chilled observatory.

"Actually, sir, they are tortoises. Galapagos, in fact," I say. "I have a special place in my heart for the tortoises." I glide my hand across the glass separating us from the giant specimen on the other side.

"Oh yeah?"

"There's something about going at your own pace that really speaks to me. The tortoise is strong, stable, protected.

It doesn't let anything around be a bother. Just lives life to the fullest, you know?"

"Is that how you live your life, Theo? Going at your own pace, living your life under a hard shell?"

"I try." I run my hand through my hair. "Life throws too many curveballs at you. One minute you're young, running through sprinklers, then the next minute..."

"You're emptying out your father's bed pan," he finishes my sentence, but in a direction I wasn't going to take it... necessarily.

"Exactly! I mean...we all go through our own different shit, but you need to be ready for whatever mud you have to trudge through. Life is unexpected and will always find a way to slow you down."

"I don't think you've told me what happened to your dad? You said he was injured, but I don't really know the extent of it."

"He was in a motorcycle accident. It's been eight years. Eight whole years of trudging slowly through mud, just to keep the family together."

"Slowing down can't be the only option though," he says. "Take it from me. After I got back from deployment, I realized I already missed out on so many things. You have to strike when the moment comes, and quick-pounce on opportunities, because one of those opportunities could be the one that changes your life for the better. Your family did what you had to do at the time. It doesn't mean you have to keep trudging."

We walk into the next room, and we're surrounded by schools of fish and several stingrays circling us. The glass between us and the sea creatures starts from ground level and makes its way up to the ceiling before curving around to the other side. I look up and see the bottom of a giant angelfish swimming across the bend. I press my hand against the glass, and the angelfish swims downwards, finding my hand. It stops, its whole body turned so I can see its head, trunk, and tail. Its black-and-yellow-striped scales glimmer as its fins tenderly wave back and forth.

"I think angelfish are my favorite." I gaze in awe at the creature's beauty.

"They're the angels of the sea, from what I've heard." Randall comes up from behind me and places his hand on top of mine, against the glass. Another angelfish, this time full of beautiful black and baby-blue scales, swims next to my already established fish friend. It's hard to tell if both fish are staring at each other or us, but, either way, they have found something to stare at.

"Look! I think they're in love." Randall's thumb caresses the back of my hand, and through the soft fabric of my shirt, I feel his lips and the hardness of his chin against my shoulder. He whispers in my ear, "I have a surprise for you," and summons me to follow him into the next room—the dolphin observatory.

He finds another light switch against the wall when we enter through the double doors. A spotlight shines on a podium sitting on a stage facing about twenty rows of theater seats. Randall skips down the steps, toward the giant tank behind the stage. He reaches behind the podium and grabs a water pail filled to the top with what looks like floating dead fish and shrimp.

"How in the world?" My jaw drops for a moment. "You must bring your other dates here, because you know this place way too well."

"No other dates! Promise! I just know a guy," his voice carries.

Randall slides on a glove he finds behind the podium and takes a handful from the bucket. He walks around the edge of the tank and drops single shrimp onto the surface. Some sink, but others continue to float. About ten seconds tick by, and a dolphin majestically paddles its way to the surface. Its snout breaks the stillness of the water, and it greets us with a melodic clicking noise. According to the plaque, this dolphin is female, and her name is Rosie. She takes off around the edges of the tank and collects the floating shrimp, flapping her tail in excitement.

"I feel like this is highly illegal, Randall," I speak up. "Don't the dolphins stay in another part of the habitat? I can't imagine the aquarists just leave them in the show tank."

"Let's just say I've spent the day planning this rendezvous and meeting you at your house. I took a little time to prepare." He laughs. "And, plus, I know a guy."

"You keep saying that." I shake my head and smile. "Someone who works here trusted you to do this? I feel like they should be fired."

Rosie sinks down below the surface and, within a minute, splashes through the water, jumping several feet above the threshold, and then she elegantly dives back in the water. A gentle splash hits the glass retaining wall, and a mist finds its way across my face.

"I think you're in the splash zone, cutie pie," Randall calls out.

"Yeah," I patting dry the droplets on my face, "I figured that one out."

Randall slips off his boots and rolls up the bottoms of his jeans above his ankles. He starts to climb the ladder against the tank. With each rung he takes, my throat closes, making it more challenging to breathe. He looks back at me as if he knows exactly what I'm thinking, and tells me to stop worrying because he knows what he's doing. I don't know if I'm pissed that he thinks telling me to stop worrying is going to make my panic go away, or if I'm happy because he stopped to think about how I was feeling.

He makes his way to the top of the ladder and sits on the last rung. He sinks his feet into the water and moves his legs from side to side, tapping the top of the water with his palm. "C'mon, Rosie girl. Come to good ole Randall. I got your favorite meal here."

Rosie resurfaces, a mixture of air and water spraying out of her blowhole. She makes a clicking noise and drifts over to Randall, skimming her slick body across the bottom of his submerged feet.

"That tickles, silly girl." Her tail slaps the surface of the water, and Randall lets out a boisterous cackle as a splash of water sprays his face. "I double-dolphin dare you to do that again, missy."

Randall's laugh is a bright, happy sound, floating above Rosie's chirpy whistles as she circles around him. He's got his arms out like he's playing a game of tag, reaching toward the dolphin each time she passes. His face is wide open in joy as she plays right back, swimming close enough to brush against his legs, like she's in on the private joke.

It's his laugh. That perfect, ridiculous laugh of his that makes me forget where I am, what I'm even doing, just... everything. It's like he's lit up, and I can't tear my eyes away, can't stop feeling this tug in my chest every time he howls so vivaciously.

Then Randall turns, his eyes beaming and playful.

"Theo!" he calls, stretching out a hand. "You comin' over, or are you just gonna stand there gawkin' all night?"

My heart trips over itself, but I can't help grinning back.

After his third wave begging me to join him, I kick off my shoes, roll up my pant legs, and make my way to the ladder, which is large enough to hold the both of us. I swing my legs around and sink my bare feet into the water right next to Randall's. Rosie swims away, but Randall assures me she'll be back. He tosses her an entire fish he grabbed from the bucket before he climbed up.

At this moment, I feel safe with him. I'm doing this absurd thing I don't think I'd ever do with anyone else, and I don't even really know the guy. I just know I'm starting to feel something for him I've never experienced before.

Under water, I rub my right foot against Randall's left. He returns the gesture by locking our legs together. He takes off his glove and runs his hand through my hair, swiping strands away from my face. "You're beautiful. Do you know that?"

"Oh, stop." I feel the warmth rise up from my neck and fill up both of my cheeks. "Thank God you took your stinky glove off first before you started touching my face."

"You're lucky. I almost forgot to," he laughs, "but I'm serious, Theo. I've never met anyone like you before." He bows his head as if what he's saying to me leaves him vulnerable.

The surface of the water ripples, indicating Rosie is on her way back up, this time to greet me. Her large gray body become clearer, and suddenly, a firm, slick sensation brushes across the front of my legs. "Whoa!" The tenderness surprises me. I wasn't sure how Rosie's body would feel to the touch. "I hope this means she likes me."

"It definitely means she likes you. One time, I brought this guy here, and she bit him. I think she thought he was a dead fish. He did stink a little." He smirked.

"Another guy, eh? I thought you said you don't bring dates here?" I bump my shoulder against his, hoping he doesn't hear the jealousy in my voice.

"Nah, I'm just joshin' with you." He returns the romantic shoulder bump. "I promise, you're the only feller I've been interested in since Marc..." he stops himself from finishing the name.

Joshin' with you? Feller?

His old soul is so endearing.

I wrap my arm around his back and place my chin on his shoulder. "You can talk about him with me. You don't have to avoid saying his name."

"Yeah, and be the guy who talks about his dead ex on a first date? No thank you."

"First off, I would never want you to censor yourself around me. Secondly, Marco wasn't your ex. He died during a time you loved him, and I'm one hundred percent sure you still love him, and I'm okay with that. We all have our baggage." We lock gazes, taking in the moment we just had.

In a matter of seconds, Rosie interrupts us and begins slapping her tail hard against the water repeatedly. Not only do the splashes break us out of our romance trance, but the waves Rosie makes in the tank send panic vibrations up and down my spine. She senses something wrong, maybe even senses someone else in the building besides me and Randall.

Randall quickly swings his legs from the other side of the ladder and starts making his way down. He reaches for my hand and invites me to do the same, requesting I hurry down the ladder fast, just as he is.

We make it to ground level and both grab our socks and shoes. Randall walks up to the glass of the tank and places his hand to it, meeting Rosie's face on the other side. "Thank you, *silly girl*. You really outdid yourself tonight. Head on back, will ya?"

I take back what I thought earlier: *This* is hands down the most adorable thing I have ever seen.

The overhead lights of the observatory turn on, and a rich, husky male voice calls out, "Who's down there?"

Randall and I don't answer. Instead, we sneak out the double doors we entered from and make our way through the rooms we once visited.

When we enter the employee break room to return Charlie's keys and badge, the man's voice rings loudly again, this time through the intercom, "If there is anyone here without permission, I've already called the police. They are on their way. If you do work here, please press *45 on the intercom and enter your three-digit identification number to let me know this is not an emergency."

Randall and I let out a boisterous laugh, then quickly cover our mouths to avoid making more sounds. The coast is clear, so we exit the building the way we came in, through the back door. We make our way across the empty parking lot and quickly climb into my car.

The man who almost busted us is the aquarium's security guard. His golf cart, labeled *Security*, has flickering blue and red lights and is parked near the main entrance.

"You don't think he saw my car, right? My license plate number?"

Randall reaches in the back seat and pulls out two license plates. "You mean these?"

I gasp, "Oh, you're bad. You are really naughty! When the hell did you have time to take those off?"

"Don't worry about that. Let's get out of here. We'll pull over in a couple blocks and put these babies back on."

I start the engine, shift into drive, and press my foot to the gas pedal. "Let's go!"

As we pull into my driveway, I look at the clock on the dashboard. I have approximately a half hour before my mom gets home from work. I see the lights in the house are off, which means Aunt Kay must have fallen asleep on the couch after putting my dad to bed. I don't know what I'd do without her. I'll have to figure out how I can repay her for giving me the chance to have this amazing night with Randall.

"I had fun tonight," I say, unbuckling my seatbelt. I look at him, and he's already staring into my eyes. He shifts his body toward me. I hold my own, but I sense his warm, minty breath on my lips.

"Me too." He leans in closer, so close I can feel his lips bounce softly against mine. He's stopping himself from making full contact, but I know he wants to pull me in and take me. He breathes in and places his hand on the side of my face. He whispers, "I want to kiss you good night."

"Why haven't you?"

Our lips join together. His warm tongue finds its way into my mouth, caressing the inside ever so gently. His breath tastes fresh, and I can smell the dabs of cologne he placed behind his ear. His aroma is intoxicating, and I don't want this moment to end.

I pull back, savoring the magic of his touch and smile. "Thank you for tonight." Out of the corner of my eye, I see the living room light flick on. Aunt Kay must have woken up, wondering who is parked in our driveway. "I'll see you in class tomorrow?"

"I reckon you will." He nods. "And you're welcome, cutie pie. Thank you for joinin' me."

We both get out of the car, and I press the lock button on my key fob. "How are you getting home? I can call you an Uber."

"Name-callin' ain't cool." He smirks.

"You don't know what an Uber is either?" I roll my eyes in jest. "It's like a taxi, boo. I can call a taxi to come pick you up."

"Ah, I see. Nah, I'm good. I think I might want to walk home. It's chilly out, so hopefully that will cool down all this heat in my body from that kiss."

I smile and shake my head. "Well, be safe. I'd tell you to text me when you get home, but..."

"Don't worry. I'll be okay." He tips his invisible hat. "Tell your aunt thank you for me. She helped give me one of the best nights of my life." He starts walking down the road, humming a sweet tune.

I make it to my front porch steps and turn around, trying to get one last glance at Randall walking away. I extend my neck but don't see him in sight.

I open the front door, and Aunt Kay asks how my evening was, but she makes a passive aggressive comment about how she didn't think she'd be watching my dad all night. She hates getting him a shower and putting him to bed.

"Well, I thank you very much, Aunt Kay. So does my date. You came through for me tonight, and I owe you one."

"Maybe next time you can stop and get me a hot fudge sundae from the ice cream shop on your way back. That'll make it up to me," she says.

Before she leaves, Aunt Kay tells me my father's been sleeping for an hour and might need to wake up to go to the bathroom when Mom gets home. She agrees to keep this night a secret between the two of us because she knows how guilty my mom will feel if she finds out she spent the whole evening here.

After my shower, I crawl into my bed, pulling the covers across my chest. I pat the bed beside me, and Hamilton makes his way up using the doggie steps I have for him. His little paws dig their way under the sheets, and he burrows comfortably next to my side. I kiss his sweet little forehead and wish for him to have the best of dreams.

Staring at my popcorn ceiling, I take a heavy breath. For the first time in a long time, overwhelming feelings of happiness set in, and I can't stop smiling. To me, thoughts are not permanent unless they are said out loud. You can take back anything you think, but once it's out into the world, it's hard to deny it. As I lie in bed with my eyes closed, I whisper to my audience of none, *"I think I might be falling for Randall Stevens."*

TWELVE

The smell of fish oil invades my nostrils, and my forehead gets lathered in slimy drool before I push Hamilton's snout away from my face. "Gross, Ham! Get off, you cute little dumpster truck!" My fur baby knows he has my whole heart, and I'd do anything for him, but dammit does he have horrendous kissing etiquette.

My feet ground themselves on my carpeted floor as I reach above my head to stretch last night's hard sleep out of my system. I must have crashed hard from the adrenaline of breaking and entering last night, because I haven't slept that soundly since Lianna and I crashed her neighbor's backyard wedding and danced the night away with two of the caterers.

As I stand there, looking in the bathroom mirror with a toothbrush sticking out of my mouth, a flash of warmth travels from my neck to my cheeks. The thought of kissing Randall awakens a fist pump toward the ceiling, causing me to accidentally hit the glass globe around the light fixture above the mirror.

Nothing broke, but holy hell that hurt.

A text comes up on my phone, Lianna confirming our early lunch at Cristella's—Baltimore's popular new taco joint. It'll take me about twenty minutes to get there, so I send her a quick reply with clock emoji equaling the number forty, just in case there is traffic.

Before I make my way to the living room, I slip on my leopard-print Sperry's because I'm feeling sassy and confident. Today is going to be a good day. Nothing is going to ruin it.

Mom is kneeling on the floor in front of my father's wheelchair, wrapping his leg up with some gauze and medical tape. With every ounce of me wanting to ignore this and just keep walking, my internal guilt takes over, and I ask what happened.

"Your father must have hit his leg on something. He has a pretty large gash, and I need to doctor it up before it gets infected. Where are you going out to?"

"I'm meeting Lianna for lunch, and then I have class at 4:30 p.m." The idea of leaving her alone to deal with my dad's leg sends a swarm of guilt-ridden butterflies throughout my gut. I look for a reaction from her, but she's so intent on my father's open wound. "Is it alright if I leave a little bit earlier?"

"Yes, why wouldn't it be, sweetie?" She readjusts the tape on my father's leg, pulling a little bit of hair. He jerks his leg and lets out a short flare of aggravation. "A meal out sounds really nice."

I can't tell if that's a genuine comment or some deep-rooted feeling about not being able to go out to eat when she wants to.

"I don't have to go, Mom. I'll call Li and cancel with her." I bend my neck to the side and sigh.

"No, no, no! You go. Have fun! I'm just saying, maybe one day, me and you could have lunch?"

"Why didn't you just say that then?" I shake my head, knowing somewhere, deep down inside, she knows her comments bother me. "We can do lunch on Saturday, before I go to Lianna's bonfire?"

"No, it's okay, sweetie." Her rejection stabs me in the gut. "I wouldn't know what we'd do with your father, anyway. You know he's too difficult to manage in restaurants."

Going to a restaurant with my father is one of my least favorite things to do. For starters, he's a messy eater. He'll get crumbs and gunk everywhere, from the corners of his mouth, on his hands, and then down his shirt. Secondly, he tries to make conversation with the servers and invites them to go shopping so he can buy them things. We always have to speak up and tell the servers about his brain injury, giving them permission to ignore him. Especially when Dad asks to see their bosses so he can tell them to give the server a raise. Most people find it endearing, but my family and I find it embarrassing.

"We could have Aunt Kay stay with him, and we can go have a day together, including a nice lunch. I asked her to come over last night to sit with Dad, and she was fine with it."

"You called my sister and asked her to take care of your father without telling me? Where were you?"

"I went out...uh...with a friend. It was fine. Aunt Kay didn't care. We have to get comfortable with asking for help. Especially from our family, Mom."

"I wish it were that simple, sweetie." She pauses. "And next time, please speak with me before you ask my sister to come over and sit with your father. She has her own life to live." She lets out a breath. "Now, I want you to go have fun with Lianna, okay? I'll be here until I have to go to work. Your sister is off tonight, so she'll be here to help with your father." She wraps the final piece of tape around Dad's leg, and when she's done, she pats her hands together.

The thought of Haley helping me take care of Dad later this evening is laughable. We still haven't spoken since our fight, and my fear of her possibly abusing my father's medication is still floating around in the back of my head. Just the idea makes me sick to my stomach. I let out a groan. "Yeah, sure she'll help."

"Theo," Mom's voice sharpens, "give your sister a break. The hours at the hospital are catching up with her. You'll realize one day when you get a full-time job that it's not easy doing that along with what we do here with your father."

I guess now would be the perfect time to let her know about the graduate assistantship position I start next week. "Now that you bring that up..."

"What's wrong?" Her right brow shoots up, and her lips purse like a 2001 runway model.

"Nothing is wrong!" Something being wrong is always her first response to everything. "I think I may have found a job. At school."

"Oh really?"

"With my professor. She's looking for a graduate assistant, and she asked me if I wanted the job."

Her eyes sway to the side, and I see her pondering the types of questions she needs to ask in order to get a clearer picture of what is expected of her.

"So is this during the school day? What are the hours?

Are you still going to be able to sit with your father at nighttime?"

There it is. It always comes back to Thomas Branson.

"I just need to stay two hours longer on Tuesdays and Thursdays for my office hours." I pause and evaluate if this response answers all of her questions, hoping she can piece together what she needs in order to make arrangements for Dad.

She straightens her pants as she stands and shuffles her way toward the kitchen. She calls back, "It is what it is, Theo. I'm proud of you. I'll talk to your sister and Aunt Kay, and we'll see what we can do."

I give her a kiss on the cheek and say my goodbyes. She tells me to be careful, but the look in her eyes tells me she'll be worrying for the next several hours about finding coverage on the days I'll work late.

An hour later, I meet Lianna at Cristella's. I order a brunch-aco, which is a giant taco made up of an egg, bacon pieces, diced tomatoes, and spiced ground beef, with a side of cinnamon donut rounds with a creamy sweet glaze drizzled over top. Lianna orders a taco salad, but instead of meat, she orders scrambled eggs.

When the food is delivered, I dig in, stuffing my face like a farm animal.

Or even worse, like my dad.

"Girl, I haven't eaten since yesterday morning. All that crime can make a boy hungry!"

"Yes, tell me everything. Tell me all about this crime you speak of," she demands as she pushes her salad forward and slides my plate of cinnamon donut rounds in front of her. I don't mind sharing.

"There's not much to say besides that it was," I breathe in, "...amazing."

"I'm going to need more details than that, jackass."

Lianna's jaw drops, and her eyes frost over when I tell her about the aquarium's unlocked back door and the adorable bond Randall had with Rosie. She asks a couple of questions I wasn't sure how to answer, like how Randall knew about the lack of security and why his connection with Rosie seemed to be so strong. She asked if I was scared at all, to which I told her I absolutely was not, even when the security guard essentially chased us out of the building.

"So, yeah, I was captured and turned into a common-rate criminal, and I think I'm in love with the man who lured me into a life of crime." I look up and sigh as if I'm waking up from a dream full of wondrous splendor.

"Okay, slow down, Patty Hearst." She laughs. "Oh my god, you need to bring him to the bonfire on Saturday."

A large gulp of anxiety pushes its way down my throat. "Do you think that's too soon? Introducing him to my friends?"

"Hell to the no. He needs to see what he's working with." She pulls her salad closer and stabs her fork, picking up bits of lettuce and egg.

Thoughts of Damien flash through my head. I threw the aspects of my life in his face, and he couldn't handle it. I thought being completely honest and open about everything, including the shit about my dad, was the best approach. Yet, all it did was push him away. I'm not in the business of being hurt anymore because the love interests in my life can't accept I have responsibilities and a life outside of them.

"We'll see. I'll give him the option to come or not." I spoon the last cinnamon donut in my mouth, chew for a couple of extra self-conscious bites, and swallow. "But I am very excited about Saturday. Are you bringing any boytoys?"

"The only man I'm bringing to the fire is Eugene Levy." As my eyes widen, she continues, "I'm writing the chapter on how genuine his chemistry is with each and every cast member. He's all I've been thinking about these past couple of days."

"Speaking of, how's the book coming along?"

She nods and tells me, even after watching *Schitt's Creek* thirty times, she is still able to find little pieces new to her. She's in awe that a show can be fresh and new every time she watches. It seems as though both Lianna and I have found our muses. It's just hers is a fictional family, and mine is a Southern veteran who loves to swim with dolphins.

All of the sudden, Lianna gasps so loudly, I almost drop my fork.

"Lianna!" I clutch my chest like she just shaved at least two years off my life. "What the—"

"Don't. Look." She grips my wrist like she's trying to anchor me to my chair. Her eyes dart toward the counter.

"Don't look at what?"

"I said don't!" Her voice dips into a harsh whisper, but it's too late. The curiosity is too strong.

I look.

And there he is—Javier. The tawny skinned dreamboat has a black strap over his shoulder attached to a hanging guitar across his abdomen. He's standing at the counter, casually cool, waiting for his carry-out order, the sleeves of his navy henley pushed up just enough to show off his fore-arms—lean, strong, and faintly dusted with dark hair.

There's an ease to the way he leans against the counter, like he owns the space without even trying.

Our eyes meet, and panic sets in.

Gay panic, to be exact.

I spin around so fast, my knee hits the underside of the table. My face burns hotter than my underarms in a wool sweater on a summer day.

"Oh my God, he saw me looking," I groan, hiding my face in my hands.

Lianna cackles. "Of course he saw you. You weren't exactly subtle. I legit told you not to look."

"He smiled at me." My voice is muffled by my hands.

Her laughter stops. "Wait, what?"

"When he looked at me—he smiled. Like, faintly. It was cute," I admit, peeking through my fingers.

Lianna practically vibrates in her seat. "You *have* to go talk to him."

"No way!"

"Yeah way! T, this is perfect! Go say hi!"

"But what about Randall?" I blurt. "We had a really nice date last night, and I don't want to ruin that."

She rolls her eyes. "I thought you weren't trying to be serious with anyone. Now's your chance to spice it up. Date as many people as you can! It's the buffet of life, T. The main course is dick. Enjoy the dick, Theo."

I shake my head furiously. "No. Absolutely not. And don't you even—"

But she's already out of her chair.

I watch in horror as she strolls up to Javier, waving like they're long-lost friends. As if she was more than just his student's sister. I see them talking, laughing, Lianna gesturing toward our table.

Oh no.

Javier walks over with her, his carry-out bag in hand and a smile on his face. "Well, well, well. If it isn't Mr. Caramel Vanilla Chai," he says, that adorable grin sparkling—literally. There's a little glimmer on his teeth, and I'm left helpless. I'm no more good.

"You two have already met?" Lianna asks.

"Yes. Um, hi," I manage to squeak.

"It's nice to see you again," he says with effortless smoothness. "Theo, was it?"

"Yes. Um, Javier?" I try not to sound robotic but also make it seem I forgot his name. Lianna always suggests playing *dumb*, but she never told me how hard it would be in the moment.

He chuckles before shaking his head. He turns to Lianna. "I can't stay long. I've got to get home and prep for a charity event at the fire department."

Leanna smirks. "Ahh, my mom told me you love to volunteer. Theo, he volunteers at a fire department."

"And a hospital, as well as a retirement home."

"Aren't you just a good little Boy Scout?" Lianna jokes. "Well, enjoy your food. Are you going home to anyone in particular to share your meal with?"

His pearly whites poke out, and he shakes his head. "Nope. Just me, myself, and I. When it comes to Cristella's cinnamon donut bites, I don't share with anyone."

"Same. I love donuts," I say awkwardly, my volume raised just a bit higher than I'd prefer.

Javier's gorgeous smile continues. "That's good to know." Before leaving, he hugs Lianna, tells her he'll see her this weekend and warns her to wear ear plugs. "I plan to bring the amp with me. I promised Trevor."

"Sounds good! I'll see you then."

Javier turns to me, and before he says anything, he taps my shoulder with a sharp edge. I look down and see him holding a business card above my shoulder. "*Llámame alguna vez*, Mr. Caramel Vanilla Chai. Maybe I can take you out for a real *café* sometime."

I take the card and nod, unsure of what to say, deciding it's safer to stay silent rather than risk embarrassing myself further. He walks away, leaving behind a trail of smoked vanilla and subtle black pepper. The scent lingers, hovering around me, and I can't help but take a deep breath, trying to hold on to it as long as possible.

Lianna grabs my hand as he walks out the door. We're both grinning, giddy, laughing like kids on a playground. Everyone's staring, but who cares?

Then the thought hits me.

What about Randall?

Yes, Javier is perfect, and he just asked me out *and* gave me *his* number with ease, unlike Randall.

But I still can't seem to shake Randall. I still want to see where that goes.

Last night, Randall showed me what life would be like if there were no limits. Today, I embraced that lesson from Randall and took a number from Javier.

If these two guys can give me the kind of life with no limits, then why do I still feel so trapped?

THIRTEEN

The loud bass from Haley's car sends vibrations to my ears. I move the curtain with my finger and peek through, trying not to be obvious. She takes a fast, sharp turn into the driveway, giving zero fucks that she almost hit my car. Not even P!nk's angry hits of the early 2000s blaring from her speakers can make me accept this type of behavior.

I begin to wonder if calling her out for her reckless driving would even be productive at this point. My blood is already curdling as I sit here listening to my father chew on his vegetables like a goddamn rabbit.

Oh, rabbits?

Randall.

My level of calm just increased by forty percent. I can work with that.

The door swings open, and in walks aggression. "What are you looking at?" Haley scoffs as she makes her way up the steps from the foyer.

My hard stare at the front door breaks as soon as her

second or third heavy grunt slices through the room. "Oh, sorry. I was just thinking. Didn't even realize you came in."

"Whatever. I just figured you were already judging something about me as soon as I walked in." She loops her key lanyard around the knob of the banister and frantically kicks off her shoes, which land in the middle of the hallway before she walks into the kitchen.

I lift my hand toward the misplaced shoes and tip an imaginary drink. Here's to hoping Thomas won't trip over them on the way to the bathroom.

"How was your day?" I shuffle myself to the edge of the couch, peeking my head in her sight from the other room. I want her to know I care and actually want to hear about how her day went.

The silence in the room ends as Thomas puts a crunchy celery stick in his mouth. I stare at Haley, waiting for her to respond. For as warm as it was today, the sun definitely hasn't touched her cold bitterness.

After unwrapping the miniature frozen pizza, she crinkles the trash in a ball and throws it away. According to the last beep on the microwave, I have at least three minutes to try again with the conversation, this time louder. "Haley, did you have a good day at work?"

Staring straight through the microwave door, she cooks the pizza with the heat from her eyes. She grumbles, "Why do you care? Honestly."

"You're not supposed to get that close to the microwave, you know?"

"Of course you'd say that. Theo to the fucking rescue." She slams her fists down on the stovetop. An agonized grunt escapes as she turns around to face me. "Leave me the hell alone."

"What is your problem, Haley?" My face reddens. Adrenaline pulsates through my skin. "I don't deserve to be spoken to this way."

"I don't deserve to have my little brother treat me like a child." She opens the microwave, grabs her pizza with her bare hands, not caring about the heat, and throws it on the counter. She slams the door harder than needed and lets out a rough breath.

Her temper tantrum ends as soon as her phone illuminates on the counter. It's not possible for me to see who it is from where I'm seated, but I can tell whoever it is distresses the hell out of her. She runs her hand through her hair and g,ives the fistful she has a quick tug before she stomps away toward the bathroom.

Her phone's screen is still bright, begging me to hurry to touch it before the display light goes dim. I tap the screen and see the green phone icon with a small red number sixteen perched at the top right corner. She has numerous missed calls, but I'm not sure if they're from the same person or not. I can't tap the icon because the number sixteen will vanish, and she'll know I was on her phone. So I do the next best thing and swipe down from the top of the screen, allowing all of the recent notifications to show.

There it is. Two voicemails and fourteen missed calls within a two-hour timeframe.

One name appears, and it's one I've never seen or heard before.

Jesse.

This Jesse person has called her seven times to no avail. Above Jesse's name are seven more missed calls from an *Unknown Caller.* Under the notifications is a text message that only allows me to see the first line before showing a set of ellipses that taunt me. If I tap that text button and open her chats, she'll know. I can't risk that. I'll settle for the first line: PLEASE GET IT FOR...

The toilet flushes from down the hallway, and I hurry to click the side button of the phone to turn it off. The distance between the couch and the kitchen is too far for me to rush back to my place, so instead, I leap to the refrigerator to make it look as if I'm grabbing something cold to drink.

She turns the corner into the kitchen, and with her bloodshot, watery eyes, she gives me one of the most menacing looks I've ever encountered. She knocks her shoulder into mine as she walks by, which has become her new favorite way to greet me and say goodbye.

Her movement stops abruptly. I sense her turn to me after she realizes her phone has been left alone with me for far too long. She reaches for her cell and presses the four-digit code to access the main menu. The next steps she takes are backward, side-stepping out of the room. She must have read the remainder of that text I so desperately wanted to click on.

A breathy sniffle slips out as she takes off down the steps and into her basement room.

I stand there, speechless. Confused. What just happened? Who texted her? All I want to do is figure out what is going on, why she's so hostile. But I can't do that if she won't speak to me. Whatever trouble she's in, she's going to have to go through it by herself, as much as it pains me to say. There is nothing scarier than the secrecy of an isolated soul.

My cell phone rings, and Lianna's voice is on the other end, "Hello, darlin'!"

"Hey, what's up?" I let out a small cough, readjusting to a new interaction.

"How would you feel about going on a double date? Remember that guy I was telling you about? Yu-en?"

"Not really." I furrow my brow.

"That Taiwanese man who took me for a ride with his tongue. Yu-en!"

"Oh, yes! I do remember your little friend; however, I don't remember him having a name, and I also don't remember that detail about his tongue, so feel free to keep those details to yourself next time." I smile.

"Whatever, Theo," she returns with a laugh. "Do you want to double, or what?"

"Sure, let me ask Hamilton."

"You are nothing but jokes today, aren't you, Mr. Man? But I'm serious. We can make it official tonight at the bonfire. Yu-en is coming, and you're bringing Randy-poo, right? You're going to ask him to come with us."

Shit.

"Lianna! I forgot to invite him," I wail. It's been two days since our date, and he didn't show up to class yesterday. Which I found odd, but didn't think anything of it at the time. With him not having a cellphone, it's extremely and annoyingly difficult to talk to him. Even though there's nothing I want more.

"Theo!" she gasps. "What is wrong with you? I gave you ample time to invite him."

"I didn't get to see him yesterday and..." The doorbell to my house interrupts my excuse. "Hey, I have to go. I'll text you in a little bit. Someone is at my front door."

I swing open the door, and Randall stands there, his big smoldering hazel eyes staring back at me, holding two beautiful stems of vibrant orange roses. I get an intoxicating whiff of his cologne, and my entire body freezes in place. I'm both happy and shocked to see him.

Hamilton, on the other hand, is not happy to see him. His short, compact body is tense and guarded, a soft growl slipping through his teeth. He stands frozen at the top of the stairs above the foyer, like an overprotective gargoyle.

"Were your ears burning?" I ask, shooing away my guard dog.

"Does that mean you were talking about me?" His smile breaks his suspicion because he knows damn well I was at least thinking about him.

"You could say that. Also, not to be rude or anything, do you normally just show up randomly at boys' houses? Why are you here?"

"I was in the neighborhood and figured I'd mosey on over and say hi. I can go if you'd like?"

"No! I'm glad you're here."

"Well, alright then."

I let out a random word I really wish was accompanied by a sensical sentence, "Bonfire!"

Randall widens his eyes. "Was that a question or a statement? Do we need a fire extinguisher?"

"Hardy-har-har," I mimic hilarity. "No, it was a question. I'm just excited to see you because I forgot to ask you on Thursday if you wanted to attend my best friend's bonfire with me tonight."

"Well, in that case..." He pulls both of his hands behind his back, holding them together. His chest puffs out slightly, and he says in his most Southern drawl, "I'll be there if the creek don't rise. I love me a bonfire."

Attempting my own Southern accent, I say, "Burning shit is your thing, ain't it?"

"I reckon you can say that." He chuckles. "May I come in? I don't want the bugs gettin' in. It's gettin' to be that time of night."

"Oh, yes, come in!" I step aside and chauffeur him upstairs and into the living room. Hamilton lets out a bark and scurries to my room, where his cage sits. My dad sits in his corner, next to the breakfast bar, awaiting his dinner. "Dad, this is Randall. Randall, this is my father."

"Hi, Mr. Branson, I'm Randall! Are you gettin' ready for some dinner?" Randall calls out.

"Howdy! You're right and tight!"

Along with his brain injury, my dad is also cursed with casual rhyming. The doctors say it's normal, and we've accepted it over the years. However, when he rhymes around new people, things usually get pretty awkward. I turn to Randall and begin to explain this is a part of his brain injury, but Randall puts his hand up.

"I bet your dinner is going to be smokin', Mr. B!"

Randall's response to my dad takes me back. There's something genuine, even gentle in his voice. He's not letting the awkwardness ruin the moment. He's just...going with it. Randall reaches for my dad's hand, lifts it, and shakes, holding his hand in both of his. "It's a pleasure to meet you, sir."

Is this what it feels like to have your worlds collide? No one I've cared for the way I care about Randall has acted this way toward my father before. My dad has always just been a responsibility to everyone else. He's never been...a person. At this moment, watching Randall make actual conversation with Thomas Branson sends an overwhelming sense of calm over my body. I don't hear the thumping in my chest. I don't feel the jitters in my fingertips the way I normally would.

I don't want this to end.

Don't let go of this moment, Theo.

A minute goes by, and I realize I've stood there watching Randall have a full-on conversation with my dad and politely disregard my presence, which couldn't make me happier.

I glance at the clock in the kitchen and see that the time is getting close to when I was hoping to leave for the bonfire. I definitely don't want to be late, especially if I'm bringing some military man candy on my arm.

I ask if it's okay if I go into my room to change, to which Randall waves his hand and says, "Of course! Take your time. Your dad's telling me how he's going to take me shopping."

The both of them laugh, which makes me laugh.

I pull my cell phone out and text Lianna.

> It's confirmed. Randall is coming tonight. I think he's actually here to pick me up.

> No shit! What a charmer!?! Yu-en literally just bailed on me. Kinda relieved. Looks like I'm going solo tonight.

> I know, right?! And what the hell, dude? I'm already not a fan of this Yu-en. Be there soon!

ONE OF THE many things I love about my bedroom is I have a giant closet. All of my XXL sweaters and shirts hang snugly but perfectly, just waiting to be chosen for wear. I drag my fingers across the fabrics with hopes an outfit will magically jump out. The longer I'm in here picking something out, the more my father has a chance to scare Randall away.

I throw on a gray tee-shirt, some washed-out jeans, and a black cardigan. My Converses slip on easily, and I tie the laces tight, just the way I like them.

I look in the mirror above my dresser and rub some whipped hairstyling mousse in my hair and mess it around with my hand. It lies exactly how I want it, so I spray a third of the can of hairspray on it to keep its hold.

I hear my sister's voice from the living room. My heart immediately drops. She usually doesn't come upstairs to watch my dad until I leave the house—or at least that's what she's been doing lately.

"Dad, come over here to sit down," her voice croaks as she demands for him to take the seat next to her on the couch. "You're not getting dinner yet."

Randall steps up to me. "You ready to go, babe?"

"Did she introduce herself to you? Did she even say hi?" That protective feeling quickly consumes me.

"She has a lot going on. Don't worry about it. Let's get out of here, okay?" He begins taking steps down the stairs to the front door.

"Haley, Dad's dinner is in the refrigerator. Remember, heat for two minutes. He likes to eat it with a spoon because he drops too much stuff with the fork." I follow Randall down the stairs.

"I know, Theo. Leave. *Have a blast.*" Her sarcasm settles in my mind.

"Mom should be home around..."

She interrupts me with a raised voice, "Eleven o'clock. I know! Go!"

I shut the door behind me. I see Randall standing by my car as I press the unlock button on the fob. As I approach him, he opens the driver's side door for me. Hope for a fun evening washes over me, and Haley cannot take that away right now. Even if the text she got from that Jesse person is going to be on my mind for the rest of the evening.

"Why thank you, sir." I quickly check the time on my phone. "Seven thirty. A little late, but I'm sure we haven't missed much."

Randall's shoulders stiffen like he's just remembered something important. "Oh? It's later than I thought it was." He rubs the back of his neck, glancing at me with a hint of hesitation before stepping back.

"Everything okay?"

"Shoot, Theo, something just came up I gotta handle," he says, his voice tight but steady. He taps the glass of the car window with two fingers, avoiding my gaze for a second before looking me in the eye. "But I promise I'll be at the bonfire. Swear it."

I tilt my head. "Okay? But you don't know where Lianna lives."

His hand grips my shoulder for a quick squeeze, then he's already halfway down the driveway, moving like he's racing the clock.

"It's 54 East Pine," I shout, unsure if he's heard me.

"Got it! See you there!" he yells back, throwing both of his thumbs up in the air without looking back.

I scratch my head, watching him disappear farther down my street. I climb in the driver's seat and pull the seatbelt across my chest. Feeling confused is the understatement of the century.

Did Haley scare him off? Did my father say something that was too awkward? A piece of me feels like I'll never know what happened here tonight, but a bigger piece of me knows I will probably not see Randall at the bonfire this evening. At this moment, I'm just not sure whether I should feel acrimonious or just...plain heartbroken.

FOURTEEN

The smoke from the bonfire billows in the sky above Lianna's roof. As soon as I step out of the car, the scent of roasted marshmallows wafts in my direction. The crackling from the wood burning echoes from the backyard, not to mention the familiar voices laughing and hollering in jest.

Ms. Gloria opens the front door and spreads her arms to welcome me. "Oh my goodness, well, if it isn't my second-born coming to grace us with his presence!"

I wrap my arms around her and see Lianna's little brother, Trevor, poking his head out from inside the living room. He rolls his eyes and shouts, "How many times do I have to tell you, Mom, *I am* your second-born. It's like I'm not even here!"

"Oh, he's just jealous," she whispers in my ear and squeezes tighter. "Don't mind him."

"How are you doing, Ms. Gloria?" Our embrace ends, and she invites me inside.

"I'm doing well, Theo. More importantly, how are *you* doing? I heard about this Randall fellow."

I already knew Ms. Gloria was under the impression Randall was coming this evening after I received a text from Lianna apologizing in advance. Ms. Gloria has always been invested in my love life. When Damien broke up with me, it was Ms. Gloria who wanted to egg his car. She has even gone so far as to try and set me up with the receptionist at her podiatrist's office.

"So when is he coming? I'll need to pull out the good china." Ms. Gloria pulls back the front window curtain with two fingers, looking side to side.

"Who are you kidding?" Lianna interrupts her mother's investigation. "The only 'good china' we have is paper product and has the word 'Dixie' written on it." She throws her arms around my neck and pulls me by my hands toward the back door. "Theo, baby! I'm so glad you came!"

I close the sliding glass door and see the flames from the fire igniting the yard as if the sun never set. Tristan is holding a green beer bottle to his mouth, singing along to Bruno Mars' "Billionaire Song." His pitch is off-key, but he doesn't seem to care. There is a recycling can right next to the fire, full of those green bottles that must have helped him prepare for his sold-out concert. His audience consists of a roaring duo, Shelby and Kelly, whose laughter echoes as high as the trees, their arms waving from side to side, cheering on our friend.

It's Kelly who first notices my presence and jumps out of her lawn chair to embrace me. "I'm so happy to see you! It's been way too long!"

"I know!" I mirror her excitement and pick her up,

swinging her around in a full one-eighty. "You have to tell me all about your brother's wedding."

Kelly's brother, Caleb, is two years older than us and the first gay person I knew. In high school, Caleb who made history in our town by bringing his boyfriend from a neighboring school to prom. I remember seeing the two of them pose for photos, standing by the pink azalea bush out front of Kelly's parents' house. Caleb is tall and muscular, like a model for *Men's Fitness*. His sharp jawline had both girls and guys wishing they were the ones he was taking to the dance. No one had issues with Caleb because of his sexuality. Jocks never messed with him, and even those jocks' fathers were always impressed with how agile and athletic Caleb was.

The only person that had an issue with Caleb was his father, Mr. Henry. One year at the end-of-the-year sports ceremony, Mr. Henry publicly shamed his son for being a disgrace to their family when Caleb thanked his boyfriend, Anthony, for helping him during their gym workouts together.

Kelly's mother, Ms. Anne, was so embarrassed by her husband's reaction to their son, she asked him for a divorce the next day. Kelly wasn't all that upset about the news, since Caleb was the person she looked up to the most—and no one, not even her father, was going to put him down and get away with it. After the divorce, the judge granted visitation every other weekend for Mr. Henry with, specifically by his request, just Kelly.

Not Caleb.

Caleb's story was one that stuck with me prior to my coming out. To know someone can be loved and have the support of many, but still have that one important person in their life not accept them was scary.

Luckily, Caleb outgrew his father's abandonment. He persevered, which was evident by his and Anthony's destination wedding held in Hawaii one year ago.

"Oh, Theo, that wedding was a lifetime ago. Caleb and Anthony are going to be adopting a child soon. I'm going to be an auntie!" Kelly flips her hair and gives me the most curious smirk. "But let's talk about Randall. I hear he's Southern and wears camouflage. He sounds sexy as hell."

"Oh?" I try to force a smile. "I didn't know that about Caleb." I should have known that fact about my friend's life. "That's exciting!"

"Yeah, yeah! Thanks! But...Randall," Kelly redirects.

"If you think having a Southern accent and wearing camouflage are the only two characteristics that make a man sexy, I worry about you, Kel." I laugh.

"That was so funny, I forgot to laugh!" She wraps her arm around my shoulders. "But seriously, when is he coming? I want to meet the man who makes my friend happy." Kelly peeks through the sliding glass door as if Randall is inside the house already being harassed by Ms. Gloria.

"I'm not sure where he's at, honestly," I mimic her curiosity.

From her lawn chair, Shelby presses pause on her phone, stopping Tristan's strange and very pitchy rendition of Katy's Perry's "Roar." She shouts at me that she's not going to get out of her seat to say hello to me, and I'll need to *walk my ass* over to her for a proper greeting. My nervousness about Randall not showing erases with Shelby's assertiveness and beckoning.

On my way over to Shelby, I connect with a drunken Tristan, who attempts one of his fist-bump-handshake-thumb-tug-of-war greetings I always fumble over. He pulls me in for one of those manly-man hugs he likes to give to prove he's not afraid to show everyone he's okay with being intimate with another man.

During our embrace, Shelby dismisses her previous stance and stands up, walks over to us, and begins to rub her hand through my hair. "We missed you, slugger."

I roll my eyes and let out a chuckle. "Thanks, Dad."

"Speaking of dads, how is good ole Mr. Tom?" Shelby asks.

Before Randall, this was the question I typically got from people I haven't spoken to in a while. They always want to know how my brain-injured father is doing. Is he still rhyming? Is he still being aggressive behind closed doors? Is he still eating raw food from the freezer?

Once people realized my father was going to survive long past his accident, the fascination of such a medical miracle, on top of how my family could possibly deal with such a traumatic event, was so intriguing that every conversation I had started with *How is your dad doing?*

"He's hanging in there, still being a pain in my ass." My typical answer usually causes a nervous giggle from the other party; however, I revel in the fact that I cause them a slight panic. Who in their right mind would talk about their disabled father that way?

"You're so mean to him, T." She shoves my shoulder. "Make sure to give him a big hug from his girl, Shelbs."

"You want one, buddy?" Tristan shoves a golden, oozing marshmallow in my face.

I shake my head. "Only if it comes with chocolate and a graham cracker."

"Are we having smores?" a voice cuts through the crackles of the burning wood, soft but clear. For a split second, it's Randall's voice, low and inviting, the way I hoped he'd come across to my friends all evening when they officially met him.

My breath catches as I turn. My heart stutters for reasons I can't pin down, and I freeze. Bright cerulean blue eyes meet mine, the firelight flickering against their shine.

It's not Randall. It's Javier.

His hair is the first thing that locks me in place as a sudden comfort washes over me. That singular gray streak cuts through his rich black hair, like someone painted it there on purpose. He's standing a few feet away, hands tucked into his jacket pockets, his guitar case casually slung over his shoulder.

"Hi," I say, my voice caught somewhere between excitement and timidity, like I can't decide whether to subtly wave or jump up and down. Choosing to wave, my arm wails more like the *Forest Gump* GIF than it does anything that resembles subtly.

"*Hola*," his Latinx cadence is sharp but leaves an impression that lasts. "Trevor didn't say there was going to be smores tonight."

"Trevor?"

"Yeah." He smiles and puts his hand out toward me before I take it into mine. "Sorry I couldn't stay and talk earlier at the restaurant. I don't know if Lianna told you, but I'm Trevor's guitar teacher. That's how I know her. I give Trevor private guitar lessons every Wednesday and Saturday. Before Lianna told me about it, Ms. Gloria already invited me to stay for the bonfire tonight."

"Oh, cool!" Shelby's excitement goes unnoticed since Javier's stare hasn't left mine. "I'm glad you could stay, Mr... Javier! I'll start toasting you a 'mello."

"Please," Javier's attention breaks before he waves his hand, "just call me Javi. I save the *mister* for the kids I teach. I'm pretty sure I'm y'all's age."

"My bad, Javi," Shelby shouts. "My name is Shelby. This drunkard is Tristan," she points at Tristan playing air guitar around the fire.

"And I'm Theo if you didn't remember from earlier," I say, still thinking about how soft but firm his hand was. "I'm glad you could join us."

"Of course I remember. You're pretty hard to forget." His wide smile shows his top lip broadcasting a small but starkly defined scar. *God, I love a lip scar.* He thanks me and begins to pull his guitar strap from his shoulder over his head. He leans it on a lawn chair before taking a seat. He lifts his head, and his eyes give off a flirtatious gleam accompanied by a seductive smirk. "I hope it's okay I sit here?"

"Of course." I grab another beer from the cooler stationed next to the other empty lawn chair I claim for my plus one who hasn't showed. "I'm going to get a chocolate bar for my smores. Want one?"

"*¡Definitivamente! Gracias!*"

Maybe it's the confidence boost from the beers tonight, but I don't feel as nervous to speak to him as I have the past two times I've met him in real life. I'm not sure what this means, but at least for just one moment, I forgot I was waiting for someone else.

~

I'm FOUR BEERS DEEP, and Randall still hasn't shown. Maybe he's lost? Maybe the smoke from the bonfire will signal him here? I did give him the address, but God knows if he remembered it with how fast he was high-tailing away from me earlier. It's eleven o'clock, and the longer we go into the night, the more I feel I'm being stood up. It's hard.

I keep checking my phone thinking he's going to message me or something. Every time I see a blank screen, I'm reminded he doesn't text. He doesn't use social media. How in the world do you get ahold of someone these days without those two things? I'm starting to think his refusal to use technology to communicate is just his subtle way of telling me he doesn't want to commit. Or he was simply scared away after meeting my dad or Haley tonight.

Fuck. I should have been in the room when Haley came upstairs.

We had a phenomenal first date, and he promised he'd be here tonight, but he doesn't even have the courtesy to tell me he's going to be late, or not going to show.

"He had to have gotten lost. Got fed up and went home," I slur my words, sensing Lianna coming up from behind me.

"I'm sorry." Lianna hovers over my shoulders and whispers in my ear, "Maybe he's a jerk and makes empty promises." She hands me another beer. "This is strike one for him."

"We had such a good time..." I start, but Lianna covers my mouth with her hand.

"You know who doesn't have any strikes? Javier. Good ol' sexy music teacher, Mr...I don't know his last name because Trevor just calls him Mr. Javier. Look at him over there.

Going to town on that s'more." She positions my head to the right.

Javier is sitting by the fire, chatting with Kelly and Tristan. With each bite of his s'more, his lips wrap around the cracker without letting any crumbs fall. I don't know if it's the last beer I chugged or not, but whatever his mouth is doing is making me quite aroused...and hungry.

A HALF HOUR GOES BY, and I hear a metal jingle from the fence surrounding Lianna's yard. The metal lock slides, unlocking the gate. At first, I think it's Randall finding his way through the door for the hundredth time tonight, but knowing my luck, that's not going to happen. Four bodies walk through the entrance, tugging along coolers, chairs, and black plastic bags filled with loud, clinking bottles.

"Ronnie!" Tristan stands and jumps over the flames of the fire like a complete idiot. He runs over to the four newcomers.

The girl standing next to Ronnie laughs. "This bromance is going to be the death of me!"

Tristan hugs the guy with the long brown hair shimmering in the moonlight...or the back porch spotlight. My bleary eyes can't tell the difference at this point.

Kelly pulls her chair closer and tells me Ronnie works with Tristan at the farmers market on the weekends, and they've become close.

I feel like I don't know who my friends are anymore. Their lives have drastically changed. I had no clue Tristan even worked at a farmers market. I thought he was taking over his father's antique shop in Rivera Park. With going back to school and focusing on helping my family, I feel like I've placed my friendships on the back burner. My stomach curdles with the thought. If there is anyone to blame for the separation between myself and Shelby, Kelly, and Tristan, is it all on me?

With throwing myself into school, spending my nights taking care of my father, and trying to find out ways to provide for my mother and sister, I have lost all sense of connection I have with my chosen family: the friends who got me through my coming out, my break-up with Damien, and even my father's accident. They were the ones to support me through the hard times, and what did I do? Phase them out of my life so much, I don't even know what they do for a living or that they are going to become aunts.

I look over to Lianna and give her a pouty face. "I think I'm going to head out. I'll call an Uber and leave my car here tonight."

"No, please don't go." She puts her hand on my lap. "My mom is going to bring out her famous Jello shooters."

"How are you okay with Yu-en just bailing on you at the last minute? I'm sitting over here taking Randall not coming so personally."

"You know what your problem is, Theo?"

"Tell me," I mumble.

"You don't live your life for you. You say you want to. You set limits with people. You put up a hard exterior. But when a guy comes around and gives you attention, you give everything you have back to him. You forget about living life for you." She shakes her open beer bottle at me, splashing me with drops of her IPA.

"I'm feeling attacked," I say dryly.

"As you should," Lianna says. "Jello shooter?"

"You know how much I love your mom's Jello shooters," I remark, pulling back my resistance to fun. "Thanks, Li."

"No problem, babe. Let's drink."

Ms. Gloria comes from behind the group and lays a tray of assorted Jello-filled cups on the table, replacing the bag of marshmallows and box of graham crackers. The blue, red, lime-green, and orange colors of gelatin distract me enough I don't even realize two hours go by.

"You're staying the night." Lianna points her finger.

From what I can tell, that was a demand and not a request. My vision is even blurrier, and my face is warm. My bladder is full, and I'm at the point of the night that I need to break the seal. "I have to go to the bathroom."

"Oh my gosh, I need to go to the bathroom too! Let's pee together," Lianna hollers over the blaring music, a song I've heard a bajillion times, but have no clue what the words are.

In college, there was not one bathroom Lianna and I didn't christen together. It was a known fact that if Lianna had to pee, then so did Theo. We considered it a safety precaution. There were so many stories we heard about girls getting abused or taken advantage of during solo pees that we didn't want to risk it. When we would go together, there would not be any need to worry, which made the stream seem effortless.

There is a bathroom in the hallway right between Lianna and Trevor's individual bedrooms. It's spacious with cold, white tiles. A steel-gray paint covers the walls surrounding the matching tile backsplash and dual mirror set-up that hovers over his-and-her sinks. There are two standing showers on each side of the room, which Trevor probably enjoys because he doesn't have to worry about stepping in

Lianna's hairball-clogged drain, which I know for a fact she never cleans. It's so gross.

The only thing they fight over when it comes to this gigantic bathroom is the one toilet that sits opposite from the sinks. I check myself in the mirror and immediately see the one giveaway that I'm tipsy. Bright red blotches circle my neck and down my chest. I turn the sink on and pat some water on my face and under my chin.

After Lianna finishes draining, I take my seat on the throne and begin to break the royal seal. Mid-pee, Kelly comes bursting through the bathroom door—a door I thought I locked behind me. Kelly comes barreling in with three half-filled shot glasses. "I brought us double shots of cinnamon whiskey, bitches!"

"I feel like you miscounted your fingers with those pours, Kel." I stand to my feet.

"Or I just might have whiskey stains on my carpet after she spilled it coming upstairs." Lianna pulls her tucked-in blouse from her pants.

"Oh, shut up! You're lucky I thought of you both, since you never think of me when you go do this awkward-ass pee thing," Kelly slurs her words between hiccups. "Where is Randall, Theo? I want to meet your army daddy."

I roll my eyes, tightening my belt buckle. "You would know just as much as me. I have no clue where he is."

"He stood you up?" Kelly hands both me and Lianna a half-empty shot glass, and on the count of three, we shoot back what's left.

I return to the mirror, and my reflection illustrates a messy, frizzy situation on top of my head, where usually a combed and hair-sprayed side-do perfectly sits. I run my finger through my hair and lay it nicely toward the left. I turn to Lianna, who is bent over Kelly's face flossing our friend's teeth—something I'd rather not inquire about.

My audience is preoccupied as I ask, "Do you think I could just take a shower and go to bed?"

Lianna's cackling and Kelly's loud groaning leave my request unanswered.

Once the girls leave the bathroom, I slip off my clothes and jump into the shower. I close the glass door and twist the knob in the direction of the red line. It takes a moment for the water to change from a brisk chill to a warm heat, which always does the sobering trick for me. I close my eyes and embrace the steady stream.

The door creaks open, and I assume it's just Lianna or Kelly coming back in to grab the shot glasses left on the sink. I hear a belt buckle loosen and heavy jeans drop to the floor.

"Kel? Li?" I turn the water off. A chill surrounds my body as I stand in the shower dripping.

"Oh, sorry." A manly cough clears the throat of someone I wasn't expecting to walk into the bathroom while I was in the shower. "It's Javier. I just really needed to go to the bathroom. You can keep showering."

I stick my arm out and grab the towel hanging on the rack beside the shower. I pull it behind the closed curtain and begin to dry my body from head to toe. "I was just getting out anyway. I was going to head to bed. I think I've had enough for tonight." I step out, the towel wrapped around my waist.

"Very responsible of you." He flushes the toilet before pulling his shirt up. He tucks it under his chin while he buckles his belt tight. I subtly sneak a peek at his exposed midsection. His muscles are well-defined, shaped to perfection. His skin is soft and glowing, tanned in a golden fashion.

"You could say that." I clear my throat and look away before he catches me staring. "Or I'm just running away from my friends out of embarrassment over being stood up."

"Someone did say you had a date coming." He turns to face me. "I'm sorry he didn't show. For what it's worth..." He pauses.

I hang on his last word, wondering what he was going to say next. He shakes his head and lets out a hesitant exhale. He aborts his sentence until I push a little, "Worth?"

"For what it's worth, he's an idiot for ghosting someone like you." He walks over to the sink and starts to wash his hands. "That's all I was going to say."

"Someone like me?" I blush.

"I've been teaching Trevor guitar for two years now, and you are the only thing Ms. Gloria and Lianna talk about. They say how amazing of a person you are and what you do for your family. It's quite impressive, to be honest," he pauses, "plus, you're super cute. So, he's an idiot for not showing up tonight."

"Oh?" I'm taken back by what he says. "Well... thank you. I guess?"

"No problem. I'm gonna catch an Uber home. This twenty-four-year-old body feels older than it is. It's been a long week, but it was nice seeing you again tonight, Theo. Hope we can do it again another time soon."

"Yeah, definitely. Maybe next time, we won't end up in the bathroom together at the end of the night."

"Or maybe we will..." He gives me a slow, appreciative once-over before stepping out of the bathroom and shutting the door behind him.

As I brush my teeth with a disposable toothbrush Ms. Gloria keeps in the cabinet, I ruminate on the interaction I just had with Javier. I'm at a genuine loss of thoughts. I keep replaying his words in my head. *Or maybe we will.*

What the hell does that mean?

Does he want me?

Do I want him?

But Randall...

I make my way over to the corner shelf where I see clean, folded clothes lying. I find a giant t-shirt, which is probably way too loose for Trevor, and some boxer shorts.

When I leave the bathroom, I drag my hands across the walls of the hallway to make sure I don't fall, even though I'm certain my steps are fairly stable. I end up in Lianna's bedroom and crawl into her bed. I pull the covers up to my shoulders and turn my body to its side to look out the window.

Before I fall asleep, I tell my brain over and over again, about twenty times, that I just want to dream about hot, naked Javier. I try to imagine myself cursing out Randall in our next class together and telling him I met someone else. I tell myself to dream about forgetting who Randall Stevens is.

I close my eyes and start falling in and out of sleep. From what I can tell, my dreams are disobeying me.

They show me confronting Randall, but the outcome is peaceful. He broadcasts his bright smile, and everything seems to be better again.

Goddamn these dreams.

FIFTEEN

My head throbs when I pull myself up from Lianna's soft pillows. Dryness coats the insides of my mouth before I reach for a water bottle on the bedside table. The bottle most likely belongs to Lianna, but at this point, we've shared at least one bodily fluid or another over the years, so I don't even care.

The floor creaks as I put my weight on my feet and make my way downstairs. The smell of bacon and French toast lures me toward the kitchen, where Ms. Gloria stands and flips over-easy eggs in the frying pan.

"Good morning, party monster!" Ms. Gloria's cadence slams back and forth in my head like a ping-pong tournament.

"Morning, Ms. G," I mumble.

"I want to say thank you for not throwing up in my living room last night. It seems like you did the responsible thing and put yourself to bed." She pokes her head over my shoulder and glares at Tristan as he's sprawled out on the couch with a car-washing bucket in hand. "Unlike *some people*."

My temples throb, and nausea flutters in my stomach like the fizz from a shaken soda bottle. With my hangover being so bad this morning, it makes me never want to drink alcohol again. Until the next party I'm invited to, that is.

Once I realize Randall never showed last night, resentment runs through my gut. Warmth circulates through my body, leading up to the deep furrow of my eyebrows that I can't seem to shake.

Not only am I pissed off I was stood up, but I feel deeply embarrassed knowing all of my friends were under the impression he was coming. They asked about him repeatedly last night, and I had no clue how to respond.

This is exactly why I don't bring guys home to meet my friends and family. I'm tired of the insecurities men have with me when we get too close. I'm not sure what it was this time with Randall. It could have been that I introduced him to my dad too early, Haley's coldness, or even asking him to meet my friends so early on in our relationship. Whatever it was, I was left wanting something I know I'll never be able to have. Again.

I feel stupid.

Worse, even.

I feel angry. I'm mad at that mahogany-haired, strong but sensitive, muscly liar. I'm mad he took me on the most romantic date—one I couldn't have even dreamed of before—and then chose not to follow through with my invitation to meet my friends. I'm mad he tricked me by being so genuinely nice to my father—so much so, he made me think he could be the one who could handle all my baggage.

I'm mad. I'm so mad.

But mostly I'm hurt.

"Good morning, everyone." Lianna struts into the kitchen looking like a lingerie model taking a ten-minute break from a luxurious photoshoot for *Women's Health*.

"How do you look so perfect, even after the night we just had?" A placemat from the dining room table flies past my face and hits Lianna in the chest. Shelby, appearing exhausted, lets out a moan as soon as she realizes throwing it at Lianna took way too much energy for her this morning.

"How many times do I have to tell you all my secrets for hangover prevention?" Lianna reaches into the refrigerator. "Before you go to bed, drink one of these," she pulls out a cold sixteen-ounce Deer Park water bottle as if she is Vanna White, "take two Tylenol," she twists off the plastic cap to the giant bottle of vodka sitting in the middle of the counter, pouring it straight into a clean shot glass she takes from the drying rack, "and take a shot of clear alcohol in the morning. You'll be good as new." She tosses back the mini glass and swallows the warm vodka. Her face is left unbothered, like a champion.

"Are you trying to make me throw up?" I let out a bustling laugh, which I regret as soon as the random burp surfaces as actual vomit in the back of my throat.

I stand up and swiftly leap into the vacant guest bathroom. I cup a handful of sink water and splash my face, hoping to get myself together this morning. As the faucet runs, the thought of Thomas Branson intrudes into my mind, and I immediately remember today is my day to sit with him while my mother goes grocery shopping.

Every Sunday.

After working nights and taking care of him all week, my

mother needs a vacation, and if grocery shopping is her getaway, then I will be sure to make it happen.

I step out of the bathroom and make my way to the living room closet to grab my set of keys. Ms. Gloria keeps everyone's car keys in a lock-box in the closet with her being the only source to unlock it. The number of lives this woman has saved by doing this is actually phenomenal to think about, especially on sobering mornings like this one.

"I'm going to head out," I shout. "Thank you, Ms. Gloria, for hosting this fantastic fire-filled rager."

"No problem, sweetie. Next time, bring your mom. I'd love to see her," Ms. Gloria answers.

The fact she has to ask me to bring my mother, instead of calling herself tells me Ms. Gloria already knows what answer Mom would give her. I can't even recall the last time my mom mentioned a friend's name, let alone an event she went to without wheeling around her husband.

Mom and Ms. Gloria would actually hit it off. Both are hilarious, nurturing, and they would call you out on your bullshit real quick. It's a dream of mine to get my mom *out there*, per se, allow her to see the world, experience new things—something I'm sure she has no idea where to even start if you ask her to suggest something.

The door closes behind me, and beams of sun flash me. I immediately throw my arm over my hungover eyes to block the rays blinding me. The car door shutting at the end of the driveway triggers me to rub my eyes to see who it was. I wipe away the bright chaos, and the blurriness begins to clear.

It's Javier.

He's carrying a brown paper bag and a carton of what seems to be several iced coffees. "*Buenos dias.*" He walks toward me.

"Good morning," the scent of his colognes strengthens, "did you bring breakfast? Ms. Gloria is already in the kitchen catering to all the leftover inebriates."

Javier scoffs, "If I recall, you were one of those inebriates last night." He smiles. "Plus, Ms. G asked me to go out and get some croissants and coffee."

"Did you have fun last night? You didn't stay very long."

"As I recall, you were showering and getting ready for bed when I was heading out. I'm not the only one who left the party early." We share a mutual laugh before Javier continues, "Plus, I thought it was best to sleep in my own bed. I wouldn't want to wake up to any Google reviews from Ms. Gloria saying, '*Horrible teacher. He got drunk and passed out at my house. 0 out of 10, Do Not Recommend.*'"

"Smart decision. We don't need to see your beautiful face on *Dateline*," I say as my body begins to shut down. My heart continues skipping beats as I quickly realize I just blatantly flirted with this man with no censorship. What the hell just slipped out of my mouth?

"You think I'm beautiful, eh?"

My face reddens a deeper shade, similar to the color of fresh blood. I look away, avoiding his response. "I really need to hit the road. It was nice seeing you, Javier."

"Did you want one of these coffees for the road?" He takes the only caramel vanilla chai and hands it to me.

"Thank you," I say, taking the drink, "I feel bad taking the only fancy one."

"Nah, don't. I got that one for you. I thought of you when I saw it on the menu." He notices a stickiness on his hand from dripped caramel and brings his fingers to his mouth, softly licking each one of them clean.

I could watch him lick between his fingers all day, but

after just a couple of seconds—and a quick swipe of my tongue to catch the bit of saliva pooling at the corner of my mouth—I ask, "It's my favorite. How'd you remember?"

"I take note of what matters." He smirks. "Plus, *es una bebida dulce y hermoso*. Just like you."

My cheeks warm as I fight the urge to smile. "I only took two years of Spanish, but did you just call me a sweet and beautiful drink, Javier?" I laugh.

"For two years, your Spanish is pretty good. And, yes, I did. I wouldn't mind having a taste." He raises his eyebrows briefly, giving a playful expression. "And feel free to just call me Javi."

"Oh, well, *Javi*, it looks like the only thing you're going to have a taste of is that caramel on your pretty little face." I point to an area on my own face, right underneath my nose.

"Why don't you get it for me then?" He grins and quickly jerks his head back, teasing me to get closer.

I slowly shake my head and suck in my cheeks as I contemplate what I would do to him. Surprisingly, I don't feel any anxiety in this moment. His looks, his beauty, don't seem to faze me the way they did before the bonfire. Without too much hesitation, I crane my neck toward Javi and find the sticky spot above his lip. I glide my tongue across his skin, and before I pull away, I give him a small kiss on his cheek. I whisper in his ear, "I guess you are pretty sweet too."

"What was the kiss for?"

Astonished by my sudden confidence, I answer, "Take it as a *thank you* for the chai tea."

He takes a couple of steps past me, gently grazing my arm with his. "Anytime, *bello*."

I pull my phone up to my lips. "Hey, Siri," two beeps

come from its speaker, "what does the Spanish word *bello* mean?"

Even though I say it loud and clear, of course she doesn't understand.

"It means *handsome*, you nutball! Be careful driving home," Javi calls out as he reaches the steps of Ms. Gloria's porch.

Leaning back on my heel, I spin around to make my way to my car. I hear Ms. Gloria's excited voice greeting Javier and welcoming him in. Before she shuts the door, she loudly apologizes for the mess and blames the *hungover twenty-somethings* lying across her furniture like tree sloths.

HALFWAY HOME, I hear the alarm go off on my cell phone sitting in the middle console. Siri cuts in to make an announcement, "Thomas Branson's testosterone shot is due today."

After his injury, my dad developed hypogonadism, which led to weakened strength. Because of his low testosterone levels, we need to give him a shot once every two weeks. I am always shocked when that alarm goes off because it tells me just how quickly those past two weeks went. I press the volume button on the side of my phone to silence the alarm because, if I turn it off, I will most likely forget to give him the medication when I get home.

As I'm walking into the house, my mom rushes past, sending an air kiss my way. "Hey, sweetie, did you have fun last night?"

Before I can get an answer out, she interrupts me and tells me my dad's sandwich is in the refrigerator right next to his dinner and peanut butter cracker snack. She keeps every food item for the night huddled on the second shelf of the fridge and never ceases to remind me about the evening meal routine, as if I haven't been following this routine for years.

I yell out to Mom that Ms. Gloria sends her hellos, but her perplexed facial response shows me she has no interest in building any relationships outside of her grocery store alone time. I'm not even sure she has any clue or care in the world who Ms. Gloria is.

I take steps down the hallway, and when I get to my parents' bedroom, I see a pile of clothes on the bed. A sweatshirt, a pair of socks, a t-shirt, sweatpants, underwear, and a stick of deodorant. Those items remind me that tonight is *shower night*. Mom hates to leave this chore to me, but I promised her that since Sundays are her day of rest, where she has time alone by herself, I would do the one task that takes a lot out of her.

My dad is an absolute pain-in-the-ass to help shower. He gets irritable really quickly when the shower seat is *freezing* or when the shower curtain doesn't close all the way. It takes about an hour to get him fully washed and dressed, and that's only because he loves to pick fights at this time. Mom doesn't need the added stress, especially when grocery shopping, a chore in itself, is her only getaway. So I take one for the team and just do it.

I hear Haley barge into the house and throw her belongings in the closet. My plan is to just keep to myself and let her go do her thing downstairs. I'm not in the mood to fight with her tonight.

"Dad," I call out from his bedroom, "make your way to your room. We're going to get you in the shower."

A whimper comes from the kitchen. It's the sort of cry

that demands to be consoled. I make my way toward the sound and poke my head in the direction it's coming from.

It's Haley. She's bent over the breakfast bar, with her forehead lying across one arm. It appears she's holding one of our father's hands as he gently caresses the back of her head with his other.

"Haley? Everything okay?" my voice shakes in preparation for what feels like a dark truth about to be revealed.

"Theo..." She lifts her head from her arm, and her back straightens a bit. Snot hangs from her nose, and she wipes away slobber from her mouth with the collar of her scrubs. Her eyes are blood-red, full of tears. "I think I fucked up. I think I fucked up really bad."

SIXTEEN

The steam from the cup soothes me as I stir the tea with the spoon. Haley's face is buried in her hands, and her tears vibrate the dining room table. I slowly walk the teacup over to her and place it in front of her on the round green placemat. In case she needs to wring out the teabag, I leave the spoon submerged in the hot water.

Her wails echo in the palms of her hands, and she repeats the phrase, "I can't believe I did this," over and over again until her voice croaks and her throat dries out completely.

I give her a moment. It pains me to see her this way. I want to hold her, to hug her, but if I want to get anything out of her, now is not the time.

I tuck the box of teas back into the cabinet along with the squeeze container of honey, and push the giant sugar bowl in the corner of the draining board. Haley's cry quiets, and I slowly turn myself around because I get the feeling she's about ready to talk.

I can see through the wall Haley has up protecting her

from her fear of my judgment and ridicule. She knows what she's about to admit to me is going to come at a price.

"Don't look at me like that," she says, staring off at the wall.

"Are you going to tell me what happened, or do you want me to guess?" My assertive tone sets the mood that I'm not here to let her wallow, but to actually help her. I shuffle my way closer, taking a seat on the barstool at the breakfast bar.

"I swear to you, it's not my fault," she pleads.

To risk her getting defensive and shutting down, I bite down hard on my tongue. I try not to be a stereotypical counseling student by using what I've learned in class on my family, but the technique of reflecting Haley's feelings might help her continue to open up. "You seem really nervous to talk to me right now."

"Nervous? You could say that."

Her resistance is inviting. "Talk to me, Hales. I'm right here."

She huffs her breath, rolls her eyes, and gathers herself in her chair. She clears her voice with a cough and straightens her back, placing her arms on her lap. "I'm worried you're going to judge me. You're my little brother. You're supposed to..."

"Nothing you say will make me love you less. I promise."

"My boyfriend, Jesse. He hurts me." Her quick statement comes matter-of-fact, like she's ripping off a Band-Aid.

I don't know what to say. My fingers curl into tight fists, and I feel the veins in my wrist pulsate.

She stares at me with a look in her eye, begging me to say something.

Anything.

A moment goes by, and I need clarity. "I didn't know you were seeing someone. What do you mean, '*hurts you*'?"

"I've been seeing him for the past two years. I didn't tell anyone about him because I'm not ready to bring him home to meet Mom and Dad. I thought he would change, but he's not changing. I've tried to break up with him before, but it never sticks. He has a hold on me. He makes me feel..." she looks down, "needed."

"Oh, Haley."

"To add just how messed up things are between us, he forces me to do things. When I don't do them, he..." Haley's voice drifts off.

The cat is out of the bag now. There isn't any more time left for reservation. "He *what*, Hales?"

She slowly lifts her head and looks me in the eyes as if what she's about to tell me is what will tear us apart forever. "He hits me."

There was only one other moment in my life that caused my world to come crashing down around me before I heard this news. It was when Haley told me about our dad's accident.

Yet this? This is on a whole different level. The worst thing about this is the victim, my beautiful sister, is standing right here, with her big blue eyes staring straight back at me, afraid of what my response will be.

"What does he make you do?"

Haley slides her hand into the pocket of her scrubs. She pulls out a clear plastic bag and throws it on the counter. Small, round, white pills spill out from the weakened zip lock at the top of the bag.

"Another nurse caught me taking them from the drug lockbox. She threatened to tell my supervisor if I didn't turn myself in." She slams her fist on the table. Her outburst penetrates the room as she shouts, "That stupid bitch has always had it out for me."

"You stole medicine from the hospital where you work, Haley." I throw my hands up in the air, and they fall quickly back to the sides of my body. This revelation ruins me. My thoughts are running aimlessly, trying to figure out what to say next. I whisper with the gentlest tone I can muster, "You were right, Haley. You fucked up."

"What am I going to do, Theo? Jesse needs..."

"I don't give a shit about what Jesse needs. Are you using this stuff too, Haley? Are you using drugs?"

The question comes out before I can think of the repercussions, before I can even tell if I want to know the answer. We were raised around an alcoholic grandmother who always chose to buy herself a wine bottle over buying us birthday cards, and a cousin who was so strung out on heroin, she ended up homeless for two years before she finally admitted herself into a halfway house. We know what drugs and alcohol do to people, what they do to families. Before Dad's accident, Haley and I promised our parents they wouldn't need to worry about us when it came to drugs.

And now this.

Haley's stone-faced expression gives me the answer I didn't want. But it's still not enough. "Tell me the truth, Haley. Are you using drugs?"

"I've tried them." She quivers. "I'm a nurse, Theo. I know better than to take them routinely like Jesse does."

"Like I said, I don't care about Jesse. I'm not talking about Jesse. Stop bringing him up. I'm asking you, Haley Branson. What does '*I don't take them routinely*' even fucking mean?"

A knock on the door cools the heat I feel flushing up my neck and encompassing my entire face. My stomach drops, and Haley and I lock gazes, attempting to use telepathy and guess who could be at our front door right now.

The door creaks open. "Hello?" a familiar voice calls out. "Theo? It's Randall. You home?"

Haley takes the sleeve of her coat and wipes the tears from her face. "Whoever just opened our front door, can you send them away? I can't take letting someone see me this way."

I make my way toward the entrance in hopes that Randall doesn't decide to break more boundaries and begin walking up the stairs of the house he just let himself in without permission.

"What are you doing here?" I put my hand on the door, blocking his ability to come past the frame.

"I just wanted to swing by..."

"And break into my house?" I interrupt. "You should go. I wasn't expecting company."

His bottom lip pushes up his top, and the corners of his mouth sink into the cutest frown I have ever seen in my entire life. But I am not going to let that distract me. I don't want him here right now. He stood me up at the bonfire, and now he's interrupting me finding out Haley's an addict, or drug dealer at best. I don't have it in me to hear Randall's excuses as to why he wasn't there last night.

"Look, I'm sorry I didn't make it to the bonfire. I got held up with something and lost track of time. Once I realized, it was way too late, and I had already messed up."

I run my fingers through my hair and rub my hand down the side of my face, across my open mouth, and down off my chin. "Randall, I appreciate you coming here to tell me this, but I really don't have time to talk with you right now. I'm in the middle of something."

"I can come back," he takes a step backwards, "I just didn't want any more time to go by before you..." Randall stretches his neck and listens as Haley whimpers from the dining room. His attention returns to me. "Is everything alright with your sister?"

"It's none of your business," my response is as sharp as a knife. "You should leave. I'll see you in class tomorrow."

Randall takes the hint and shakes his head. He knows he's not going to get anywhere with my mood being like it is. "I understand you're upset with me, but please try not to let it spill over onto anyone else. I'm not sure what's going on, but it seems like she really needs you right now. I just don't want you to wake up tomorrow feeling regretful."

He takes a step back, and my impulsivity makes me close the door on him without saying goodbye. His message is ringing loudly in my head, and I can't help but stand in place, losing myself in the blandness of our closed front door.

He's right, though. I am mad at him, and I think those feelings are rolling over to this confrontation with Haley. I'm coming at her with full persecution, thinking she's some addict who can't control herself, but instead she's being controlled by some asshole boyfriend we've never heard about before. That's not the Haley I know.

She needs me.

She's coming to me for a reason.

I need to do better.

Respond better.

"Who were you speaking to?" Haley switched from the dining room to the couch in the living room, her feet curled underneath her, a fleece blanket over her lap.

"This guy I'm, I guess...talking to? I don't even know. But he did say something that resonated with me."

"What's that?"

"I'm not being a good brother sitting here questioning you about what you're doing wrong. You already know what you did wasn't the greatest idea. So, I apologize." I pull back the fleece blanket she's using and crawl underneath it with her.

"Yeah, believe me. I'm punishing myself enough as it is."

I lay my head on her shoulder, using her long blonde hair as a pillow. "So what do we do?"

"We?" A single tear falls from her face, landing on the back of my hand holding hers on her lap.

"Yes." I rub my hand against the blanket, wiping away the wetness. "Whatever you decide, I'm here for you. But I'm going to need you to be honest with me about everything. You think you can do that?"

"I promise I have only used painkillers twice since being with Jesse. One night, I couldn't sleep after I pulled my back lifting a heavy patient. Then I used them again the other day..." she trails off.

"What happened the other day?"

"Jesse pushed me to the ground after I told him I didn't want to steal anymore. Then he kicked me in my ribs." She gently leans back and pulls up her shirt to her midriff. She pulls away a layer of tape wrapped around her torso, showing a large dark purple blotch on her side.

My throat locks, and I can't seem to find any gumption to speak. Anger flushes through me but is masqueraded by pure sadness, an emotion that begs me not to let it escape, because if it does, my façade of a supportive rock will crumble. How could anyone do this to another person and get away with it?

"I'm sorry, I shouldn't have shown you." She re-wraps the tape as if she regrets showing her little brother a scene from a gory horror movie.

Even though I'm still pissed off at him, Randall stopping by and checking in totally saved me from going postal before I had all the facts. He reminded me to listen, which I wasn't doing, and I could have easily caused strife between me and Hales. The pain in her eyes is evidence enough she feels backed into a corner. A corner she's been punched and kicked into so many times. I'll be damned if I let it keep happening.

"No," I place my hand over her bandages, "I'm glad you showed me. We're going to handle this. We're going to get through this as a family."

"Mom and Dad are going to be so disappointed in me," she says. "Well, Mom will be. I'd rather her not know anything."

I'm not sure how to respond to her comment about our father being disappointed. I hardly ever think about how he would react to anything related to us these days. The silence in the room breaks when I ask a random question, one Haley wasn't prepared for, "Out of curiosity...do you regret asking Mom to keep Dad alive that night?"

"Whoa," Haley says, letting out a breath, "I think about that a lot. Knowing what we know now? I think I would have advocated more for us to let him go. He loved us a lot, and I know he wouldn't have wanted to see any of us in pain like we have been in. How about you?"

"I agree," I say, "I think he would have been happier if we let him go." Silence returns as we sit and think about what we've put into the atmosphere.

A couple moments go by, and Haley and I talk about her

next steps in telling her superiors what all she's done for Jesse. She cries, but she knows it's the right thing to do. I continue to remind her I'm not going anywhere, and she's brave enough to survive any consequence that may follow.

Everything she's worked for over the years, dealing with our father's brain injury.

Every long night studying for exams or prepping for nursing position interviews.

Every patient she's put so much energy and knowledge into saving, and every patient's family member she's delivered both bad and good news to.

It might all be for nothing.

But at least we'll figure out how she can survive this.

Survive Jesse.

She's my sister. And in this family, we can survive anything.

A FEW MINUTES pass as I settle into my room for the night, the exhaustion shedding itself off me like a second skin. I've changed into an old T-shirt, tossed my shoes into the corner, and now I'm sitting on the edge of my bed, trying to shake off the weight of everything my sister and I discussed. Downstairs, I can still hear her voice as she talks to Dad, steady and present. It's comforting, in a way, knowing she's here, doing what needs to be done.

I reach for the journal in my bedside table, the one I always think about writing in but never do. Tonight, though, I can't ignore the urge to shake off some feelings and put something down.

Flipping to a blank page, I start writing to Randall. At

first, I vent about him not showing up for me and jot down all the names I wish I could call him. But as I write, my frustration twists into something softer.

Something kinder.

I find myself thanking him for not coming to the bonfire, realizing it reminded me why I don't want to get into anything serious with anyone right now. Then I thank him again, for giving me the space to spend time with Javi instead, which was an unexpected and welcomed surprise. And then I find myself thanking him for suggesting what he said tonight about not wanting to regret saying anything harmful to Haley.

By the time I reach the end of the letter, I'm still at little to no resolve, torn between wanting to hold my ground and feeling this raw, aching need for someone to share moments like these with.

Someone like Randall.

Or even someone like Javier?

After tonight, I just need to rest. The boy drama can wait. Although, I have a feeling I'll still be lying here for a while, stuck between Javi's bold reliability and Randall's unpredictable pull, wondering why neither one will leave my mind completely.

SEVENTEEN

I'm awakened by a string of texts from Haley this morning outlining the consequences she's been given after declaring to Human Resources and the Board of Nursing that she's stolen medication twice from the hospital.

> Two weeks' suspension

> Three years' probation and re-evaluation when that time is up

> Random urine tests twice a week

> A job relocation within the medical center that has no direct patient care

> It's strange to say, but I'm so relieved I'm not hiding from the truth anymore.

I'm happy to know she's taking the outcomes positively, and she feels good about her decision to confess. Although it's probably nice to have the truth out there, staring her in the face, it also has to be a consolation that she hasn't been completely banned from the field she's worked so hard in.

All because of *that* abusive, manipulative asshole.

Last night, I promised Hales I wasn't going to share her story with Mom. Haley doesn't want to put more things on Mom's plate, additional things that will most likely keep her up at night. It's not the decision I would make, but this experience is not mine to make decisions about. It's not my story to tell. Haley will tell Mom when the time is right, and she'll do it in her own way.

I'm not going to take that away from her; however, I will most likely ruminate on it until she does it. A part of me is jealous. Even though she doesn't know it, Mom has been graced with not having to deal with the new anxieties about Haley, like I have.

I have to trust the process.

I have to trust my sister.

For the next two weeks, Haley is going to leave the house at her normal time, and she's going to spend some time with friends she hasn't seen in a while since being with Jesse. Over their time together, he's isolated her from everyone she's ever loved, which honestly explains her constant irritability toward Mom and me. We're the two people she couldn't isolate from, even though Jesse probably wanted her to.

Before I went to sleep last night, I sent Haley a link to a free domestic violence group that takes place in a small church two neighborhoods over. She said she'd check it out, now that she has two weeks of time to recharge and prepare for her new nursing job as a cardiac transplant coordinator.

Another concern I have is how Jesse is going to take this news. I'm scared to death about what he has the ability to do or make her do. From what Haley told me last night, she doesn't think she's ready to be finished with him completely, which hurts my heart, but she is going to demand they take a break from their relationship until he either goes to rehab or seeks outpatient substance abuse treatment. I, for one, think he needs all the above—mental health treatment for his anger and aggression, substance abuse treatment, and a clean break —away from my sister or his neck—either one will work.

If he doesn't leave her be, or if she ever feels in danger, we hashed out a plan. If he shows up, she calls the police first, no matter what. If calling the police takes time or makes things too obvious for her, she will call or text me instead. Even if the phone rings only once, I'll drop everything and use my *Find Me* app to locate her, while I call the police myself. We came up with a code, something simple: if she says or texts "Easy Peasy," I know she's in trouble and can't talk. We chose something seemingly positive just in case that can throw Jesse off. Not to mention, she and I both know nothing in our lives is ever *Easy Peasy*.

The plan has its flaws, but it's the only one Haley approves of. The thought of her needing to use a code to signal danger makes me sick, but at least now she knows she's not alone in this.

Two hours later, I get settled into my seat and get ready for class to start. Images of my sister's taped and bruised ribs flash in my mind as I look around the room and see a post on the wall with a giant circle and the words *Power and Control* written over top of it. The graphic explains several different tactics abusers use to gain power and control over their victims.

Financial abuse.

Physical abuse.

Sexual abuse.

These are just some of the words plastered around the circular image.

A cool wave of air touches my neck as Randall quickly comes from behind to take the seat next to me. His military attire has returned, combat boots and all.

"How'd everything go last night with your sister? I was worried 'bout ya." He clasps his fingers around a pencil poking out from behind his ear.

"Everything's better. Haley is taking some much-needed time off work the next couple of days. Thanks for asking." I keep focus straight ahead, refusing to look at him. Deep down, I hate that I'm thanking him after he completely embarrassed me by not showing up to the bonfire. How could I be so stupid to let a guy's lack of communication and care affect me so much? I've set boundaries for so long to protect myself from having these exact thoughts and feelings, but this Southern piece of man pie just swoops in and makes me forget the walls I've put up were built for a reason.

Men will always run. They can't handle not being my full attention, and I refuse to put aside my friends, my family, *my dad* for just one person. If Randall knew exactly what he walked into last night, if he knew exactly what my sister was confessing to me, he'd regret ever coming over.

My life is not...

"Normal?" The end of Randall's question catches me off guard as it echoes my thought.

"What?" I growl.

"I was askin' if things over your house are ever normal? Like, whatever it was, it seemed like your sister was really going through it, and, once again, it fell on you to fix it."

He's right. Things at my house are never *normal*, and I always find myself in the middle of it.

"Someone has to do it, right?" I attempt to give the fakest smirk I can muster. "By the way, I appreciate how you were able to calm me down last night when I needed it, but I really would like you to start letting me know somehow if you plan to show up to my house uninvited."

"Oh? I guess I was right when doubtin' my decision to come over."

My eyes continue to peer into the distance intently. "Hmph, I wonder why." I shuffle my notebook and papers together on my desk and straighten them up as if the organization means more to me than what he's about to say.

Keep it cool, Theo.

"Well, I fucked up." From my peripheral, I see him scratching the back of his head. "I should have been there. At the bonfire."

The bones in my neck couldn't have cracked loud enough, turning my head quickly toward him. "Then why weren't you?"

"I...I just couldn't make it. I'm sorry."

"At least I wasn't alone. I had my friends. I met some guy named Javier though." A small choke surfaces from my throat. I wasn't expecting to throw in the name of Trevor's music teacher to see if it would make him jealous. I guess my subconscious had other ideas. "It was a lot of fun. You missed a really good time."

"Javier?" The name slips off Randall's tongue with an air of envy and regret.

Dr. Ambrose makes her way into the classroom with her fancy brown leather briefcase strapped around her shoulder and her Gucci high heels strutting as if she owns the whole university. Her entrances typically cause conversations to stop, so I'm appreciative of the reprieve.

"Theo?" she calls out as she unpacks her bag on the podium. "I finally have your first GA assignment. I apologize it's taken me so long, but I promise work will pick up for you this semester. Can you meet me after class?"

Nodding first with appreciation, I respond, "Of course, Dr. Ambrose."

She straightens up and focuses her attention on the rest of the class. She requests that we take out our textbooks and turn to page one hundred sixty, the chapter on Cognitive Behavioral Therapy. Not a minute past the class's start time, she asks aloud, "Who here can tell me what CBT is?"

"It's a therapeutic modality in which the therapist focuses on changing cognitive distortions and behaviors in hopes of improving emotional regulation and developing effective coping strategies," the blonde know-it-all in the front of the class calls out without raising her hand.

"Yes, thank you for that, Alexis. What are cognitive distortions?" Dr. Ambrose gently lifts the palm of her hand toward Alexis, indicating she doesn't want her to respond, to let another person prove they've read today's chapter before class.

"Inaccurate and negatively biased thoughts," Randall mumbles to the left of me.

Not hearing his answer, Dr. Ambrose asks, "Anyone?"

I speak out, "Inaccurate and negatively biased thoughts." I look over at Randall, gesturing for him to take credit, but all he gives back is a smile and sense of pride that I echoed what he said a moment before.

"Yes, thank you, Theo." Dr. Ambrose makes her way to the other side of the classroom. "A cognitive behavioral therapist believes clients come to their session with a severe lack of understanding and knowledge of how much power our mind has over our mood and behaviors. Let's say a client has a strong dislike of mice, and the only thought they have is that *all mice are bad.* How likely is it that person will ever buy a pet mouse?" She takes a moment to let the question soak in before she answers her own rhetorical question. "Not very likely. You see, the client's cognitive distortion here is called an overgeneralization. The client's overgeneralization for all mice is an inaccurate assessment that causes the client to dislike all mice."

"Cinderella's mice aren't that bad," Alexis says, looking around to see if anyone takes pleasure in her silly joke.

Completely ignoring her, Dr. Ambrose continues, "CBT theorists tell us there are at least ten cognitive distortions. They are all listed on page one hundred sixty-two. I would like you to either join with a partner to discuss, or if you feel having a partner is too distracting, you may consider this information alone. Pick one and be prepared to give an individual presentation on it by the end of class. And everyone," she pauses again, "please try not to pick the same one. Think outside the box. Have a second choice. Think about your life. Your own thoughts. Your inaccurate cognitions. If you don't challenge your own beliefs, how do you expect to challenge your clients'?"

Chairs push out, and desks pull together. I look over, and Randall's head is cocked, giving me the most adorable puppy dog eyes. In his Southern twang, he asks if I'd like to work together, to which I can't say no. I want to, but I can't seem to. The corners of our desk tap, and we both flip to the next page and begin to read the list of distortions.

"How 'bout we make this interesting?" he asks.

"How so?"

"You pick one distortion you believe I have, and I get to pick one for you."

This could go one of two ways. On the positive side, we both learn something about the other. On the negative side, we might end up hurting each other with how we perceive the other. I don't know Randall as well as I'd like, but I do know he blames himself for what happened to his partner, Marco. If I suggest the *personalization* distortion for him to focus on, would he take offense? On the other hand, if I suggest it, it might help him begin to work through whatever feelings he has that obviously inhibit us from working out as a couple.

"Fine. For you, let's go with," I act as if I haven't read the entire chapter the night before and scan the page looking for a better option, "personalization."

"Ah, when someone takes an inordinate responsibility for an event or situation. Damn, has it taken me a long time to realize I can't control everything that's ever happened in my life. Even if I want to."

The fact he knows exactly what he needs to work on doesn't surprise me. With his experiences, he's probably learned so much about himself, more than anyone would be able to enlighten him about. Especially some boy he just met a couple weeks ago.

"I think you should present on polarized thinking." His eyes cautiously widen in hopes he didn't offend.

"Black-or-white thinking?" I tilt my head to the side. "And why do you think that's a good choice for me?" I don't want to show him I'm taken back by his abruptness. He didn't even look at the textbook page. There were no finger scans or reconsideration. He went straight for the jugular.

"I don't know everything about you. I get that. However,

I do know the way you see some things makes you closed off and not willing to experience new things. Take us, for example." He plants his feet under the desk and straightens his back in the chair. "I'm a horrible boyfriend because I stood you up one time."

My face reddens. "Whoa, you're not my boyfriend."

"But you want me to be."

My pen flips in between my fingers. "How dare you assume—"

"I wish I could be."

I glare, not knowing what to say. "I'm sorry?"

"See? You aren't able to move past your distrust of my one fuck-up to see how much, even in such a short time, I really care about you." He clasps his fingers together and places his palms on the desk as if he's just proven a point.

"No," I swallow, "you've got it all wrong."

"Oh? Interesting." He breathes in a sharp breath. "Did you or did you not think that because I didn't show up the other night that I didn't want to be with you? That you don't deserve someone to love you?"

"Randall, I don't think that's fair."

"Tell me I'm wrong. Why try to make me jealous by bringin' up some guy named Javier? Why give me the cold shoulder when I'm tryin' to apologize for not being there for you?"

Sweat collects across my brow. "No, I'm not going to play this game. The assignment is over."

"I get it. It's totally black-or-white with you. Because I didn't show up, I'm a horrible person, and I'm not good enough for you. I couldn't possibly have had somethin' else come up, right?"

"That's not it." I collect my breath and hold it in. My leg

starts to aggressively bounce, and I place my hands on my lap. I look around the room. The noise from everyone's discussion is getting louder, and it appears no one can hear Randall calling me out for things about myself I don't want to hear right now.

"Then tell me. *Don't go easy on me.* Stop holdin' back."

I bite the air just to keep myself from shouting louder before I erupt, "I don't have it in me to get hurt. To lose everyone I love. I've sacrificed everything to take care of my father after his accident. There is literally no one in this life who will understand that. There is no one in this life who will love me the way I want...the way I *need* to be loved." I bite down on my words, trying to keep my voice level. My hands clench and unclench at my sides, and I feel my jaw tighten as I look at him, willing him to understand.

A muscle in my cheek quivers as I try to keep control, but my whole body is a taut wire, pulled too tight. "Is this what you wanted, Randall? Did you want me to confess my deepest darkest fears here in this class? Do you want to break me?"

"No, I want you to be honest with yourself. You refuse to think there is someone out there who will find you good enough. You spend so much of your life takin' care of other people that you don't even know how to let someone in to take care of you. Because of that, you think you don't deserve love. Someone broke your heart because they couldn't handle what you brought to the relationship. I get that. I really do. But you don't need to be scared to let another person in. You can't be mad at me because I fucked up one time. I came to you to ask for forgiveness, and you've been sittin' here shuttin' me out and givin' me the cold shoulder, even though I know deep down inside you don't want that."

"What do you want from me, Randall?"

"Another chance. I want to show you how much you deserve to be taken care of." He reaches under my desk and lays his hand on top of mine.

"People get hurt when they love me." A sudden chill brushes across my cheek from the single tear that falls down my face.

I catch a movement out of the corner of my misty eye— Dr. Ambrose, glancing over from the front of the room, her brow raised. She takes a moment, assessing the commotion between us, then starts walking over, her heels clicking against the tile like a countdown.

She bends her knees in front of my desk and meets me at eye level. "Not sure what's going on over here, but it sounds like a lot of overgeneralization happening. It can't be *all* people." She stands up and walks past to the next pair.

Randall lifts up his hand and straightens his desk as Dr. Ambrose asks for everyone's attention. Throughout the noise of everyone getting back to their seats, he leans over and whispers, "By the way, it would be impossible."

"What would be impossible?" I whisper, wiping away a tear from the corner of my eye.

"To break you."

EIGHTEEN

I stay behind to collect the stack of essays Dr. Ambrose needs me to grade by the end of the week. Randall stands by the exit as he waits for Dr. Ambrose to finish explaining the grading rubric to me. The outsole of his boot props up against the door frame, leg bent, and the loose ends of his camouflage pants tucked into his boots.

"No pressure, but I definitely need these back by Friday morning," Dr. Ambrose says, packing up her briefcase.

"I'll keep him on task, ma'am!" Randall calls out.

My attention goes from Randall back to Dr. Ambrose. I step backwards, dodging the desks. "I'll have them done by Thursday, and I'll place them in the bin outside your office door."

She thanks me as I leave the classroom.

"Professor Branson," Randall smirks, "will you be giving me an *A* on my paper?"

"Oh hush," I shove his shoulder, pushing him gently into the hallway, "I'm still mad at you."

He laughs and apologizes with a flirtatious wink and blows me a kiss. "So, who is this *Javier*?" He holds the door for me as we step outside. Autumn leaves rustle on the path leading up to the building's entrance.

"That is none of your business, *sir*."

"Ah, I see what you're doin'." He clasps the dog tags around his neck and nervously pulls them from side to side on the necklace.

"And what am I doin'?" I respond, mocking his Southern accent.

"You're still trying to make me jealous."

"How do you figure?" Warmth touches my neck. I'm not the best at playing it cool.

"It's okay. I get it. I wronged you. You want to keep your options open. All I'm saying is I want you to do what makes you happy, and if this Javier feller makes you happy..."

"You want me to do him?"

"Yes...I mean, well, no. Not *do* him."

We both share a laugh as we step into the parking lot. "Well you don't need to worry about that. I don't know if I'll ever see him again, and plus..." I pause, "I want to keep giving us a try."

"I'm glad to hear that. It's just...you deserve so much. You need to live your life, and I don't want to be one more thing that holds you back."

"Oh my gosh, will you stop it?! Also, walk straighter, you're running me into parked cars here." I sigh, rolling my eyes.

A piece of paper crinkles underneath my shoe, and I bend over to pick it up. It's a flyer outlining an evening of entertainment at a local pumpkin patch. The flyer reads *Hay*

Rides, Pumpkin Decorating Contest, Caramel Apple Creation, and So Much More.

"We should go." Randall opens my car door for me after I press the unlock button on my key fob.

"This weekend?" I climb into the driver's seat.

"No," Randall shuts the door, waiting for me to put the window down, "let's go tonight. I'm in a fall mood. The weather is colder; I got this really cute sweater and some tan corduroy pants I can wear. It'll be a grand ol' time!"

"I'm not sure I can go tonight. I—"

"—have to call your sister and ask her to watch your dad first, so you can come? Since she's taking some time off work, she's home now, right?" he interrupts.

Usually, at this point, I'm coming up with an excuse as to why I can't rely on my sister to watch Dad all by herself, but after spending all evening with her coming up with how she was going to break out of the toxic pattern she's been in, I think she owes me a night out.

"Fine, I'll call her and ask if it's alright. But no guarantees, okay?" I shoo Randall away from the car and press the button to put the window back up. I reach for my phone and find Haley's contact information. I press the green phone image by her name. Three rings vibrate my ears.

"Hey, everything okay?" she answers the call.

"Yes, I'm fine. What are you doing tonight?" The age-old habit of a caregiver: ask what the other person is doing first, just in case they already have plans, and you have to cancel yours.

"Well, since I'm on suspension, blocked my boyfriend's number, and decided tonight was a good night to bake some brownies, I was thinking about using this time to finally watch the rest of *The Big Bang Theory*. Why, what's up?"

"I'm sorry, Sis. Did you want to call a friend and go out tonight?"

"Eh, not really. I don't think I'm ready for all that just yet. I have plans with some people this weekend, but tonight I need some *me* time."

"That makes sense. Um, so, in that case..." I hesitate, knowing *me time* during the week usually includes our father and is not really *me time*.

"Tell me what you want to do tonight, Theo," she says, her tone bordering on exasperation.

"Randall invited me to a pumpkin patch and—"

"Theo, you can go, boo. I got Dad. Mom gave him a Seroquel before she left for work, so we're good."

"Bad day?" I ask, dreading the answer.

"Supposedly he was getting mouthy because she asked him to get his hands out of the sink. He called her a *bitch* and told her he was going to hit her. He's napping right now. I'll wake him up around seven o'clock for dinner and to give him a shower."

"Are you sure? You know I hate when he gets like this."

"Yes, Little Brother. I'm sure. You need to let me be the big sister every now and then. And plus, after you helped me get my shit together last night, it's the least I can do."

There is something clear in her voice, sounding maternal and peaceful. It reminds me of when I was in the fifth grade, and I came home and told her some boy was making fun of my fringed and stressed shoelaces. The protective look she gave me was all I wanted in that situation. I didn't want to talk about my feelings. I didn't want to rehash what the boy said to me. I just wanted to be heard and wanted a solution. She went to her room, got a pair of fresh shoelaces, and taught me how to tie them where the laces went straight across the shoe without intersecting. She told me everyone would be jealous of my fashionable lacework, and she was right. The next day at school, all the kids in my class wanted to learn how to tie their shoes like me.

"Thanks, Hales."

"Tell Randall I'm sorry I wasn't in a good place last time he came over. I'm getting my life together. I hope to officially meet him one day soon if he's taking my little brother out on these romantic dates and shit." She laughs.

"I will. Love you, Hales." There's a brief silence on her end. "Hales?"

"Yeah, I'm sorry." She sighs, irritation suddenly consuming her tone. "Dammit. Someone keeps calling me from an unknown number." Without hesitation, she rushes me off the call. "I gotta go, Little Brother. Love you. Have fun!"

I fight every anxious ounce of me that wants to call Haley back to find out who was on the other line, but I choose not to. Not today. Today, I'm going to choose me. I'm going to go on a date with a hot military stud and simply trust my sister to take care of our father without any issue.

I owe her that.

I put the car window back down and wave to Randall, who's kicking rocks in the next parking spot over. He saunters over and leans into my open window. His smile is wide, and his eyes are impatiently waiting for the outcome of the call.

"I'm warning you now: I take my pumpkin decorating very seriously." Randall jumps into the passenger's seat and leans over, planting a kiss on my cheek. He whispers in my ear, "Butter my butt and call me a biscuit, I'm so excited."

~

Trudging through rows of pumpkin vines, between an orange pumpkin with a smashed-in black hole and a smaller, premature green pumpkin, we set our sights on a large, round white one. Randall bends down, using his knees to pick the giant squash. He puts out his muscled arms and shows me at all angles that our pumpkin has no dings, scratches, holes, or scuffs, "It's pretty darn perfect, if you ask me. She's fuller than a tick."

I don't think I'm ever going to fully understand his Southern phrases, but damn he sounds sexy saying them. He hands me the pumpkin, and I rub around its edges. "It's the perfect shape to decorate it as a head."

"Oh! Can we do Dracula? With fangs?" He gnashes his teeth like a vampire.

"No, that's not going to win us anything. Everyone does vampire pumpkins. I'm thinking of a mummy head."

"I can go to the bathroom and get some toilet paper?"

"I applaud you for your efforts in thinking about your resources, but I have a better idea. I saw a pie contest over yonder." I point at the booth with a wooden sign reading *Pies*.

"Hot damn!" Randall gasps. "We can steal one of the cans of whipped cream!" He grins, missing the fact I was mocking his Southern twang.

For the next ten minutes, we map out our *Oceans 11* thievery. We share notes on who looks suspicious, who we can outrun, and how many cans we need to lift. Randall says we need two, but I'm confident we only need one to complete our mummy design.

The woman guarding the condiment section of the booth seems to be a napper, taking increments of two-minute catnaps before she's awakened by a customer asking for a serving of whipped cream or cinnamon sprinkles. As soon as she closes her eyes, Randall quickly shuffles behind her, reaches his arm over the booth and grabs a can of whipped cream from the shelf underneath the sleeping condiment guard. He makes his way back toward me, jerking his head from side to side, front to back, ensuring he's not spotted by anyone.

"I don't know whether to be turned on or check my pockets to see if my wallet is still there. You're a ninja!" I throw myself into his chest and wrap my arms around his neck.

"Now let's make a mummy!" He returns my squeeze with a tighter one. I feel his fingers lock in place across my lower back. His hold on me dawdles, but I'm not complaining.

I rub the side of my face against his, feeling the smoothness of his cheeks. I grip the back of his collar and gently squeeze. I breathe him in. His scent is masculine and makes me want to drop to my knees. I feel him burrow the top of his head into my shoulder. He knows he needs to stop because, if we keep touching each other like this, we'll need to shorten this date and find somewhere quiet. Somewhere private.

Not wanting to, I pull away and place both hands against his shoulders, forcing a small distance between us.

"I really want to kiss you, Theo."

"I really want you to kiss me." I stare at him, his beautiful hazel eyes shining in the leftover light from the sun setting across the field. I take his hand. "But we're in public, and there are so many people around. Let's keep focus on the task at hand. We have a mummy to make."

We gather the rest of the decorating supplies from numerous things we have in our possession and things we find around the patch. For our mummy's goofy eyeballs, we use extra buttons Randall popped off the bottom of the flannel I was wearing. For the mouth, we use a pin I found on the ground. On the pin were a set of lips made famous by the movie *Rocky Horror Picture Show*. It was a miracle we found an item with the actual body part we needed to put the finishing touches on our mummy pumpkin. Though, I'm starting to realize that miracles, even the smallest ones, tend to happen when I'm with Randall.

"Last call for the seven p.m. pumpkin decorating contest!" a male voice calls out on a loud speaker hanging from the surrounding light posts around the patch. "Any submission after seven will need to wait for the eight p.m. contest."

"You think we're ready? I reckon we can put a fork in it." Randall turns the pumpkin around using the visible brown stem at the top.

"I think you're right. We gotta make the seven p.m. contest, or else this little guy is going to be a puddle of melted dairy."

We take our pumpkin and stand in line behind a mother and her son. Their pumpkin is decorated in a red curly wig, with white paint around it. I assume there is a red nose, a creepy smile, and the figment of my nightmares across the front of it. Clowns are my least favorite thing on earth, and I will fight anyone who says they aren't out to steal your soul.

Randall laughs at the side-eye I give the clown pumpkin as he digs around in his jacket pocket. He pulls out his rabbit's foot, immediately giving me chills. "Here, you're going to need this." I open my palm, and Randall places the keychain in the center of it.

"Clowns and small rodents. Two of my favorite things." I squeeze my eyes shut in horror.

"It's my good luck charm, remember? Hold on to it for me. We're going to need it to defeat the scary clown." He smiles at the little boy in front of us, giving him a nod of approval for his pumpkin design.

As I place the keychain in one pocket, the other vibrates, signaling for me to reach for my phone. My mom's name comes up on the screen, and my heart drops. She should still be at work, so I'm not sure why she's calling me right now. I answer, "Hey, Mom, what's wrong?"

"Hey, sweetie. I know you're out with your friend, but your sister had to call the ambulance for your father. I'm on my way to the hospital now. Supposedly, he slipped and fell in the shower."

"Oh my god, is he okay?" I look at Randall. A little piece of me is hoping she says my father is fine, and I can continue my date. However, in my heart, I know that's not what a call from my mother means.

"He's stable, maybe? I don't know. The EMTs said he broke his brow ridge and mentioned he hit his shunt, so they are taking him to the hospital to make sure he didn't damage it too much. You know how important his shunt is," she says. "You don't have to come now, but I do hope go see you at the hospital soon, Theo. I need to go. I hate driving and talking on this car speakerphone thing. You don't need two parents in the hospital tonight." She hangs up.

Of course she'll see me at the hospital.

It's my obligation.

My duty to be there.

Like it was Haley's duty to take care of Dad and not to let him fucking fall and bust open his head. What the hell was she even doing?

"What's going on?" Randall's face is long and curious, full of dread for what I'm about to say.

"It's my dad. He fell. Haley had to call the ambulance, and they took him to the emergency room. I gotta go." I step out of line. "I don't want to assume, but are you alright to come with me to the hospital?"

Randall looks away, his jaw tightening. "I don't think that's a good idea."

"What?" My voice comes out sharper than I mean, but I can't help it. "Why not?"

He hesitates, flicking his thumb against the stem of our mummy pumpkin. "I just... I can't. I don't know how to explain, but it's not a good idea for me to go. You need to be with your family."

Frustration flares in my chest. "Are you serious right now? My dad's in the hospital, Randall. I need you..." I catch myself. "I would like you to come with me."

"I'm sorry." He looks at the ground. "I'll catch a bus home."

"A bus?" I stare at him, shaking my head in disbelief. "Fine," I mutter, pulling my keys from my pocket and turning toward the parking lot.

I make it two steps and hear Randall speak up, "Theo, wait."

I turn around, hoping he's changed his mind.

"You'll have all the support you need at the hospital. I'll just get in the way. I promise."

"Yeah, okay. Thanks for the date, I guess." I wave him off

before turning back around. I swallow hard, pushing down so much disappointment. No one's ever going to understand what it's like to live this way and always be on alert for my family. To always feel the need to be on-call when something bad happens.

But he's right.

I need to be with my family.

And he's right again.

I don't need him to get in the way.

He's right.

As I pass the voting booth, I glance back. Randall's still standing there holding the pumpkin, his shoulders slumped and his face twisted with something that looks an awful lot like regret. For a second, I almost run back to him, beg him to come with me. But the confusion in my chest is too heavy.

So, I turn and leave without another look back.

A HALF-HOUR GOES BY, and I arrive at the hospital.

Walking in the building with my hands buried in my pockets, I turn Randall's rabbit's foot over and over between my fingers. I hate to admit, but it's surprisingly calming once you ignore the fact it belonged to a rodent before.

As I approach the front desk, I give the receptionist, an older black woman with the name *Abby* written on her pinned name badge, my name and the floor and room number Haley texted me on the way. She writes my name down on the sign-in sheet. The gentleman behind her, wearing a navy-blue security guard uniform and a mustard stain on his shirt calls past me, "Mr. Javier! It's so good to see you. Going to 4-North this evening?"

"Just call me Javi, sir," a familiar voice answers, "and, yes, I hear the kids were requesting to play with the guitar again."

The receptionist wraps the visitor's bracelet around my wrist. I thank her and turn around to face Lianna's brother's music instructor, catching the attention of his bright cerulean-blue eyes. His smile widens, and he says my name like it's been on the tip of his tongue since the last time we met.

"Theo! It's nice to see you again, but I hate to ask why in a place like this." He sticks out his wrist so the receptionist can loop the visitor's bracelet around. "Thanks, Mrs. Abby."

"You're welcome, sweetie. Go make those itty-bitty babies smile, honey."

Javier simultaneously nods and winks at the receptionist and waves goodbye to the security guard. He looks at me. "Walk me to the elevator? Talk to me about what's going on."

I tell Javier everything from my dad falling in the shower to my date being cut short. I tell him about my anger toward my sister for letting this happen, and the feelings of selfishness and guilt taking over my own mind.

We come up to the elevator and prepare for our separation. Without expecting it, he takes my hand. "Listen, I'm scheduled to sing for the kids for about an hour. If you're still here when I'm finished, I'd love to come find you and sit with you while you wait to see your dad."

"Oh, Javier, you don't need to do that."

"I know I don't need to, but I want to." He hands me his phone after unlocking it with his fingerprint. "Type your number in, and I'll text you."

Wow, a man with a cellphone.

I enter my number and return his phone. "Thanks, Javier. I appreciate you being here for me."

He wraps his arms underneath mine and around my back. He holds me for a moment and whispers in my ear, "I really am glad to see you again, and I hope everything with your dad is okay. I'll see you in an hour and some change." He makes his way toward the elevator and presses the up arrow.

The elevator doors open, and Javier's smile sends me off as I make my way down the hall toward the emergency room. I see my mom and Haley sitting in the waiting room chairs. Haley, in sweatpants and a long-sleeve shirt stained with orange cheese puff dust and what looks like chocolate ice cream, stands up to greet me. Tears fill her bloodshot eyes, and she mouths *"I swear I didn't leave him for more than five seconds,"* but I dismiss her and walk right past her to comfort our mother.

I don't know why I feel so hostile toward her, but I can't help it. Call me triggered. Call it distrust. I don't care. I just know my gut is telling me there was something else that happened tonight as to why my dad was left alone long enough to fall and end up here. If she watched him like she was supposed to, our night wouldn't have wound up like this.

Mom wouldn't have had to leave work early and have her pay docked. I could have continued to feel good about finally being able to rely on her to help with our family. And Randall...Randall wouldn't have shown me, yet again, that he's not ready for the life I lead.

I ask my mom for an update on Thomas, but she doesn't know anything. She said a doctor hasn't been out since they took him back. I sit next to her and rub her back. Haley's arms are crossed as she paces near the K-Cup coffee station. She sounds tired, and there are bags under her eyes. She's more exhausted than when I last spoke with her.

I hope to see Javier soon. I don't even know him all that well, but I do know he seems to be a man of his word. Let's hope he doesn't leave me hanging like Randall did.

An hour goes by, and I look at my phone to see a text from Javier.

Are you still here?

NINETEEN

Javier delivers me a scalding but comforting cup of coffee. He added two sugars and two creamers to it, just the way I like it. His charm was evident when he asked my family and me what we wanted from the café as we waited to hear from the doctor.

To keep her mind distracted from what was going on with my father, a fidgeting and anxious Sarah Branson sparked conversation with Javier. She asked him about his volunteer responsibilities with the kids on 4-North, the floor designated for pediatric cancer. He shared that he started singing and performing for the kids last Christmas, and in February of this year, he received a letter from a little boy's parents. In the letter, they thanked him for his volunteering and told him their son looked forward to his singing and guitar lessons every week. The little boy passed away in January, and the parents credited Javier for helping give their family one last holiday to spend together.

"That is the most tragic but inspiring story I've ever

heard." My mom sheds a tear from her cheek. "It really goes to show you how powerful music can be."

"Yes, it really does, and thank you," Javier replies. "I hope I didn't put a damper on an already nerve-racking night."

"Oh, not at all, sweetie. In fact, I feel like you gave me… us…a little bit of hope." Mom lays her hand on top of his knee before standing up and walking over to check on Haley.

While listening to Javier's story, along with seeing his kindness for my family, I can't help but think about Randall. I don't want to, but Randall's empty promises continue clogging my mind, and I can't seem to shake my frustration.

On top of worrying about what additional caregiving responsibilities I'll have after tonight, Haley's distressed pacing isn't making anything better for me. I feel my heart beat faster and my head throb like it's about to explode. There is no more room left in my mind for Randall, let alone the idea of him always leaving me when I need him the most.

That's what I have to keep telling myself, at least.

"Hey you," Javier's soft, raspy tone interrupts my internal self-pity. "Are you doing okay over there? Are you still thinking about that guy?"

"Randall? Yeah. Sorry," I say, wondering if I should dignify his name.

"No, don't apologize. I didn't know his name was—"

"You're right." I stand up. "Let's forget about him for tonight. I have more important things to focus on." I walk over to the nurses' station, off to the right of the waiting area. "Hi, do you think we can get an update about my father? We've been waiting here for almost two hours with no update from the doctor."

"Patient's last name?" the nurse asks.

"Branson."

"Thomas Branson?"

I nod.

"Yes, actually, we were just given the confirmation that he's now set up in his room and can have two visitors at this time."

"That's great! Thank you so much!" I turn and see my mom and Haley making their way to meet me at the station. I focus on Haley, with her hunching shoulders and a face covered with apprehension. She rolls her sleeves the closer she gets and takes ahold of my mother's wrist.

A few steps away, she says, "I'd like to see him first. If that's okay with you, Theo?"

"Yeah, that's fine. Just as long as Mom gets to see him; that's all I'm worried about."

"I figured." She lets go of Mom.

"Can we talk for a second before you go in?"

"I think that's a good idea, you two." Mom places her hand on Haley's arm and gives her a nod that it's okay to talk with me. With the nurse leading, she walks away.

"Tell me what happened tonight."

She hesitates before she begins to share, "I haven't given him a shower in such a long time. I didn't think it's gotten so bad that you and Mom wash him yourselves now. Like, when did that change?"

I look at her, deadpan.

She continued, "I just gave him the soap and went out to the kitchen to wash the dishes."

"We wash him because he doesn't know how to wash himself correctly, Hales. He barely knows the difference between his legs and his arms these days. Also, he can't be left alone in the shower because he'll try to stand, and if the floor is soapy, he'll fall. I just don't understand why you don't know this about him yet."

"I fucked up. I know, Theo. I haven't been around a lot, and I just forgot how much attention Dad needs all the time. This is all my fault. I have too much on my mind with work and Jes..." She runs her hand through her hair.

"Jesse? Is that who called you earlier when we were on the phone? Is that why you weren't paying attention to Dad? You were too busy talking to *him*." My body begins to tremble from the anger exploding inside me.

"No, Theo," she huffs. "I knew I shouldn't have told you about my situation. At least Jesse trusted me. You're never going to," she says, shaking her head.

I can see how badly she wants to walk away from this conversation, but to compare Jesse's trust to mine? That's a low blow. "Jesse only trusted you when you did what he wanted you to do for him."

"If you say so, Little Brother." She rolls her eyes. "Whatever. I need to go see if Dad is okay. I can't stand here and keep talking about how I'm the reason we're all here tonight."

I know I shouldn't blame her. In all reality, Dad falling could have happened on any of our watches. I get that. There have been many moments where I've messed up with him. There was one time when I took out the trash and began a conversation with the neighbor. During that five-minute conversation, Thomas found Hamilton's box of dog treats and started to eat them because he thought it was a snack. When you step away or don't give our father all your attention, he will find himself in trouble. It's inevitable.

"Hey, Theo. Let's let your sister go in and see your dad."

Javier walks up and places his palm on my shoulder. Reminding me he's still there. Still here for me.

We sit back down in the seats we've been keeping warm since we arrived. Javier's phone rings, and he hits the side button, making the vibration go silent before shoving it into his pocket.

"You can take that if you need to." I gesture to his jacket.

"Don't worry about that. It's not important. What's important is that your dad's stable. How are you holding up?"

"I think I'm better. I just hate we all had to drop everything to be here. Like, we could have easily avoided all of this if she just fucking took care of him correctly." I struggle to keep my volume down. A custodian mopping up some spilled coffee in the waiting room sends a sharp glare in my direction.

"Can I be honest?" he asks.

"Sure."

"You need to go easy on Haley. It was an accident. She didn't intentionally push your father down in the shower. She's been here the entire night, afraid to speak, knowing she's going to be blamed for what happened. It's okay not to be so angry about this. It was a mistake."

The guy I met only once before—who doesn't even really know me—is telling me to *go easy on Haley*. My eyes widen, my chin juts out without saying a word, and a shudder erupts throughout my body. Uncertain how to respond, I shake my head. What he's saying is not wrong, but it's still difficult to hear.

A minute later, my words formulate. "You're the second person to remind me to be supportive instead of a bitch." I run my fingers through my hair.

"Oh yeah? Who was the first?" he asks.

"Randall, actually."

Javier repositions himself in the chair, turning his body more forward-facing.

I continue speaking, "He came over the other day during a very tense moment between Haley and me. He told me to listen to her instead of saying something I'd regret. Knowing me, saying something I regret is exactly what I'd do. So, I'm happy he was able to defuse the situation before I made an ass out of myself. I actually heard what she was saying, and we figured out her issue together."

"Sounds like good advice," Javier says, his lips reverting to a straight line.

"I suppose," I sigh. "Very much like your advice just now."

Javier nods, but the conversation goes quiet for a moment. "So about this Randall..." He pauses. "Man, it's weird saying that name."

"Why's that?" I ask.

"Oh, no reason. It's just, I used to know someone named Randall. Let's just say he broke my heart," he simpers, but I know it's not genuine.

"In that case, then all Randalls must be jerks." I notice Javier fidgeting with the silver necklace around his throat.

"They aren't all that bad." Javier crosses one leg over the other and turns toward me again. "Tell me about your Randall."

"To be honest, it's surprising my Randall ever liked me in the first place." I shrug. "I just don't see what other people see in me. Randall is strong, intelligent, and direct. He's also super kind and makes me feel like I deserve...more. Like I deserve better."

"It's because you do."

"Oh? Well, thanks." I sigh. "I just never saw myself with someone like him, or even you, for that matter. I look at myself in the mirror sometimes, and I'm just appalled by the way I look—the way I feel about myself."

"Nah, don't say that." He reaches over and cups my chin in his hands. The calluses on his fingertips, textured from his guitar strings, are warm and gentle against my skin, a rough tenderness that steadies me. "You're beautiful."

I swallow hard, knowing he's the second person in several weeks to call me beautiful. A little part of me fights to believe it. "You don't mean that."

He slides off his chair, crouches down in front of me, and looks into my eyes. His stare begs for my attention, my focus. "Take a walk with me? There's a small walk-through garden outside. It's lit up at night, and it'll be nice for you to get some air."

I agree, taking his hand as he leads me to the elevators.

ONCE OUTSIDE, I see the garden glowing under soft but warm string lights. Its pathway is lined by muted blooms and lanterns casting a gentle ambiance over each step we take. A stone fountain in the center ripples with illuminated water, while the scent of lavender drifts through the cool night air. Its quiet respite offers a moment of peace outside the gloominess of the hospital.

"Since meeting you, my world refuses to be the same as it once was." Javier takes my hand into his. "I don't know this Randall person, and to be honest, it upsets me that, after several empty promises he's made to you, he still has a chance to win your heart. I want you to know I feel a real strong connection with you, and if you give me that same chance, I would love nothing more than to show up for you and be the man you need. I won't disappoint you like he does."

We turn to face each other. There is a sincerity in the look he gives me, such passion. I wrap my arms around his neck and lightly nuzzle my forehead against his cheek. The tiny hairs of his beard tickle my skin, and I feel his sweet breath caress my face. "I think this is the part of the story where we kiss."

His whisper lingers in my ear. "I think you're right."

I lift my head parallel to his. Our noses meet, and our eyes close at the same time, as if we know exactly where we want to align ourselves next. A soft tremble waves through my nerves before he draws me in with his succulent bottom lip. His warm tongue seizes the inside of my mouth with a touch I want to experience across my entire body.

Something comes over me, and I take hold of his face with both of my hands, repositioning my lips. I nibble his lower lip faintly, trying not to hurt him. I want him to feel just as good as he's made me feel at this very moment.

Breath from his light laugh grazes my chin as he pulls away after a minute of our embrace. "Let me take you out."

"We are out," I say, keeping my eyes closed and holding on to every ounce of gravity I can muster, not wanting our kiss to end.

He lets out a snicker and places his hand on my cheek. My eyelids open slowly, and I realize, in this instant, everything is real. I'm not dreaming.

"No, silly. I want to take you out to dinner or something."

He looks around. "This garden is pretty romantic for a grief garden, but I don't want to count this as our first date."

Still simmering from our kiss, I find myself speechless. I'm unable to do anything else but move my head up and down, except quickly wiping my mouth with my sweater sleeve to check for any drool.

You know, just in case.

"I'll take that as yes." He leans in and gives me a soft, lingering kiss on the cheek. "Once your dad gets home, we can set something up."

I take his hand and pull it toward my mouth, pecking his hard knuckle with a delicate kiss.

Not a second later, an image of Randall flashes through my thoughts. For weeks, we've been chasing each other, playing this flirtatious game. We've been strengthening our bond by sharing major parts of our lives with one another—parts we don't share with everyone. Can I give that all up for Javier?

Randall wants what's best for me. He's told me he wants me to live my life for me and only me, to not hold back. On the other hand, he really hasn't been there for me like I want him to be. Like I need him to be. It's like he pushes me away during the times I fall for him the hardest.

"We've been out here for a bit, and your mom is probably waiting for you upstairs." Javier points over his shoulder with his thumb. "I'll make sure you get back upstairs safely so you can see your dad, and then I think I'm going to head out so you can be with your family."

"Thank you, Javier." I recognize the difference between his goodbye and Randall's this evening. "Thank you for being with me. For being my random guardian angel tonight."

"Anytime."

When we step off the elevator, Mom is pacing back and forth near the nurses' station. Before he leaves, Javier reaches in for a hug. His delicious fougère, woodsy aroma clings to me like a warm blanket, and I take it all in.

"I'll text you tomorrow." He squeezes me a little harder before finally letting go.

Mom sees me and waves me over as a nurse behind the counter presses a button under her desk, opening the locked doors into the hall of emergency rooms. While Mom and I make our way back, I ask her how Dad is doing.

"He's doing fine. He didn't hit his shunt, which is what the doctor was worried about. But they did have to bandage up his eye socket and forehead. He has some bruising and some internal bleeding the doctors were able to stop. Haley—"

"Where is Haley? I thought the nurse said we were only allowed to have two visitors at a time. I didn't see her come back." I look behind me to see if I missed crossing paths with her.

"She left already." My mom furrows her brows. "I thought she would at least say goodbye to you." She takes a sharp breath between her closed teeth. Wrinkles and worry consume her face.

I nod, thinking the same thing. I wanted to tell her I don't blame her for Dad's accident tonight. I feel like she needs to know, in just one day, I've seen how hard she's working to make up for the mistakes she's made these past couple of months, and I, too, have stuff I need to work on as well.

My mom pulls back the curtain, and we step into my dad's hospital room. "Thomas, your son is here to see you."

My father gargles and mumbles something I can't comprehend. Cathy, the night nurse in the room, tells us my dad's speech is actually normal after a fall like his this evening. She assures us his vitals look good, and he's up-to-date on his pain medicine. Soon after she leaves the room, my phone buzzes, and I look at the screen to see a text from Lianna pop up.

> Supposedly, Javier canceled Trevor's music lesson tonight because he was at the hospital with you. Should I be worried, sir?

TWENTY

Hamilton is pulling at the leash a little harder this morning on our way to the park two streets over to meet Lianna. He stretches his upper body so far ahead of the rest of him so he can sniff each leaf we pass by. From afar, I see Lianna sitting in the swing, her legs dangling in the air like she's seven years old again.

"Is that my Hammy?!" Lianna jumps off the swing into the wood chips that fill up the landscaped park, catching Hamilton's attention. I throw down the leash, and the two run toward each other like a 1980s romantic comedy. She takes Hamilton into her arms and rolls around on the ground with him, wood chips sticking to her shirt and Hamilton play-growling at her, trying to nibble at her hands.

I step closer. "You don't act like this when you see me."

She ignores me, but I don't mind. I love when Hamilton gets his love.

"Okay, Hammy, let me get up." She gets to her knees, debris falling off her clothes. She wipes away the extra that doesn't naturally come off. "So Javier, eh? How did that fucking happen?"

"I don't really know. I think we had a connection the night of your bonfire. Maybe?"

"What does this mean for Randall?"

I contemplate how to respond because of the same dissonance I have spiraling through my own head. "That's a long, complicated story I'm not interested in rehashing at this moment."

"Well, I'm here for you when you're ready. How's Mr. Tom doing?" She plucks a twig out of her hair.

"He's doing well. He'll be home tomorrow. Thank you for asking." I bend down to tie Hamilton's loose leash to the leg of the bench we've found to sit on. Even though I know my Siamese twin, Hamilton, is connected to me by the hip and won't run away, it'll be nice to be able to talk to my best friend without fear of him chasing a squirrel.

I'm still stuck on Lianna's question about Randall. With him, not once, but twice, leaving me stranded, things are being put in perspective for me. I wanted Randall to be this new, enigmatic source of spontaneity, adventure, and self-love in my life, but, in reality, he leaves me like a baited, dried-up swordfish, left ashore from the hooks he's dug into me.

"How's Haley?" Lianna asks, checking to see if my face makes a reaction. "I heard she was there when Mr. Tom fell."

"She was there." I sigh. "There is so much I have to catch you up on, it's not even funny."

"Well, thank goodness I don't have any plans for the rest of the day. I finished my book, by the way. Sent it to the editor this morning." She excitedly pumps the palms of her hands in the air.

"That's amazing, Li! You wrote that one quickly. We need to celebrate!"

"Yes, the book just flowed right out of me. And we will celebrate this weekend. But first, talk to me about Haley." She places her arm across the top of the bench and leans her body back.

I take a deep breath before I open the emotional floodgates that were begging to be set free. I share about Haley stealing medication for her abusive boyfriend, the consequences she got at work after she confessed, and even the mistrust I can't seem to shake, which caused me to act like an inconsiderate troll toward her at the hospital.

"Holy shit, T." Her head shakes in shock. "Well, I hope your sister knows she's not to blame for your father's fall. He could have fallen on anyone's watch."

"Yeah, I'm trying to make sense of it all myself. I just can't help but think none of this would have happened if Haley..."

"No," Lianna interrupts. "Your sister made a mistake because someone influenced her. That Jesse creep was holding something over her, and yet, she figured out a way to get out of that situation." She brushes her hand through her hair. "That's strength, my friend. A strength that doesn't deserve to be blamed for an accident she had no control over."

"A huge part of me feels relieved to hear you say that. To hear another person think that way. I was afraid people wouldn't understand."

"I get that, but you never need to worry about that with me. The amount of shit the Branson family has survived... this ain't nothing."

"I just hope Haley feels that too and comes around. She left without saying goodbye. I'm worried about her."

"She'll be back. She'll be okay." Lianna embraces me, wrapping her arms around me in a tight squeeze. "Now, tell me about Javier. He canceled on my brother for you. He never cancels a session. That's huge."

I let out a deep but contented breath. "He sings for kids battling cancer, for crying out loud." I gently pinch the skin of my neck to remind myself the man who came to my rescue last night is real.

"What are the odds that you ran into him though? That's like some *fate* shit right there."

Javier does have me thinking about fate recently. Both times Randall pushed me to the side, Javier was there to pick me up. Is this the universe telling me something? I usually don't fall for divine interventions or fateful experiences that make me doubt reality, but it's different with Javier. It seems like he's being driven into my heart each moment I doubt myself. I can't ignore those signs. Right?

"But for real though?" Lianna interrupts my thoughts, loudly chewing the piece of spearmint gum that's probably been in her mouth for over an hour. "He's so fucking hot. Like, of all the times he's been at my house teaching Trevor the guitar, I could have sworn he wasn't gay. I've flirted with him several times before, and it now finally makes sense as to why he didn't want to get none of this." She rubs the palm of her hand down the side of her waist, to her thigh, in a slow motion. The words come out of her mouth slowly, trying to sound sensual.

"You know what?" I realize. "We have never spoken about sexuality. I just assumed he was into guys."

"So I still have a chance?" Lianna quips.

"Don't you have a man from Taiwan or something? Why you gotta be coming for my man?" I laugh, nudging her body off my lap.

"All I'm saying is that my mom has told me he's pretty well off financially, takes care of his family, and he's told her he wants to start a family of his own someday." She finally spits her gum in a tissue she pulls out from her purse wrapped around her shoulder.

"Lianna, if you think bringing up that he has money will seal the deal, it won't. Money isn't everything," I say before she interrupts me.

"The fuck it ain't." She softly slaps the back of my head with her hand.

"Ow! And..." I give her a stern look, "we're not on that level yet to be talking about having kids. I don't even know his last name. We're not even officially dating."

"But you want to be?" She smirks. "I'm just bringing all of this to your attention because, unlike *Mr. Randall the Mysterious*, Javier meets most of the *F's* in your whole *F Package*."

I smile, remembering the four *F's* I believe make a successful relationship. "Family, Finances, Future Planning, and..." I pause, batting my eyes at Lianna.

"Fucking!" we both say together, loud enough for the gentleman riding his bike past us on the trail to look back at us and swerve a little.

"Oh my god," she gasps. "I don't even know his last name."

"Holy Carrie Underwood." I laugh. "Why are all the guys I like so damn mysterious?"

"You know what else is a mystery we need to solve?" She pauses to let me answer what seems to be a rhetorical question. "How big their dicks are." She takes her hand and gestures smacking a grinding ass against her lady parts.

"I've said it before, and I'll say it again. I. *Can't*. With. You, Lianna Charles! I can't," I say, joining her in an uproarious cackle.

Hamilton leaps up on the bench and onto my lap, landing licks on my neck and under my chin, barking and putting his muddy paw prints all over my jeans. Between barks, he nudges his head underneath my arm, begging for me to play with him or at least keep walking him.

"Looks like he wants Daddy to pay attention to him," Lianna's playful, high-pitched tone makes Hamilton's tail wag even faster.

A ding echoes in the front pocket of my Colesville hoodie. I reach in and take out my phone, looking at the notification in the center of the screen. "It's Javier!" I say, dodging my phone away from Hamilton. He hates when he's on my lap and my hands are too busy to rub behind his ears. "He said, 'Good morning.' Aw. And he's asking how my family is doing."

"Co'mere, Hammy. Let Daddy talk to his daddy." Lianna pats her lap, signaling Hamilton to crawl over to her on the bench so I can respond to the text without getting my phone knocked out of my hands from the hardtop of his head.

I roll my eyes at her and mouth the word *"gross."*

Hey, good morning to you too ;) Family is good…I think. Haley stayed in her room last night and didn't come out before I left to go meet up with Lianna this morning. Dad should be coming home tomorrow.

> That's good! Tell Lianna I say hi. Unless that's awkward for you….

I stop texting and look at Lianna. "He's wondering if saying hi to you through me would be awkward for me. Isn't he cute?"

Lianna rolls her eyes and pretends to gag, inserting her finger midway into her mouth. "Tell him I say *hi* back and I'm suing him for leading me on for so many years. I'm still mad he prefers eggplants to tacos."

"Yeah, I'm not telling him that." I lift my phone to respond to his text.

> She said hello back :)

> What are you doing tonight? I'd like to take you out to dinner, if that's something you'd like to do?

I crack my neck, bending it from side to side. "Shit, he's asking me out to dinner tonight, Li. I have class, and I have to get home to watch my..." I pause, knowing I completely deserve the second smack Lianna lands on the back of my head.

"Bitch, you gotta watch what? Mr. Tom's *ass* is sitting in a hospital bed tonight. Go! Have fun! Go get yourself some of your own *ass*!"

"Would you stop talking about *ass*?" I look around to make sure no other bikers or runners are listening in on our conversation. "You're right. I'll just text my mom and tell her I'm going to be home late. She doesn't want me coming to the hospital tonight anyway."

"That's my boy! Go get your man! Your *fine-ass* man!"

I'd love to! I do have class tonight though. It ends around 6:15 p.m. I can meet you at 7:00 p.m. Which restaurant?

Wonderful! Let's do DiVinchi's? I'll make a reservation.

Perfect, I'll see you there. Can't wait!

This just made my day, and it's only morning ;)

I shove my phone back into my hoodie pocket and look down at the ground. Lianna is once again rolling around with Hamilton. This time, Hamilton is standing on her chest like the king of the mountain. She stops mimicking Hamilton's growl and looks up at me. "So, what's the plan?"

"Dinner tonight. DiVinchi's." I scratch my head, thinking about what I can wear at both school and a dinner date.

"Ooh la la! Fancy." She hands me Hamilton's leash before making her way up off the ground. "Now, let's go home and pick something out of your closet to wear tonight. Let's pick something real sexy so you can make Randall jealous tonight when you see him in class."

Lianna knows me so damn well.

TWENTY-ONE

The pulsating bounce between my legs is the rush of blood pumping through my thighs as they are forced to settle in these tight-ass jeans Lianna chose for me to wear. Before I left the house this evening, I made a mental note to throw this pair away as soon as I cut them off and free myself when I return home tonight. If I didn't know any better, I would say this is what a drag queen feels like after they've taped their tuck before their big performance.

Now that I've arrived at my destination, there is no turning back. My only recourse is to go into the humanities building's bathroom and do my best to readjust myself. Just in case I end up sitting on the classroom chair and popping a testicle, that is.

I cup my hands together and fill them with some cold water from the restroom sink. As the cool splash against my face dissipates, for just a moment, it occurs to me how ridiculous it is to try to make Randall jealous on the same night I'm going on an official first date with Javier. I've never been one to play games with people. I like to consider myself a straight-shooter, but with feeling like Randall has already been toying with my emotions ever since I've met him, a part of me doesn't feel bad about causing a little chaos in his mind. That is, if he even notices the effort I've put into my appearance tonight.

Hopefully, he at least notices the new blue tone to my skin due to the lack of circulation in my body from these fucking jeans.

Feeling ready, I dry my hands with some thick paper towels, the same one I use to grab the handle of the bathroom door to open it, and I make my way to class. According to the syllabus for tonight's Introduction to Counseling Skills class, we're talking about the Father of Psychology, Daddy Freud, and his psychodynamics theory. The supreme topic for any psychology nerd who wants sex to be at the forefront of their mind. Bringing up Freud's psychosexual stages during foreplay could be what gets the party started. It could also be what compels people to recognize their mommy and daddy issues, turning their intimate moment into the perfect nightmare.

I take my seat and begin to pull out my notebook. A body comes up from behind me. A chilled air lands on the back of my neck as Randall takes his seat at the desk next to me. "How's your dad doing?"

His question is abrupt. No hello. Straight to the point.

"He's doing better. Thanks for asking," I say, refusing to look at him. If there was anything colder than the air against my neck when he sat, it's the shoulder I'm giving him.

Randall lets out a small cough, clearing his throat. "You're not mad at me for not going to the hospital, right?"

I try to think of a response that doesn't sound completely passive-aggressive. I know if I want to accomplish that, whatever comes out of my mouth needs to be short. "Not mad at all." I give myself a mental pat on that cold shoulder of mine.

The class begins to fill. Dr. Ambrose follows the last student in, closing the door. She introduces the lesson for the day and invites three students to the front. She gathers three chairs and places them in a diagonal formation between the white board and the rest of us who are sitting in the audience, anxiously waiting to see what happens. Two of the chairs are facing us, while the other chair is facing away, toward the white board. She assigns the students to their designated seats.

She puts her hands on the back of the middle chair and addresses the student sitting in it, "I want you to tell both of your fellow peers here about your biggest fear."

"What? For real?" the girl in the middle chair asks.

"Yes. It doesn't have to be anything deeply personal, but it needs to have some substance. Now, talk to them." Dr. Ambrose points at the students in the experiment with her two index fingers.

The girl begins to open up about her fear of taking elevators. She shares that when she was younger, she got stuck in one, by herself, for two hours when she was visiting her grandmother in hospice. She described the smell of antiseptic and bleaching powder and how she can't take an elevator without having those memories pop back up. She looks at the student facing her and appears validated, but when she begins to turn her neck to look at the person behind her, Dr. Ambrose interjects and reminds her she cannot reposition herself.

"How do I know if they are paying attention to me?" she asks.

"That's a good question. What's it like to think the person you're speaking to may not be listening?"

"It doesn't feel good. I want to know if the person I'm talking to is understanding me."

"What if I said that's not the point of psychodynamic therapy? According to Freud, the therapist's presence is unimportant, and the only way for clients to bring their unconscious to the conscious mind is to freely associate their words with memory and action. It's about the client's willingness to be open and honest about their own thoughts and motivations without interruption from the therapist." Dr. Ambrose thanks the three students and sends them back to their seats. "And that is how Freud used blank space as a clinical tool to help his clients build insight."

A quick jingle comes from my bag as Randall kicks it to get my attention. His rabbit's foot keychain dangles from the shoulder strap, and for a second, I just stare at it. The last time I saw that thing was when he gave it to me at the pumpkin decorating contest. I could've sworn I never put it on my bag. But before I can figure it out, Randall smirks and says, "Freud is a kook."

"You know what else is kooky?" I whisper, "Taxidermy key chains." My lips almost curl into a smile as I point to his keychain on my bag.

"Whoa, low blow, Branson. Low blow," he says with the tone of a flirtatious purr.

Keeping my voice low so I don't disturb Dr. Ambrose, I mutter, "Please take this back." I unclip the keychain from my bag and quickly attach it to Randall's duffel strap.

"No, I wanted you to keep it for a little bit. It's all for good luck, remember? I'm tryin' to catch my luck with you."

"You're going to need to give me eight more of those

things if you want to get back in my good graces, sir." I can't help but smile. "Actually, please don't. One dead foot is enough."

"Can't blame a guy for tryin'." He pauses and looks around to make sure no one can hear him. "Listen, I know I haven't really shown you the kind of boyfriend I can be, but if you just give me some more time and another chance, I promise to..."

"I have a date tonight," I say abruptly and a little louder than expected.

Dr. Ambrose stops speaking and looks in my direction. Her lips pucker as she sucks at her two front teeth. Her glare snaps me in place as I mouth an apology to her. She continues on with the lesson, but the class know-it-all, Alexis, obviously annoyed by my interruptive outburst, turns around in her chair, two desks in front of me. She gives me a drab thumbs-up gesture and follows it with an eye roll.

"I was wondering why you showed up to class looking so sexy," Randall mutters with his neck bending down and his shoulders slouching, twiddling a pen in between his fingers.

My heart skips a beat, and I swallow hard. "Thanks?"

His flirting will not win me over today, even though it feels really good to hear it. My goal for this outfit was to turn some heads, and it's nice to know he was one of them.

"Is your date with Bonfire Javier?"

"I'm not sure it's any of your business, but..." I pause, letting my healthy boundary with him sink in for a moment, "yes, I'm going to dinner with Javier."

His voice still has a soft, quiet inflection, "It makes me happy that you're happy. You deserve to meet someone who will take care of you. Javier seems like a good guy."

I make it a point not to respond because he doesn't even

know Javier and what kind of guy he is. *I* don't even really know what kind of guy Javier is. I don't even know his last name.

I spend the rest of the class listening to Dr. Ambrose and participating when necessary. An hour later, Dr. Ambrose excuses the class and reminds us about our paper due next Wednesday. Before I leave the classroom, she gives me another stack of papers to look over. This time, she asks me to separate them and make small packets for each of her students.

After she's done explaining my task, I leave the room, running into Randall standing in the hall. It seems as if he's waiting for something, most likely me—to inquire more about my date. I attempt to ignore him, but he has the most adorable puppy dog face staring at me, desperately trying to get my attention. I wave my hand toward him, but the speed of my walk doesn't slow down. I don't want to be late for my first date with Javier.

I get about twenty feet away, but a pull in my chest urges me to turn around and give Randall one more chance to plead why I should choose him. If that's what he wants, of course. If he doesn't, then I need to know why we wouldn't work out. Is it me?

"What about me didn't sit well with you?" I ask, pivoting back around, still feet away.

"Excuse me?"

I step closer to him so there is no misinterpreting what I'm asking. "What about me didn't sit well with you? Something had to have changed for you not to want to be there for me."

"Theo, I promise, it's not about you—"

"It's you, right?" I cut him off. "The whole *it's me, not*

you bogus-ass storyline people say when they don't want to be truthful with the other person."

"Holy Moses, will you hush the hell up, Theo?" Randall raises his voice.

A tingle starts at my ears and travels down my neck. A sudden feeling of surprise takes over.

"What did you just say to me?" Immediate anger spills out. My chest shakes, and I'm afraid to say anything else because I don't know what will come out next.

"I said hush the hell up. Just stop treating yourself like *you're* the problem. You seem to do this every time. You think because someone has a hard time explaining something, it's automatically your fault. You either want to fix it, solve it, or act like you have it all figured out. But in the end, you're just left assuming life is, once again, beating you down. Like you don't deserve happiness." Randall comes up to my face and plants his feet.

My hands, hanging by my side, feel his warmth as he grabs them and pulls them up, placing them between our chests. His intimate aggression sobers all frustration inside of me.

"Theo, you are the best person I have ever met, and I wish you could fucking see that. You care so much about everyone else, and you always forget to put yourself first. I hate you don't see this.

"I'm happy you're going out with Javier. I actually want you to. Maybe you'll let him see you're more than just a stressed-out, lonely person waiting for someone else to come around and tell you how to live your life. I get it, Theo. You have responsibilities. But stop using that as an excuse. Go live your fucking life. You have no idea how lucky you are to still have one."

His words stun me. I stand still, gazing at the brick wall behind his head, afraid to look him in the eyes in case I explode with tears. I don't know where any of this is coming from. I did what he asked me to. I went on his dates. I opened up with him. I leaned on my family for support.

For him.

What more does he want from me?

"Well, there's that." I slowly back away. "I don't need this right now. I'll see you tomorrow in class."

"That's it? I call your ass out, and then you just...walk away?"

"Me walk away? What about you, Randall?" I point a finger at him. "You chose to make me want you. You chose to walk away first. You chose to leave me hanging when I needed you the most."

"That's exactly what I'm talkin' about. No one can *make* you do anything you don't want to do. The choices you make are yours and yours alone. I can't be the knight in shinin' armor you want."

"Yeah, you couldn't be Marco's either."

In an instant, regret seeps through my pores, knowing I shouldn't have said what just came out of my mouth. His cheeks sink into his face, and his lips fall. He furrows his brows. Confusion washes over his face. How could anyone be so cruel?

Understandably, Randall's not in a space to accept my insubstantial apology. He picks up his duffle bag and wraps the strap over his shoulder. The strap to which his rabbit's foot was attached before it flings off. He proceeds to walk past me. Our shoulders graze one another, but as I reach for his arm to stop him, it's too late. It's like my hand goes right through him with how fast he's trying to get away from me.

"Randall, wait! I'm sorry," I say, begging. He continues ignoring me and keeps on walking. If my disgusting display of impulse and self-deprecation wasn't the nail that seals the coffin, then I don't know what will. It's moments like these that make me realize how careless I can be with others' feelings.

~

HOLDING my phone so tightly in my hand, I feel it vibrate. Javier's name pops up on the screen. I swipe right to unlock the message:

> I can't wait to see you. I'm here. Want me to order you a drink?

I take a moment, trying to collect myself and figure out what exactly went wrong with Randall. If we're not meant to be together, I can accept that. What I won't accept is him not taking any accountability for why we can't be together.

What he said to me, though, isn't wrong. I do push people away because I don't want to be hurt anymore. I'm just so tired of losing people I love.

I press the buttons on my phone screen to text Javier back.

> Yes, order me all the drinks. It's been a day. Be there soon.

> You got it 🫶

I slide my phone into my backpack. My step forward is interrupted by a lump on the ground. I lift my foot and see a furry brown thing underneath.

Randall's rabbit's foot.

I bend over and pick it up. My thumb caresses its edges, feeling the hardened cartilage and bone surrounding it. I wrap the keychain around my finger, clinging to it like it might anchor me somehow. But all it does is hang there, lifeless and still, a piece of Randall I'm not sure I want but can't seem to let go of.

I stumble over a bent corner of an area rug as soon as I push through the thick, heavy wooden door leading into the restaurant. The lights are dim, but Javier's chiseled jaw is illuminated by a tall candle on a table across the fancy eatery. When the hostess asks if I need assistance, I point in Javier's direction and nod before I make my way toward him.

I walk through the dining tables spread fairly equidistant from one another. The lighting is not getting any better the farther into the restaurant I tread. I watch my feet on the floor to avoid tripping and falling on someone while they eat their pea soup and linguine.

Javier stands before I can reach the table. He leaps to the other side and politely pulls out the chair I was planning to sit in, then extends his body toward me and gives me a strong squeeze. This embrace is one I don't necessarily want to end. His cologne gives off a floral but masculine scent, leaving me salivating seconds after our hug. His cheek touches mine, and a soft kiss vibrates the hairs on the side of my face.

Javier returns to his seat and fluffs his napkin onto his

lap. "I ordered you a pinot noir. I hope that's okay? I didn't know what type of wine you like, but I figured pinot noir goes well with the caprese salad I ordered for the both of us."

"I love caprese salad, and I also love wine. Honestly, if it has any amount of proof, I'll take it." The corners of my mouth curl into a smile. It's strange to say, but the aura surrounding him brings me immediate comfort, like he's a weighted blanket lying across my body.

"I just want to start by saying how handsome you look tonight in that outfit." His cerulean eyes land on several intimate places across my body, judging me from head to toe. "How am I going to take my eyes off you?" He licks his lips.

Warmth consumes my neck and travels to my cheeks. I feel the need to fan myself, but the only thing I have available are my hands and this napkin. Neither would be attractive.

Lianna was one hundred percent correct when she chose this outfit for me. Both Randall and Javier took note, which was exactly the goal we wanted to accomplish tonight. With Javier licking his lips like he is, it makes me want to rip my clothes off, clear off this fancy-ass tablecloth, and take him right here, right now. His brawny neck pulsates, and with every *thump,* a shiver goes up my spine.

If only I could ravage him the way I see it playing out in my head. For now, though, I'll just settle for showing his kind words my appreciation. "This ole thing? I just found it in the back of my closet, but thank you. You're too sweaty...sweet. I mean, sweet." I cough, covering up my ridiculous Freudian Slip. Another thing I learned about in class this evening.

His bashful smile lights up the restaurant just a little bit before the waiter comes over to our table and tells us our caprese salads will be out shortly. We confirm we're ready to order when the server asks us if we know what we'd like for dinner.

Javier orders a filet mignon with sides of asparagus and mashed potatoes with gravy. I ask Javier if he likes his filet rare, medium, or well done. He chuckles and tells me that, at this restaurant, you don't really have a choice in the matter. You get the steak however the chef decides to prepare it. "But, to answer your question, I usually like my steak medium rare. They do a pretty good job with getting it just right at this place."

I order the same as Javier for two reasons: 1. I drooled a little when he said the word *mignon*. Although, from my assessment, any word that rolls off his juicy lips sounds delicious, and 2. I really hate to order food for myself in public. I'll order food for anyone else, but for me, it's always been difficult. Ask me what my dad likes to eat, and you bet your ass I'll be able to list his favorite foods alphabetically. I'm not picky, but I get anxious because I have no idea what foods I even like anymore. If I make the wrong decision, then the whole experience is ruined for me. If I let someone else make the decision for me, it's easier to move on from a bad meal I didn't really choose.

After the server takes our menus and steps away from the table, Javier places his hand over mine and massages my wrist gently with his thumb. "I know you have a lot going on right now with your family, and things haven't been easy for you lately, but I'm happy you were able to make time for yourself tonight." He smiles. "Selfishly, I'm also glad you chose to spend the evening with me."

I smile and nod before taking a sip of the lush pinot noir I've been anticipating the taste of since I've sat down. "You know a lot about my family, so tell me about yours."

"We might need to order another glass of wine for that conversation." He laughs and begins to tell me about his family, specifically his abuela. He shares that his grandmother is feisty but needs a lot of support. She often calls on him because he lives the closest to her. She lives in a condominium one neighborhood down from Javier's apartment.

He shares that he visits her about three times a week and takes her to her doctor's appointments, which is how he landed the volunteer music gig at the children's cancer center. Javier's abuela has been in remission for two years from colon cancer, and the sense of pride brewing in his baby blues warms my heart.

"So, you're a caregiver too?" I ask, taking a drink from my water glass.

"You can definitely say we have that in common." He reaches over to my side of the table and continues to softly caress his fingers against mine.

"How do you find the time to do it all? Caregiving, volunteering, and music lessons on the side. Do you have a full-time job too?"

His smile fades, but he's not melancholy. He picks up his wine glass and closes his eyes, taking in the silky cherry and vanilla tannins. "I've been graced with a hefty inheritance, so I don't need to work full-time. I only do the music lessons right now. I've been saving the money I've been making and putting it into the stock market, which has been paying off pretty well."

"Oh wow." I swallow louder than I'd prefer to at this moment. "If you don't mind me asking, who left you the inheritance?"

Javier opens his mouth to answer the question but holds off after inhaling a heavy gulp of air. Our waiter interrupts and asks if we each would like a second glass of our pinot noir. Javier thanks him, pushes his glass closer, and awaits the pour. I wave my hand, politely declining a second glass before the server walks away.

Confirming his lack of interest in answering my question about the inheritance, Javier proceeds to ask, "So, let's talk about the big elephant in the room?" He taps his fork against the sterling silver ring holding together the folded cloth napkin lying across his dinner plate.

"I don't follow?" I ask hesitantly. Do I have something in my teeth? Did one of my buttons pop off these tight-ass clothes?

"How'd it go with Randall?" He pauses. "Did you see him tonight at school?"

"Yeah," I sigh heavily, "he's in my Theories class." I feel an uncomfortable prick in between my pant pocket and my thigh. I reach in and pull out the rabbit's foot I shoved in there after Randall dropped it before storming away from me.

"Whoa, why do you have a rabbit's foot?" Javier's head pulls back in total surprise, his glare stuck on the fake rodent's limb in my hand.

"It's a long story," I say.

Javier's brow rises, and his eyes widen, subtly gesturing he wants more than just a brush off of the story. I'm not exactly sure where to start.

I let out another huge sigh and dive in, "Let's just say I pissed off Randall tonight. I said something really stupid, and he left our conversation really angry. Furious, in fact. So mad, he dropped his favorite good luck charm and didn't even realize it. When I saw it on the ground, I knew he was going to be looking for it tomorrow, or even tonight, for that matter. He carries it around everywhere he goes. I just want to be able to give it back to him."

Javier's neck starts reddening, with little claret-colored blotches traveling from his collarbone up underneath his chin and below his ears. A knock comes from under the table, and after sitting back in my chair to take a look, I see his right knee bouncing nervously. He picks the cuticles between his nails and fingers, pulling off stunted strands of translucent skin, revealing small cracks of scarlet that look as if they would burn to the touch.

I give him a moment before asking if there is anything I can do. He went from zero to one-eighty in a minute. I've never seen him like this before, which isn't saying much because I really don't know him all that well.

"I'm fine. I'm sorry. I shouldn't, um..." Again, his eyes lock onto the rabbit's foot in my hand. "Let's order some-thing." He raises his hand, still staring at mine, to call over the server.

"Javier, we already ordered," I say a minute before asking the server to refill my water glass, giving at least a small reason as to why he would be summoned over by my date. I mouth the words *"sorry about that"* to the waiter as water droplets jump out of the glass he's pouring into.

Locking his eyes on the rabbit's foot, Javier is mesmer-ized by its existence.

Its presence.

He wants to say something out loud, but something is holding him back.

"You know, I can put this away. Is it a phobia of mice, because that's what I have too, and—"

"No," Javier's stern voice silences me.

I look around, feeling embarrassed and hoping no one else heard him raise his voice.

"It's just," he speaks after a moment but stops to try and find the right words. "I used to know someone who carried around a rabbit's foot. It's been a long time. I didn't realize I'd have this reaction from seeing one again. I'm sorry." He lays his open hand across the table and kindly gestures for me to give him the keychain. I place it in his hand, and he brings it up a foot away from his face. He turns it between his fingers, studying it like he is an archaeologist who just found the fossil of a billion-year-old dinosaur.

I feel the line between my eyebrows sharpen, trying to make sense of his emotional reaction to such a strange inanimate object.

"I know this rabbit's foot charm," he rubs his thumb across it, "but it can't be."

"What can't be?" I ask, baffled.

"You said Randall dropped this? Like, your Randall?"

My Randall? What does that mean? *My* Randall.

"He's not really *my* Randall, but yes. The Randall I go to school with. The Randall who's been playing hot and cold with me. The Randall I—"

"Theo," Javier interrupts me. The way he says my name is like a question wrapped in resistance. "There's something I need to tell you." His intense fascination with the rabbit's foot finally breaks as he hands it back to me. His attention is now solely on me. The waiter returns with our caprese salads, placing one plate in front of each of us.

"Pepper?" The server shoves a giant black pepper grinder in front of my face.

"No thanks. Everything looks good, thank you." My tone is me trying hard to be polite, but still wanting him to leave our table. The waiter tells us to enjoy our salads before finally stepping away.

"I was in a serious relationship with someone named Randall once." He stops, still not sure how to continue his story.

Fuck.

"We were extremely serious, right out of high school. We were together for a long time. He...he meant a lot to me."

"Are you about to tell me you dated the Randall I know, because I'm not sure I have the emotional capacity for that right now."

"No, *your* Randall and *my* Randall," he cringes at the beginning of his sentence, "are not the same Randalls. They can't be."

"How are you so sure?"

"Because..." He pulls in a deep breath and lets out a sigh that rustles the flame of the candle in the middle of the table. "Because my Randall is dead."

"Shit, Javi," I gasp, "I'm sorry."

"It's been a long time. I've healed. I think. He died in Turkey. I never got to say goodbye to him. He was kind of my everything, and the way we ended things...it just wasn't right."

"Did you say he died in Turkey?" I double-check I heard him correctly.

"I did. My Randall joined the military. He left me right after high school graduation. Well, maybe not *left*, but he did choose to go without me having a say. To me, at the time, that was *leaving* me, you know?"

I shake my head, wondering when it'll be a good time to tell Javier that *my* Randall also was in the military. What are the odds? "What happened to him, if you don't mind me asking?"

"No, it's okay." He clears his throat. "From what I heard through the grapevine, because I really couldn't get any information from anyone, was that he was driving a Humvee that ran over an IED. He and six other people were killed instantly."

"Jesus." A heaviness fills my chest.

"Oh man," Javier rubs in a single tear before it falls from underneath his eyelid, "I didn't mean for this to happen tonight. I'm so sorry. I brought up the inheritance, and then I saw the rabbit's foot. Did I ruin this?"

"No, oh God, no." I smile and wink at him through the still dim lighting. "You didn't ruin anything. You just worried me. The way you acted when I pulled this thing out." I dangle the rabbit's foot in the air. "Do you want to continue dinner? We can keep talking about your Randall if you want," I fluff my napkin on top of my lap, "because I'm still hungry as hell, and this salad looks delicious." I laugh, hoping my hunger humor didn't sound insensitive.

"I'd like nothing more than to keep having dinner with you. My Randall is my past. It was sad, and it will always be something I need to cope with. But I'm here now. With you. I got you on a night where you don't have to worry about anyone else besides yourself. It's a beautiful thing, really."

I nod and shake my fork at him in agreement. I poke my plate and pierce small pieces of mozzarella, tomato, and basil. I bring it to my mouth and taste the sweetness of the vinaigrette glaze. "It's nice not to have to worry about anyone else for a change. So, your inheritance...is that linked to your Randall?"

"Yes." He takes a bite of his salad and swallows. "Before

he enlisted, he put my name down as his beneficiary for literally everything. I was shocked when I found out because he never said a word about it. I guess he just wanted to make sure I was okay if he wasn't able to come back to me."

I nod, trying to act like that kind of love doesn't make me a tad bit jealous. If Javier and I continue down this romantic path together, how am I going to live up to his Randall? Javier was given a gift of both adoration and sacrifice. All I've given him was a jump scare from this weaselly furry foot I jammed back into my pocket as soon as he gave it back. I take another sip of my wine before lathering a piece of buttered bread around my plate, soaking up the vinaigrette.

"I forgot to explain the weirdness with the rabbit's foot." He takes another bite, chews, then swallows. "For years, I would see signs from my Randall. I would see the cardinals, the lights flicker, the wind picking up on absurdly hot summer days, and the occasional vision of him from across the room. But the most memorable thing, the biggest sign for me, was when I came across a rabbit's foot sitting on a park bench one day while I was walking my family's dog. It was that moment when, I swear to every higher power there is, I heard my Randall speak to me. He told me I was going to be okay, he apologized for leaving me, and he promised me I'd find love again." He makes a sniffling sound, regaining his composure. "He also told me to keep that rabbit's foot because it was the only way he could communicate with me."

This time, Javier doesn't hold back his tears. Several fall from his cheek before he wipes his face with his dinner napkin. "I didn't listen to that voice because I didn't know what to believe. I thought I was crazy. So, I left the rabbit's foot on the bench, and I regret it every day. It's like I did to him what I thought he did to me." He pauses. "I left him behind."

Then, all of a sudden it hit me.

No, it couldn't be.

"Javier, when you say you thought he left you, what do you mean exactly?" I put my fork down to the side of my plate and exhale, hoping I'm not sitting on a big secret involving a fake death of a boy that both me and Javier have had feelings for.

"It's hard for me to remember, really, but Randall and I were leaving a bar after a night of partying, and a drunk driver crashed into the driver's side of our car."

It was at that moment when my heart stopped. All the air in my body hardened as every organ stopped functioning.

No, it can't be.

"You were flown to Shock Trauma," I say, emotionless.

"Yeah, the accident was so bad, they flew me to Shock Trauma. I was even declared dead for a minute, from what I was told. The next thing I knew, I was waking up almost two months later. I was told I was in a medically induced coma for seven weeks. My parents told me Randall spiraled. He couldn't deal with me being in the hospital. He left the night of my accident, and my parents didn't hear from him again until he joined the military."

No, it couldn't be.

"Javier, my Randall was also in the military."

"No shit," he exclaims. "That's oddly coincidental."

"Do you have a photo of your Randall, by any chance?" I swallow hard, preparing to run into a cement wall. Of course he doesn't carry around a photo of his allegedly deceased ex-boyfriend. Right?

"Are you going to judge me or feel weird if I tell you I do

have a photo?" He reaches for his cellphone in the pocket of his jacket hanging on the back of his chair. A shiver goes up my arm, along with the little hairs that stand erect. Javier's thumb scrolls through his phone's photo album until he finds the one he wants to show me. "This one is my favorite."

The photo shows two boys. One, barely recognizable with long black hair, his face turned to the side, and his visible eyelid squeezed shut. He has his arms wrapped around the waist of the other boy, who he's playfully kissing on the cheek.

Javier points at the photo. "This one's me, obviously."

The other boy, with a smile on his face from the kiss he's receiving, stares back at me as if I'm the camera lens. He's completely familiar and is doing my pumping heart no favors. I'd know that face and that body anywhere: strong cheekbones, mahogany-colored hair, and thick biceps I could identify were Randall's from a mile away.

"What's your beaded bracelet say?" I point to Javier's wrist in the photo.

"Marco."

My breath catches, and a rush of clarity hits me, like a puzzle piece almost connecting, but it's still not quite there.

"Everyone calls me Javi, so Randall wanted to be different and call me by my last name, Marco. He made me that wonky bracelet too." He smiles, embracing his memory. "It took him four hours. The beads kept popping out of the grips of his fingers."

"You said you died in the hospital?"

"For about a minute during one of my surgeries. Supposedly, one of the nurses got emotional and left the operating room. Somehow, the word of me dying got back to my family in the waiting room. It was traumatic because my family thought I was gone until the doctors came out and told them they were able to revive me."

Javi finishes the story with a softness about him, his fingers tracing the rim of his empty glass. "It's crazy to think about how that moment changed so many aspects of my life. But everything happens for a reason, right?"

I smile, but it feels tight, like my face isn't sure how to hold it together. The pieces are all sliding into place, and I need space to think—space away from his gentle eyes, attentiveness, and the way he makes me feel so safe.

"That's definitely a wild story," I say, my voice lighter than how I feel. "We should probably get the check, though. It's getting late."

He nods, still holding his relaxed posture, and calls the waiter over. I can tell he doesn't notice the shift in me, and I'm glad. I don't want to ruin our evening.

THE NIGHT AIR feels cooler than I expect as we step out of the restaurant, my thoughts a chaotic tangle I'm trying to sort out. Javi is all smiles, his hand brushing mine, and it takes everything in me not to pull away as we move beneath the awning.

"Thanks for tonight," I keep my voice steady and polite. Normal, even. My arms wrap around him in a hug, his scent a bittersweet longing I'm not ready to let go of, even though I know I need to. He doesn't seem to notice the hesitation as he squeezes me then steps back, his smile lingering like a half-finished story.

"See you soon?"

I nod, offering a weak smile of my own because any

words I do have get caught in my throat. Javier takes the back of my hand and brings it to his lips. He places a gentle kiss at the knuckles and wishes me a safe ride back home.

Before we separate, I want to tell Javier what I know about the boy in his photo, but apprehension rushes over me like I'm about to jump off a cliff and into a large body of cold, frigid water. So, I don't. I drop my ever-so-lightly kissed hand to my side and watch Javi walk away.

I'm left standing, knowing the boy in his photo is far from dead. He's very much alive. He's been alive for years, and he just so happens to have feelings for me now.

The boy in the photo? Yeah. *That's my Randall.*

TWENTY-THREE

"You've got to be fucking shitting me," Lianna shouts before cupping her hand over her mouth. She throws herself backwards onto my bed and kicks her legs above her head.

"Keep it down, Li!" I throw a pillow at her face. "My dad got home this morning, and my mom's been trying to nap."

Mom has not been able to sleep since my father has been in the hospital, which is completely understandable. I've been there before. Two years ago, he had an infection in his leg. One small pink sore went from the size of a penny to full blown cellulitis, swelling up his entire leg with oozing fluid.

My mom couldn't call off her overnight shift, and Haley had final exams around that time, so I volunteered to stay the night with him. Even though we were residing in the room furthest away from the nurses' station, I still heard everything. The cackles of the employees, the yells from the clients needing pain medication, and the beeping and the buzzing of every single monitor on the damn floor. Not to mention the goings-in and -out of the doctors, nurses, respiratory therapists, and housekeeping.

To say it's difficult to sleep with all of that going on is an understatement. So, I feel for my mom. Luckily, my dad didn't get much sleep either, so he's napping along with her, which is a nice change of pace because he's usually wide awake when the rest of us are sleeping. Or at least trying to sleep.

"I'm sorry, it's just insane to me. Randall has been playing dead for years, and now you're dating him on top of dating the boy he ghosted after a car accident they were both in." She flicks her fingers toward her forehead and makes an explosion noise.

"I think Randall thought Javi was dead, Li." I shake my head. "That's the only thing I could think of to make this whole situation make sense. Also, Randall and I are not official. We went on two dates. We're not *dating*."

"Dating, schmating, mating...whatever you wanna call it." Lianna waves her hand. She sits herself up on my bed, takes the pillow I threw at her and places it on her lap. She throws her arms up in the air and sends her fists pummeling into it. A feather or two floats out from the pillowcase. "So, what are we going to do next? Are you going to tell Javier? Confront Randall? Can I confront Randall?"

I scratch my head. I have no clue what I'm going to do with this information. If I tell Javier, then I run the risk of him not speaking to me anymore. Would you want to speak to the boy your presumably dead ex-boyfriend is trying to date? That would be a *no* for me.

"I think I want to confront Randall about it first." I wipe my brow. "I mean, I have to eventually tell Javier. But that will have to wait until Randall is completely out of the picture. Right?"

"Yes! Genius!" She snaps her fingers together. "You want to be able to tell Javier that, once you found out the truth, you had to run Randall off so he couldn't hurt him even more. You'll be like Mr. Javi Daddy's own personal superhero."

"Mr. Javi Daddy? Really, Li?"

"What? It feels weird to call him by his last name now that we know it." She sticks out her neck, and the whites of her eyes widen. She seems shocked that I'm still surprised by what comes out of her mouth.

"I'm going to ignore the fact that you call the guy I want to be with a *daddy*." I grimace and shake my head.

"I'm not the only one that calls him that. My mom does too!" She winks at me as her tongue slips out between her lips.

A minute later, an argument erupts from the other room. My mom and Haley are yelling at one another. From what I hear, Haley is confessing to my mom about what happened with her job, and Sarah Branson is not taking it well.

"Hey, Li, can you stay here for a minute?" I stand up to walk out of my room, shutting the door behind me in hopes Lianna can't hear the rest of the argument or what else might go down between my family today.

I walk down the hall into Haley's room. My mom is standing in the doorframe, shouting about *mistakes* and *sacrifices*. Haley's clothes are laid across her floor. The doors to her dressers are open and hanging by the hinges. Her closet is completely empty. Almost all of her shoes are stuffed into a large grocery bag.

"How did you turn this into being my fault, Haley?" My

mom's voice is shrill. "You are the one who stole drugs for that loser."

"He's not a loser, Mom," Haley defends. "He needs my help, and let's face it, I'm nothing but a fuck-up around here."

"Haley, don't say—"

"No," she cuts her off. "No, Mom. I'm the one who got suspended from work. I'm the one who stole drugs. I'm the one who pushed Dad."

"I didn't say you *pushed*—"

"Jesus Christ, Mom. Whatever." Haley lets out a heavy, dramatic sigh. "I'm the one who let him fall. I'm the irresponsible one. You are all better off without me." She points to me. "You have your perfect child right there. He's all you need, Mom, and you know it." She throws her bag of clothes around her shoulder and grabs the bag of shoes in the other hand. She charges for the door, pushing past both my mom and then me. We follow behind her.

"Haley," I call out, "I know you told me you've used drugs before, but you didn't really care for them. I know you said you were just stealing them for Jesse." I take a deep breath in. "I'm going to ask you this one question before you leave this house, and I want an honest answer."

She stops, holds on to the banister, and swings around to face me.

"Are you high right now?"

"Oh, screw you, Theo!" she spits.

"Are you?"

"Does it even matter?" she chokes on the question. "No matter what I say, you're still going to doubt me. What do you want from me, Theo? You want me to tell you I'm an addict? Do you want me to fight with you and prove I'm not?"

My mom, standing behind me, lets out a whimper. I can't bear to look at her.

Haley continues, "Maybe I should start using drugs. Maybe it will make me forget about how fucking miserable it is to live here. I hate it here. He makes our lives fucking horrible."

"Don't say that about your father, Haley," my mom cries out.

"What is wrong with you?" I shout.

"That's the thing. Everything. Everything is wrong with me." She starts making her way down the steps. Her bags bang back and forth between the wall and the banister. "That's why I'm leaving. You won't have to deal with me anymore."

Mom howls, "Where are you going?"

"I'm going to Jesse's," Haley mumbles under her breath. "I love you, and if you love me, don't follow me. I need space."

So many emotions disguised as bile swirl between my throat and my stomach, fighting for a path to erupt. I want to chase after her. Grab all of her bags and throw them on the ground. Stop her before she makes the worst decision of her life by running to Jesse. I want to squeeze her tight and tell her we'll get through this. Tell her I forgive her for everything.

Though, on the other hand, am I strong enough to keep fighting for peace, something she so clearly doesn't want? I want to let her leave and for her to never hurt me again. I want to never let her blindside my mom again as she did today.

I finally turn around and see my mom. She's thrown herself against the wall, holding on to the doorframe so she doesn't fall down. Crying. Sobbing. Confused.

Before I can decide what I want to do for myself, the door is slammed shut. Haley made the decision for me. My mom's wail will echo in my memory until I can no longer remember.

Awakened from his nap, my dad walks out into the hallway. He stands above my mom and rubs her shoulders, not having a clue why he's comforting her. He senses the tone of the room for a moment and stays quiet. He does well until he asks the most insensitive question, causing my mom to let out a more forceful bawl that eventually sends her to the floor in a puddle of tears: "Can I have an apple?"

Lianna pokes her head out of my room and catches my attention. It was like I saw her, but I had no idea why she was there. I don't recall what I was doing before everything with Haley went down. Nothing else really matters right now. I ask her to leave and tell her I'll give her a call later.

"Are you sure you don't want me to stay and..." she fumbles her words, trying to figure out what she can actually do to help me.

"I just think it might be best for you to go. I'll keep you updated, Li." I shuffle over to my mom and get down on her level. Lianna walks past me before she gently rubs and then taps my shoulder blade to say goodbye.

An hour later, my mom is still crying. This time, it's at the kitchen table. The pain she's feeling shows as her body goes limp with weakness. "Why didn't you tell me she was messing around with drugs? Was she using them, or just giving them to him? Why didn't I see it? Why didn't I see any of it?"

"Mom, I don't know what to believe anymore." I blink, staring at the ripples in the cups of tea I pour for her and myself. "She told me she wasn't using and that she was just taking them for Jesse. I don't think she's been using drugs, but I just wanted to ask to be sure. I'm so confused. I don't know anymore. I thought I was helping." My throat is scratchy, even between the sips of hot Earl Gray.

"What do we do, baby? I'm lost. I don't know what to do." She places her hands on top of mine and lightly squeezes.

"She'll come back, Mom," I say, not even trusting myself enough to believe that statement. "She needs us." It comes off more like a question than a comment.

I have about two hours left before I usually leave for class, but I'm not going. It's sad, because I made the decision to skip the lecture tonight quicker than I did when trying to figure out what I wanted from Haley.

My sister just left—abandoned us, really. I can't take care of both Mom and my dad by myself. Haley promised me that would never happen. That we'd always be taking care of them together. Why does she get to choose to just walk out on us?

On me.

The thought of people walking out on the ones they love reminds me—I need to confront Randall about what I found out about him and Javier. He needs to know Javier is alive and that he's been left feeling abandoned all these years. If I can't help Haley, I'll be damned if I don't at least try to protect Javier from getting hurt.

Tonight, I'll send an email to Dr. Ambrose to let her know I won't be in class—I've come down with something. After that, I'll head up to campus to drop off the GA assignments I graded last night. The same ones I struggled to finish after my eye-opening date with Javier.

I could barely concentrate, not after realizing Randall doesn't know that Javier—or should I say Marco?—isn't dead. Unless it was all a lie, crafted to make me feel something for him?

No.

He couldn't be that cruel.

Could he?

When Randall leaves class tonight, I'll talk to him. I'll tell him what I've uncovered and see how he reacts.

Then...then I'll figure out how to bring my sister back home. Safely. Away from Jesse.

I'm done with heartbreak.

All of it.

From everyone.

TWENTY-FOUR

The minutes tick by slowly on the dashboard clock; however, my speedometer reaches seventy-five, and I'm flying down the highway. With the music turned off, the only sounds I have comforting me are the gusts of air blowing against the side of the car, the vibrations from the rumble strips on the side of the road as I struggle to keep the car straight in line, and the tick of the blinker when I transition lanes. Music would make me happy right now, but I don't want to be happy, nor do I deserve it.

My mind races with thoughts of where Haley is at this very minute, whether she's followed through with using drugs or not. Disturbing images pop into my head of her nodding out on a ripped couch, as Jesse, whom I've never met before, tries to have his way with her. I also see a visual of her throwing back a handful of white pills, choking them down with milk straight from the carton because it's the closest thing to a drink she has.

I hope my thoughts are wrong. I hope she's safe, and she doesn't turn to the one thing I fear I've pushed her to.

I barely see the car I almost side-swipe to the left of me because I'm not paying attention. I need to snap out of this, get back into the zone. Once I get to campus, I'll deliver the packet of papers to Dr. Ambrose's office, say my piece to Randall after he gets out of the class I'm skipping tonight, and then I'll be on my way to find Haley.

Luckily, her location is turned on, so my phone has been able to pick up where she's been. For the past several hours, she's traveled to and from different places, so it's been difficult to nail down a concrete location. I'm hoping once I finish my business here on campus, she'll have stopped for a while so I can go to her.

I feel guilty that I'm skipping class tonight, but I'm relieved I won't have to sit through two hours of one of Dr. Ambrose's life-altering lectures. She always finds ways to give me even more to think about than just the lesson at hand. Her teaching makes an impact, but it's one I don't have room for tonight.

I'm also relieved I'll avoid getting another stack of papers she'll want me to grade by the end of the week. The graduate assistantship has been rewarding because it's the easiest money I have ever made. But I'm not going to lie, it's daunting at times. It's just another aspect of my life where I'm responsible for someone else. Getting students' grades in the gradebook on time is stressful—a stress I don't even want to think about, especially on the night my sister just ran away from our family.

I walk up the university's giant set of steps and make my way to the humanities building. Passing the on-campus café,

I see Randall standing in line. The barista calls out a name I don't recognize and sets a coffee cup at the end of the serving bar. Randall jumps out of line and grabs the coffee cup with no hesitation. It's obviously not his order, but he doesn't seem to care.

He turns and sees me walking past the café at a quicker than normal pace. I know I'm supposed to be confronting him tonight about playing me and Javier, but I realize I'm not ready for the full-out confrontation just yet. I reach for my shoulder and tug at the strap of my bookbag. I pull out the rabbit's foot from my pocket and squeeze.

"Hey! Theo! Wait up," Randall calls out.

I stop moving forward. Anger fills my fists and sends heat through my arms, all the way deep inside my chest. I'm livid.

I bite down hard on my lip, trying to piece together the exact words I want to say to this liar walking toward me. This liar who has the most beautiful hazel eyes and the most captivating body I've ever seen in camo cargo pants.

My heart starts to race uncontrollably as if I've been running a marathon, and my body is begging to slow down, pleading with me to sit and breathe. I try to speak, but nothing is coming out of my mouth. My tongue is as dry as the crust on a burnt piece of toast.

As he gets closer, Randall's eyes find the small chain wrapped tightly around my middle finger, connecting to the damp rabbit's foot pressed between my fingers and the palm of my hand. "You found my key chain." He reaches for my hand and releases it gently from my grip. "You brought it back to me."

My anxiety is still paralyzing my body and my voice. Extreme emotions like the one I'm feeling now send messages to my mind, demanding it to shut down. I haven't felt like this in a very long time, and I'm not sure why this moment is the trigger among all the triggers today to send me into a full-blown panic attack. It's like everything that has happened has finally made its way to the surface, threatening to burst out of the seams like a goddamn shaken soda bottle.

"Talk to me," Randall whispers. "Tell me what's goin' on."

"I...I can't...breathe," are the only words I can physically gasp out.

"Come take a seat over here." He leads me over to the metal bench sitting outside the glass entrance doors of the humanities building. People walk in and out, not paying any attention to me, unable to regulate my breathing. I'm not sure if that's a good thing or a bad thing. I'd rather not draw attention to myself, but let's face it, if I saw someone struggling to breathe, I'd at least go over and check on them.

Randall rubs my back and practices deep breathing techniques with me, reminding me to breathe through my nose and exhale out of my mouth for full effect. "Is everything okay with your family?"

"No." My breath is evening out but is still difficult to catch. "My sister...she...she ran away," I gasp again, this time holding my breath longer and then slowly letting out some air. "She went back to Jesse, her boyfriend."

"Oh darlin'," he sighs, "I'm so sorry to hear that."

"Don't call me that." My breathing steadies, but my eyes glare into Randall's. "I didn't bring your stupid rabbit's foot back to you. I came to drop off these papers to Dr. Ambrose before my deadline."

"Oh, okay?" He furrows his brows, and his eyes squint in confusion.

"Also..." I hesitate. "I figured out the connection between you and Javier."

"Excuse me?"

"*Your* Javier is *my* Javier. I figured it out." I scan his face for any evidence of guilt, fear, or even relief, but I don't see any of those things. He shows no emotion. I continue, "What I don't know is why you've been lying to me."

Now I see it. His face reddens and drops, his eyes shooting down to the ground. I've caught him, and he knows it. "I didn't want you to find out like this," he mumbles.

"So, you admit it? You lied to me." Questions rapidly begin to fall out of my mouth. "What kind of game are you playing, Randall? Are you a con artist or something? Javier got your inheritance. Did you fake your death? Were you running from something? Someone? You left Javi in the hospital. Did you do that on purpose just to allow yourself to believe he was dead?"

"It's not what you think, Theo."

"Then make it make sense, Randall."

He throws his hands in the air, landing them on the back of his head. "I thought I lost him, alright?"

"But when did you realize you didn't?" I breathe in, feeling my confidence growing stronger with each shapely second I inhale. "You must have known he survived the accident because you left him a shit load of money. I still have no clue how you were able to do that, and honestly, I don't have it in me to understand at this point." I look down, hoping he doesn't see the little trace of embarrassment I have in my face, but he turns away. "What hurts me the most is that you made me think the love of your life *died*, Randall. I felt sorry for you. Your grief made me feel connected to you. What is wrong with you?"

With his back facing my direction, he whispers something, but it's difficult to hear him.

"I can't understand your mumbling."

Exasperatedly, he says, "I wanted you to meet him."

"Huh?" I ask, baffled.

"I wanted you two to meet. I did all of this to bring the two of you together," he says, this time turning his body to face mine.

"Bring who together?" I scratch my head. "Did all of what? What are you talking about?"

He shakes his head, and I see his tongue bounce across the walls of his mouth. His lips pucker, wanting to say something. But he seems to not know how. He opens his mouth and lets out a heavy sigh. "You and Javier deserve each other. You deserve to be with someone like him, and he needs to be with someone like you."

"Is this what you do, Randall? Push people away or abandon them to make yourself look like the hero?"

"If it were that easy." His tone grows more serious before he shakes his head. "You can't possibly understand."

"Don't you dare tell me what I can or can't understand."

"Please," he begs. "Can we discuss this later? There are more important things right now, Theo." He takes a moment. "You need to find your sister. She needs your help."

"You let me worry about my family."

"She'll be at the liquor store in Lotus, Maryland—on the corner of 6th and Columbia Street. I'm not supposed to be telling you this, but I need to. You need to go now and help her."

I choke on the ball of spit I try to push down my throat. "Why are you saying this?" I stumble, grabbing my bookbag to search for my keys. "You're scaring me. What do you mean *you're not supposed to be telling me?*"

"Just go!" he shouts. "I'll be right behind you."

I find my car keys in the bottom of my bag and look up from the bench.

But he's gone.

I look around. He was just in front of me a second ago, but now he's nowhere in sight.

Randall's gone.

I get to my feet and turn my head around, looking for where he possibly could have walked off to so quickly. It's like he vanished or flew away. A sudden fist-sized boulder builds in my stomach. An ache shoots up my chest, making me want to scream out loud, but I choose not to. I've already drawn too much attention to myself on campus in the past half-hour.

I make my way down the steps, leading to the giant parking lot, where I stupidly parked my car in the last row. My phone vibrates in my pocket. I struggle to pull it out of my tight pants, but as soon as I'm able to retrieve it, the call stops. I unlock the screen and see a side profile of a head with three curved lines coming out on top, indicating a voice-mail was left. It was from Haley's number.

After a five-minute walk, I finally reach my car and jump in. Before I start the engine, I decide to listen to the voice-mail. I pray Haley is calling to explain why Randall knows where she's at and why I need to come get her, but I don't hold my breath. I have to save every ounce of air I have because I'm already fighting my anxiety.

It doesn't make sense why Randall would help soothe me but then amp me up again. It had to be a ploy to get us to stop talking about his absurd statement that he did *all of this* to bring me and Javier together.

I double-check to make sure my car is still in park before typing in my passcode and pressing the voicemail button on the main screen. I turn on the speaker phone.

"Hey, Theo, it's me. Haley."

Sniffles echo in the message. She's barely able to get her first couple of sentences out.

"I just wanted to call and tell you I love you, and I'm sorry. I don't want you to worry about me. I'm with Jesse, and I'm realizing this was a mistake. He's not a good person, Theo. He doesn't love me. Right now, he's passed out in the back seat of his car, and I'm looking around thinking, I don't want this. I need to come home. I want to come home. But I need you to know I'm sorry for not being the big sister you needed. I'm sorry for lying to you and Mom. I promise you I haven't been using drugs. You've gotta believe me. I just panicked after I let Dad fall. You were right. I should have been watching him. I'm so sorry. I want to be better."

She pauses.

All of a sudden, her voice sounds distant, almost like she's underwater. She murmurs something, but the steady growl of my car's idling engine drowns out the words. I strain to hear, pressing the phone's speaker harder against my ear, but it's no use. Her breathing is heavy, but she wrestles with it to stay calm. The clearness of her voice returns, *"Sometimes, I think you and Mom will be better off without me. I'm not right in the head. I haven't been in so long. Ever since Dad got hurt..."*

More tears.

"Ever since he got hurt, I've been trying to keep it together. It's not fair what happened to us. It's not fair what

happened to you. I think I was so hard on you when you were coming out because I was so angry. I was angry you didn't have Daddy there for you when you needed a father. I pushed you because I didn't want anyone else not to get to know the real you. He would have accepted you in a blink of an eye, you know that? He loved you; he loved all of us so much, but he was taken from us during the most important years of our lives, and that's not fair. Just please, if I'm allowed to come back home, please go easy on me. Let me figure out how to be the bigger sister. I'll get help. I'll be the sister you need."

This time, a wail on the other end.

"I'm sitting in a liquor store parking lot in Lotus, Maryland. I think it's..."

She shuffles around.

"I'm at the corner of 6ᵗʰ and Columbia Street. If you can come and get me, I'd appreciate it. I'm in Jesse's car, and like I said..."

She gasps, and another, more croaky and masculine voice takes over the voicemail, *"What the fuck, Haley? Who are you talking to?"*

"I'm not talking to anyone, Jesse. I promise."

"Give me the fucking phone. I take a nap for one minute, and you call someone to come pick you up? You're going to leave me after all we've been through?"

"No, it's not what you think. Please."

She's begging.

Suddenly, the voicemail makes a loud crackling sound, and I hear muffled shouting. It sounds so far away. Haley screams my name, but, all of the sudden, her voice is strangled silent.

Then it ends.

I look in the rearview mirror and see the smoke circulating in the air from the rubber of my wheels as I speed out of the parking lot. I need to get to the liquor store before it's too late. I can't understand how Randall knew where Haley was, but now's not the time to solve that equation.

Right now, I need to save my sister.

Right now, I need to be her little brother.

TWENTY-FIVE

I make a right on Columbia Street. A mile ahead, I see red and blue lights taking up the intersection. A line of police cars, ambulances, and a firetruck stop my little hatchback from getting closer to the liquor store.

Shock and fear wash over me like I'm suddenly soaking in a bath full of cold water that once was steaming hot. It's all reminiscent of when Haley and I first pulled up to our home's driveway and saw the commotion surrounding my father's injured body after his motorcycle accident eight years ago.

This time is different. It's more terrifying. This time, I'm alone, and Haley's on the other side of the yellow tape.

The car jerks after I throw on the parking brake. My body, free from the seatbelt, leaps out of the front seat. I realize, from the incessant beeping, that I never buckled in to begin with. Getting here, to what has apparently become a crime scene, was my priority. Screw my own safety.

A crowd stands in front of the line of cars belonging to the first responders. Several officers seem to be managing the environment, answering questions, and requesting the onlookers to *get back* or *wait until more information is available.*

I force my way through a jungle of extending necks, their sweating bodies standing still to ensure they're getting full access to the drama. I scream for the attention of the closest person wearing a badge. She looks timid while she holds back the crowd. Looking around, anxiety and doubt are plastered all over her pale white face. Her blonde hair is tucked tight underneath her cap, leaving her rosy cheeks uncovered. Her name is sewed in bright white lettering into the chest of her uniform.

"Excuse me," I shout, "Officer Dawney!"

She sees my wave and makes her way down the line of people straining their ears and eyes to sense what all the chaos is about.

"I think that's my sister. I think that's her boyfriend's car." I point to the four-door sedan being circled by additional officers and several paramedics.

"Did you say you have a personal connection to the victim, sir?" she asks.

Her words hit me like a brick to the face.

Victim?

What does she mean by *victim?*

Where is Haley?

"Yes. It's my sister. I need to know if my sister is okay. Her name is Haley. Haley Branson."

The officer pulls up the tape separating us from them. I duck my head under, and Officer Dawney walks me toward someone she identifies as Detective Penderson, a tall white man with a red beard, wearing black slacks, a white button-up shirt and a thin black tie. His black trench coat hangs past his knees. He turns to me as Officer Dawney begins to introduce us. He pulls out a small notebook and takes out a pen from the chest pocket inside his jacket.

"What's going on? I need to know if my sister is okay," I say again, not caring whom I'm directing my request to. "You people need to start talking."

The circular movements of the flashing red and blue lights taunt me. My heart races, and my hands shake. My body tells me to just run to the car to see if Haley is inside, but I know if I do, I'd run the risk of being escorted off the scene, and then I'll get no information.

"So, you're the victim's brother?" the red-bearded detective asks nonchalantly.

"Stop saying '*victim*.' Her name is Haley."

"Sir, I cannot confirm her name until you confirm your relationship to her."

That's it. I'm done with this back-and-forth. My anxiety can't take it. I look between Officer Dawney and Detective Penderson, then over to Jesse's car. It's only about a thirty-second sprint away. I shift my body to make the leap. Before I jump, a hand grabs my forearm, and I quickly jerk my neck toward what's holding me back from Haley.

It's Randall.

"What are you doing here?" I look down at the fingers firmly grasping my arm. I glance around, wondering what he must have said to be able to get through the crowd.

Randall doesn't answer.

The detective looks at me with a strange stare. His brow furrows, and the line across his forehead creases. The right side of his mouth shifts upward before he says, "I'm trying to get information about what went down here between these two individuals, son. If you are Haley Branson's brother, which I hope you are, there are some details I would like to share with you."

"Yes, I'm her brother." I show him my license I slid out from my wallet.

"Theo Branson. This checks out." He gives me back my identification. "Your sister is being treated for her injuries caused by her assailant, Jesse Friedman. The EMTs are working on her over there." Detective Penderson points over his shoulder to the ambulance parked behind us. Haley's body lay on top of a gurney, waiting to be lifted and transported into the back of the truck.

I look back at Randall. "How did you know where to find her?"

Randall doesn't answer.

"The 9-1-1 dispatcher. An employee from the liquor store called it in. We've been asking him some questions as well," Penderson responds.

I shake my arm out from Randall's grip, feeling frustrated he's not speaking to the officers about what he knows. I ignore the awkwardness and focus on Penderson before letting out a giant breath. "You said injuries? So she's not..." I stutter again, "Sh...she's not dead?"

"Well..." Penderson pauses before saying, "The injuries she sustained are fairly serious. There was blunt-force trauma to both Ms. Branson's left temple and the back of her head. Mr. Friedman used a pistol he had in his possession and repeatedly knocked her until she was unconscious."

"What happened to him?" I scan the premises, and my attention goes over to Jesse's car again. I look harder, hoping to get a clearer image of who is in the backseat, but I can't seem to see through the crimson splash I'm just now noticing.

"He's dead. We suspect it was an attempt at a murder-suicide. We're assuming he pulled the trigger on himself after he thought he killed your sister," Penderson answers.

"Can I see her? Please," I beg, ignoring the news about Jesse's demise.

"I don't think that's a good idea, Mr. Branson."

"Theo," Randall says, "Theo, I wouldn't."

I take a step to my left and start speed-walking toward the ambulance. No one seems to stop me, which is good because I don't feel like going to jail for assaulting anyone at a crime scene.

All of the sudden, Randall appears right in front of me. My body crashes into his, causing me to stop abruptly.

What the?

I swallow hard. "Move, Randall!" I throw my hands against his chest. This time, different from the times I've touched him before, my body falls forward, right through Randall's, as if he was never there to begin with. He then reappears a couple feet behind me. I'm not sure if he just teleported, or if this is how my body responds to trauma. Either way, he's out of my path to Haley.

Red and blue lights continue to flash. Even though I know the sound of the sirens are turned off, I can still hear them ringing in my head. Asphalt crunches underneath my feet as I charge away from Randall. The cacophony of the horde of voices falls on numb ears.

A second later, Randall's arms take hold of my shoulders, and he turns my body toward him, away from the ambulance, as my heart rate drums harder and faster. He locks my arms against my waist, and I plead for him to let me go, for him to release the vise grip he has on me. I ignore the pain and concern in his eyes, ignore the logic and reasoning as to why he isn't letting me go. At that moment, he is trapping me. Keeping me pinned to a spot. A moment in time I want nothing to do with.

"Please," my voice breaks, tears streaming from my eyes. "Please."

His lips thin as he slowly turns me around to face the ambulance and holds me. I watch in terror as the first responders lift Haley's gurney and load her into the truck. My knees are weak, and I sense he's bearing the majority of my weight. The doors shut the doors with an audible and final click.

I tilt my head to the sky and beg for her safety, not knowing who or what is up there. My voice is a rasping whisper, raw and unfiltered. The look I give Randall is full of tears, but when I connect with him, I see his own tears leaking down his cheeks. I throw myself into the rest of his strength and just let all of my energy go. I let go of all the worry, the fear, and all the guilt held inside of me.

"Theo, I'm so sorry," Randall whimpers in my ear. "She's stable right now, but she's not gonna make it. You'll have time to see her at the hospital, and I reckon you'll say goodbye to her there. I promise."

I sob deeper into his shoulders. I lift my neck to look him in his eyes, and all of my negative feelings return. With anger being the first to show itself, I shout, "How the fuck do you know, Randall?" I look around. Everyone is gawking in our direction with perplexed faces.

"Trust me, babe. I just know." Randall wipes my wet cheek with his finger. "You need to call your mother."

He's right, I do. I have no idea what I'm going to tell her. We've been through this before with Dad. We've been a part of life-changing telephone calls. We've rushed to the hospital. We've done the waiting in the hospital chairs until they wake up. We've done it all before. But this time, I have a stronger feeling in the pit of my stomach that Haley isn't going to wake up like Dad did.

The phone rings twice before Mom answers, although it seems like a lifetime goes by. The dread in her voice when she picks up crushes every piece of me. "What's wrong, Theo? Is everything okay?"

I open my mouth to speak, but nothing comes out. How do I tell this woman who has already lost her husband that she'll lose her firstborn, her baby girl, tonight?

As the ambulance's engine starts, I drop my phone to my chin. The sound of the sirens calls out, quickly demanding a clearer pathway to transport such precious cargo. The trucks pull out of the darkening lot, leaving the non-emergency cars and the crowd of passersby alone under two giant flickering light posts.

"Theo?" I hear my mom's loud, strained voice from the speaker. I raise the phone up back to my ear. "Is that sirens? What's going on? Aunt Kay's here with me. You're scaring me, Theo."

"Mom," I say with the softest tone, stemming from having no more energy to give, "Haley's been hurt, and I think you should have Aunt Kay take you to the hospital to see her."

A deep wail comes from the other line, and the phone clicks. She's not on the other end anymore. Knowing her, she and my Aunt Kay are leaving the house as I stand here and try to piece together everything that happened this evening.

I try to put together exactly how I pushed my sister into the arms of a murderer.

Randall puts his arms around my neck and gives me a tight squeeze. "C'mon, let's get to the hospital."

I didn't hear him at first.

I don't hear anything really.

All I can hear are the incessant negative thoughts picking and poking at my mind, telling me how much of a shit brother I am. Randall told me to start listening to Haley. Javier told me to start listening to Haley. Fuck, I even told myself to start listening to Haley.

And now this.

I'm in this moment where I'm realizing I'll never be able to listen to her again.

I stare intently at the cars driving in front of me and the large green signs I pass indicating every exit from the highway. Avoiding the sickness welling up in my stomach, I blink and shake my head to keep focus on getting to the hospital safely. As he sits in my passenger seat, fidgeting with his stupid rabbit's foot, I begin to think about how Randall was not letting me see Haley's body and how he is so sure she's not going to make it through tonight.

"Javier has a music lesson at the hospital tonight." Randall places his hand on mine, cupping the rabbit's foot keychain into my open palm. Confused, I rub my free hand across my forehead and feel the oil between my fingers when I grab the steering wheel. "He'll take care of you," he follows up. "He really likes you, Theo. I'm so glad you've found each other."

I choose not to speak because I don't have anything nice or helpful to say right now.

We arrive at the hospital, and I unhook my seatbelt, straighten my shirt and look over. "Thanks for coming with me. I'd rather you not come in or wait for me. I don't know how long this is going to take, nor do I want another thing to worry about." I shut the car door and begin to walk, seeing Aunt Kay's car parked crookedly in a handicapped spot near the entrance.

"Theo!" Randall shouts as he pulls himself out of the passenger's side. "Hold on to the rabbit's foot. Don't lose it!"

I look down and open my stressed palm, forgetting the rabbit's foot keychain was what I was tightly gripping ever since he put it in my hand.

Before disappearing into thin air, Randall calls out, "It's for when Haley wants to say goodbye."

TWENTY-SIX

The hospital is becoming my second home. One I want to run far away from and never come back. So much pain and anguish fill these walls every time I step in. The smell of desperation and decay excretes from the firm plastic furniture all around the hospital to the hard, glossy floor tiles my sneakers scuff as I shuffle through the halls.

Mrs. Abby, the woman who gave me the visitor's bracelet the night my dad fell, is stationed at her desk. Warmth emits from her person. She does her best to comfort those who walk through the door. The worried look plastered on my face is one she knows well. There have been many times she's seen that look, and she has to put on a fake but believable smile to settle that type of anxiety.

She wraps the visitor's bracelet around my wrist, and as soon as she's done sticking the two ends together, she gives my hand a gentle squeeze. Although it was quick, it was exactly the amount of solace I need to take my next steps.

I know where I'm headed, but I still feel lost. The hallway is long but still completely desolate in every way. It's shared amongst doctors taking their lunches, housekeeping trying to finish their shifts, business suits making plans for the hospital, patients stepping out of their rooms to get some fresh air, and families awaiting their loved one's prognoses. It's full of sickness, empty hearts, and the common thread of people wanting to be anywhere but here.

On the wall to the right of the automatic door, I push the square metal button opening the way to the emergency room. I wait a moment until the left door opens toward me, while the right slides open in the opposite direction.

On the other side stands Javier. He has his guitar over his chest, hanging underneath his arm. Stunned, he waves me through before the doors shut themselves. "What are you doing here, Theo? Is it your father?"

"No," I wipe an escaping tear, one I couldn't hold back any longer, "it's Haley. She got attacked, and I don't think she's going to make it. They brought her here."

He takes me into his arms without asking. He didn't care if I wanted it, but he knew I needed it. All my weight falls into him, and he picks me up an inch from the ground and carries me over the side of the hallway. He rubs the back of my head and doesn't let me escape his embrace. I know I need to get to Haley, but Javier knows I'm not yet ready.

"Theo!" a familiar voice calls from behind.

Javier loosens his grip on me and turns around. It's my mom and Aunt Kay, who is pushing my dad in his wheel-chair toward us.

Javier takes the reins of my dad's wheelchair, while Aunt Kay makes her way past me, over to the nurses' station. I hear her ask for a status update for Haley and if she can have visitors yet.

My mom takes me into her arms. I hug her so tight, she

loses breath for a second. "Tell me everything that happened."

So, I do.

Everything I know.

I tell her how Haley called and left a message on my phone. I emphasize the despair in her voice when she said she wanted to come home and how she thought she made a poor decision leaving in the first place. I tell my mom how she blamed herself for Dad falling, how she felt like she couldn't do anything right.

I share that, in Haley's message, she asked me to come pick her up at the liquor store while Jesse was asleep in the back seat so she could come home. My eyes begin to well again when I tell her I heard Jesse wake up and then attack Haley at the end of the message. Then how I found out, when I got to the crime scene, Jesse used a pistol to beat her unconscious.

A young doctor, wearing his white jacket, black slacks, and a baby-blue button-up with a navy tie, comes out of the Emergency Room doors. He walks to Aunt Kay, and she then points over to my mother and me. Together, they make their way over to us.

His face is clear and tight, with bright, straight, white teeth, leaving me to think he subscribes to a Botox injection and teeth bleaching plan. He appears between twenty-six and thirty years old, give or take. He reaches for my mother's hand and shakes it after he asks if she is Haley Branson's mother.

"I'm Dr. Everett Mason. Your daughter suffered severe trauma to both her occipital and frontal lobes. Unfortunately, the damage to her skull has caused an internal bleed, known as a hemorrhage. Right now, we're supplying her medication to reduce her blood pressure, but she will need extensive surgeries to stop the bleed," he explains.

"I can't believe this. Will...will she have a brain injury?" My mother meets my eyes, and together we both turn to Thomas Branson, sitting in his wheelchair, unaware of what's going on. Javier, with eyes so brilliant but wet, hovers behind my father, trying to hide his sympathy.

"Ma'am, I don't know what the outcome will be, honestly. I will say I'm not confident in how effective her first surgery will be." Dr. Mason waves over a woman in a tan pantsuit. She's holding a clipboard and a box of tissues and introduces herself as Olivia Vanders, one of the hospital's social workers.

Dr. Mason continues, "I'd like you to go over some paperwork with Ms. Vanders. She'll provide you with some information regarding advance directives and will help you understand end-of-life decisions we'll need you to make if things in the operating room do not go according to plan."

According to plan.

What the fuck does that even mean?

According to plan.

It's as if he already knows Haley will need life support in order to survive the night. Images of Haley being intubated flood my mind. Memories of my dad being strapped to the ventilator on the hospital bed the night of his accident circulate as well, but his body flickers between himself and Haley's.

Is this what it's come to?

Again?

I hear Haley's voice in my head telling me it's not worth it. That if there isn't any way to bring her back like she was before, she doesn't want to come back at all. Our father's accident, his brain injury, and the years of hardships we've endured together as a family are the exact reasons why she wouldn't want us to keep her alive if she couldn't live a fulfilling life. I know that would be my choice if I were in the same predicament. Deep down, the members of the Branson family have all thought about this moment at least a dozen times within the past eight years, and even if we never said it out loud, we all agree.

"Dr. Mason?" I speak up, "I know you don't know what will happen in the future, but I'm asking for your professional opinion here. If we do decide to sign off on resuscitation and intubation, what is the likelihood Haley will live a normal life?"

"Theo!" My mother knows exactly what point I'm getting to, but she doesn't want to hear it. I see her head shake aggressively in my peripheral vision.

"If you want my professional opinion...the trauma is too extensive, and I don't think a normal life, as you call it, is going to be her prognosis." Dr. Mason straightens his jacket and taps his chest pocket, checking for his pen. He doesn't need his pen, so I take that as a nervous but subtle habit. Beside him, Ms. Vanders clicks the metal clip on her board. Nervousness fits her body movements as well.

In that instant, I remember Randall and what he said to me in the liquor store parking lot. His tone was confident. Certain. *She's stable right now, but she's not gonna make it. You'll have time to see her at the hospital, and I reckon you'll say goodbye to her there. I promise.*

"Haley wouldn't want any extraordinary measures."

My mother puts her hand up, silencing me. "I'm not just going to let my daughter die. Dr. Mason, please give us some time to talk about this."

"She wouldn't want life support, Mom," my volume increases. "You know this, and I know this. No machines," I point in the direction of Thomas Branson, "no machines ever again."

"Theo, mind yourself," she snaps. Her attention refocuses on Dr. Mason. "How long do we have to decide and can we please see her soon?"

Dr. Mason looks to Ms. Vanders for support. It's obvious this man doesn't have much experience delivering bad news. He looks down at his watch, as if he knows the exact amount of time Haley has left. "I would say discuss it as a family, and we can talk about our options in about an hour. But again, I'm going to leave you with Ms. Vanders to complete some paperwork. I'll see you soon, Mrs. Branson."

Ms. Vanders puts her hand on my mother's shoulder, and the two of them make their way to the empty conference room across the floor, with Aunt Kay following behind them. I don't join them because I need to take a moment. I lock my knees and lean against the wall. Closing my eyes, I replay the hurt and fear on my mother's face. She understands where I'm coming from, and she doesn't want Haley to end up like Thomas, but in my heart, I know what Haley would want.

I feel the ends of two shoes graze the side of my leg, not hard enough for me to budge, but just enough for me to know Javier has wheeled my father close to me. "I don't want to lose her, Javi."

"She'll be okay," says Thomas Branson.

I brush through my hair with my fingers and turn to face them. My heart breaks to know my father still doesn't have a clue about what's going on. His brain won't allow him to comprehend the gravity of tonight's situation.

Javier mouths the words, *"I'm sorry, I tried."* He must

have tried to explain to my father that Haley is dying, to no avail. Until now, I never realized how hard grief will be for Thomas Branson. With his short-term memory, we'll need to constantly remind him that his daughter isn't there. For him, it'll be like losing his child over and over again.

The thought makes me choke up, and another tear travels down the side of my face.

"I wanted to try something but didn't want to do it without your approval." Javier pulls out his phone and attaches a corded pair of headphones to it. "Words weren't working, so I'm wondering if music would?"

"Sure," I say with no energy.

He bends down to my father's level. "Mr. Thomas? Can I call you Mr. Tom?"

"Yeah, buddy. Tom is the bomb." The rhyme makes Javier smile, but it sends a jolt of defeat to my stomach.

"I want you to listen to this song. It's a song about losing someone you love and hoping they find happiness in heaven. I'm really sorry to tell you, but your daughter, Haley," he pauses, "Haley is in the hospital, and the doctors said there's a chance she's going to die tonight. It's really important that you understand so you can grieve with your wife and son. Can you listen to this song and try to understand it?"

"Oh no, Haley's dying?" By his tone, he appears to grasp the concept, but for how long?

"Yes," Javier continues, "I'm so sorry, Mr. Tom. But I want you to listen to this song. It's called 'Dancing in the Sky.'" He plugs the headphones into my father's ears and taps his screen, playing the song for him. He lays the phone on my father's lap.

After a couple minutes, my dad's eyes begin to well. He puts his hand over his forehead and his elbow meets his knee.

Right now, the music is helping him recognize what's happening. There are so many times I wished he could experience the same feelings we were, but I never wanted it to be about something so tragic and painful.

It's so deeply bittersweet.

"Music is a universal language," Javier says. "For individuals with brain injuries, research shows music is the one language that helps memories not fade. The patients I've worked with have been able to make connections between the lyrics of songs and reality."

I wrap my arms around Javier's neck and embrace him. "I think it's working," I say, thanking him for being so patient, so loving with me and my father. It's all I have ever really wanted in a partner. Not only do I feel safe with him, but I feel like my family can be safe with him as well.

"Also, I hope you don't mind, but I called Lianna. She's on her way," he says in my ear.

"You're the best." I squeeze him harder, showing him I appreciate everything he's done for me tonight.

"I'm just glad I was here." Javier gently pulls back. "I would hate it if you had to do this all alone." His cerulean blues take hold of me, and his hands grasp both of mine.

Blankly, I stare at him, thinking I'm grateful he's here, but I was never truly alone. Randall was there for me tonight in ways I don't think I'll ever understand.

Randall showed me there is more to him than just a Southern military boy returning to school for a second career. There's something more to him. Something mysterious. Something not normal. Randall knows too much about things he has no right to.

He knew what street Haley and Jesse were located on before I heard Haley's message.

He knew Haley was going to be taken to the hospital before I found out at the crime scene.

He knew Javier was going to be here to support me before I saw him through the emergency room doors.

And before the doctor told us his professional opinion, Randall knew Haley wasn't going to make it through the night.

He knew exactly how everything was going to play out—before I knew anything.

But what I do know is that I wasn't alone, and I have absolutely no clue who...or what Randall Stevens is.

TWENTY-SEVEN

Finding the strength, I open the door to the closed conference room. Behind the heavy oak, my mother, aunt, and Ms. Vanders sit across from one another. Papers are sprawled around the table in what seems to be an organized chaos. My mother looks at me, grateful I've decided to join. She taps the empty chair next to her.

As I sit, Ms. Vanders continues, asking my mother if she wants her to go over anything I may have missed now that I'm present. I wave my hand and tell her I know what the papers say, and I know what our signatures will mean.

My mother requests that Ms. Vanders leave the room to give our family a few moments to discuss. Ms. Vanders agrees and asks if she could bring anything back, like hot chocolate, coffee, or a snack. I can't even fathom eating right now, and I'm pretty sure that notion is shared between all of us.

Ms. Vanders shuts the door behind her, and my mother takes my hand. "Theo, I don't want to make this decision. I hate that I have to ask you for your input again, but I don't know what to do."

"It's okay, Mom. The last time you asked me, I was a child. A child who didn't know any better. I was a child who wanted his father back. And you know what? I never got that." She lets out a whimper, and Aunt Kay rubs her back to comfort her. "There is nothing I want more in this world than to have my sister wake up and be fine, but we all know that's not going to happen, and it's not what Haley would want."

"She should have been able to come and talk to me. I've failed her. I failed her as a mother."

"Don't say that," I shoot back quickly. "You are the best mother, and both Haley and I are lucky to have you. Haley... it's just...Haley is sick, Mom. There is no way we could have predicted this would happen. She was so good at holding everything in. She didn't want us to know what she was going through."

"You've lost so much. If I sign these papers, that means you're going to lose her too." She wipes her nose with the sleeve of her sweater.

"So will you. We all will." I sniffle. I'm trying to be the strong one here, but my emotions are getting the best of me. There is nothing harder than being strong for the woman who taught you what strength looks like.

"I can't believe we have to say goodbye." My mom puts her elbows on the table and brings her fingertips to her forehead as she sinks the weight of her grief into her hands.

"We're all going to miss her," Aunt Kay says, rubbing Mom's shoulders.

"Oh my god," Mom extends her head straight up, "where is your father, Theo?"

"He's with Javier. He's fine." I stand and walk over to the window, blocked by white blinds. I push one blind aside and peer out. Lianna has arrived, and both she and Javier are standing in front of my father talking with him. Lianna bends down and gives my dad a hard squeeze around the neck. Tears fill her eyes, but I know when she sees me come out of this room, she'll wipe her sadness away and support me like only a best friend would know how.

A few moments pass, and Ms. Vanders reappears, along with Dr. Mason. My mom handles the talking and tells them she'll sign the Do Not Resuscitate paperwork, but she wants her, myself, and Aunt Kay to see Haley immediately, preferably before surgery. Dr. Mason agrees to this.

Since I'm closest, I hold the door for everyone in the room to leave. As she shuffles by, I give my mom a kiss on her forehead and wipe the wetness under her eye with my thumb.

As soon as Aunt Kay passes, I see a figure standing on the opposite side of the room—a male figure who wasn't there before. His back is facing me. He's looking out the window toward the stream behind the hospital. His body glows like a blinding light, bright enough for me to pinch my eyelids together.

It's Randall.

"Hey, Mom," I call out in the hallway, "may I have a minute? You can go back. I'll catch up. I just need a moment to process everything."

She nods and continues to follow Dr. Mason as I shut the door.

I turn around to face Randall. His dazzling stature has dimmed to a normal sight. I walk over to him. His face is still turned away from me.

"Randall, what are you?"

"Cuttin' to the chase, sugar plum, aren't ya?" he asks, facing me now. "Do you have any idea?"

"I don't. Or at least I don't know how to explain it." I reach for his shoulder, and my hand moves right through as if he's not even there. My hand has an immediate chill but doesn't disappear in him. It's more like his body becomes translucent to allow my touch to pass through.

"It's pretty self-explanatory after that, darlin'." He chuckles.

"I don't get it. I've touched you before. We..." I stutter, "we...we kissed."

"And dammit, wasn't it good?" He licks his lips. "It's a little trick I can do. I can choose how you and I interact."

It's impossible. How is this happening? Words try to make sense in my head to describe what I'm feeling right now, but my beliefs—my logic—are not allowing it.

Images flash in my mind, altered clips that leave me putting the pieces together slowly but surely. I see myself sitting next to an empty chair in class. I see myself alone on the bench outside of the humanities building. I see myself in the bookstore the day I thought Randall paid for my text-books, and I see the cashier, Angelo, full of pity, observing me speak to myself, realizing now why he gave me the mints for free. I see all of the times he stood me up: the bonfire, when my dad fell; it's because he couldn't physically be there for me.

"I feel you're strugglin' here, so I'm going to help you out. Theo Branson, I'm not who you think I am. Well, I am Randall Stevens, and everything I have ever shared with you about my life is the truth. Except for maybe the fact that I'm not alive. I had some unfinished business here on Earth, blah,

blah, blah. Long story short, you're the only one who can see me. You're the only one who knows me for who I am at this moment in time."

A faint headache creeps through my temples on both sides of my head. "How is that so? How can I be the only person to see you?"

"Honestly?" He scratches his head. "It's because of that little keychain in your pants pocket. The rabbit's foot. Remember the story I told you on our way to the aquarium?"

"The story about your captain giving it to you to feel closer to Marco...or should I say *Javier*?"

"Yes, that's it. That rabbit's foot holds the power to communicate with the dead. It helps you see me."

"That doesn't make sense. You're not the only person who's died. How can I not see anyone else?

"Because I want you to see me and," he pauses, "you want to see me in return. It's gotta work both ways."

"I'm so confused," I say. "You felt so real." I think about his soft, mahogany hair shaved tight on the sides of his head. The muscles I got to feel overtop of his shirt. His smooth and delicate lips as they kissed mine. The scent of his citrus cologne tantalizing me to my core. When his beautiful hazel eyes comforted me when I needed them the most. He was always so real to me. So real, I hardly believed him to be true.

"I do apologize for *ghosting* you," he points at me and shakes his finger, "which I found out is a really rude term people use these days. Not sure how I feel about it. I feel like I should be offended. But I do think it explains what I did to you a couple of times, and I'm sorry for that."

I let out a laugh, a reaction I wasn't expecting to have today. "You did leave me hanging several times. I was so mad at you."

"Hey now! I left when I needed to. And plus, if I showed up for you, you wouldn't have found my Javier."

"*Your* Javier?" My smile subsides. "You can't claim him. Right? Oh my god, is he dead too?"

Randall smirks. "No, silly. You, your momma, the goats on that farm over there," he points out the window at a farmhouse on the other side of the stream, "you all can see him."

"Why can't he see you? You can give him this rabbit's foot like you gave me."

"Been there, tried that." Randall takes a heavy sigh. "I think he told you the story of finding the rabbit's foot on a bench? I *may* have eavesdropped."

"Yes, and how he heard, well...I guess he heard *your* voice but ultimately chose to leave it behind."

"Exactly. I thought if he took the bait and kept the rabbit's foot, he and I could be together. But he stopped wanting to see me the day he thought I abandoned him and left for the military."

"Because you thought he died in the accident. So you left. I get it. I think he understands too. Or at least that's what he told me. He misses you. He carries a picture of the two of you around in his wallet."

"Which is why I wanted him to meet someone like you."

"Wait," I shake my head, "are you telling me you played Casper the Friendly Matchmaker for me and Javier?"

"Ouch! Casper? Really?" He laughs harder this time. "The answer is yes. When I got a second chance to come back, I thought my unfinished business was me going back to school and learning how to be a therapist. Somethin' I've always dreamed about, especially since Javier didn't want nothin' to do with me. Then I met you, standin' on those steps. Somethin' bout you just blew me away. It was some-thin' I haven't felt since...since Javier."

He lets out a breath he was holding. "I thought you were my unfinished business. You were so amazin' that I got caught up in tryin' to get to know you and be with you. For a moment there, I forgot I was actually dead."

"How convenient." I smile.

"Right?! I was like, *maybe I'm supposed to fall in love again?* Who knew?" He bends his index finger up and down, pointing at the sky.

He continues, "The moment I met you, I knew you were the one. You give so much of yourself to other people—your family, your friends, everyone. But you never seemed to care the same amount for yourself. It pains me to see it because you're one of the best people I know.

"And once I realized I couldn't have you for myself, because, you know, I'm dead and all," Randall rolls his eyes in jest, "I wanted to see if you and the other best person I knew would hit it off. And that's what happened. Bringing *you* to Javier was my unfinished business. I've always wanted him to be happy, to find someone he could love just as much as he loved me, if not more.

"I had to give you a little push though—to teach you how to live your life without hesitation and to stop waiting on others to make you more content."

"And how exactly did you do that?" I ask, raising a brow. "I should've known something was up when Hamilton growled at you the first time you met."

"Yeah, your little guy almost blew my cover. Dogs are weirdly in tune with the afterlife—so are dolphins." He winks. "Let's just say I had to leave you high and dry a couple of times, if you know what I mean." He clears his throat, then adds, "But it honestly killed me—no pun intended—to know I was hurting you when I abandoned you. It's complicated, but it made sense in my head. I needed you to like me enough to hate me enough to find Javier." He lets out a long breath. "And the rest is history."

"Would Javier and I have met if you didn't interfere?"

"That's a solid question. And the short answer is *yes*. Call it a ghost power or whatever, but the moment I met you, I got somethin' like one of those premonitions, where I saw you two together. But, in order for me to move on, I felt like I had to be the one to make it happen. Selfishly."

"You seem to know about a lot of things before they happen." My smile turns quickly into a sad frown.

"Haley? Yeah," he swallows, "I'm so sorry, Theo."

"Why couldn't you tell me before it happened?"

"Because it's the rules, bub. I can only guide people into doin' things. I'm not allowed to stop things from happenin'. With Haley, if I would have told you what was going to happen, and if you were somehow able to stop it, then it would have been worse for her for defyin' fate. Just trust me when I say, I've seen it happen, and you wouldn't want that."

"What do I do now then, Randall? How do I say goodbye to her? I'm not ready for this," I cry out, not caring who hears me. I'm loud, but it feels so good to finally *feel* something.

"No one is ever ready for this." Randall wraps his arms around my body and holds my weight. He allows me to feel his skin, his soft touch, his strength. "You're gonna feel sad. You're gonna feel grief. Let yourself feel it all. Your sister will always be with you, even if you can't see her. The memories you have and the love you share with her—all of it —will never go away. I have no idea what you're going through. I've never lost a sister. I've only lost the man I loved. But take it from me: it's better to be able to say goodbye than not.

"You're gonna walk in that room, and you're gonna see her. You're gonna feel her. You're gonna remember her touch. And then you'll say goodbye, and you'll let her soul go. You'll let her soul live."

I pull back before kissing Randall on his cheek, tears flowing from my eyes without a care. The look on his face consoles me, and I take all my fear and dread in saying goodbye and swallow it.

I reach in my pocket, pull out the rabbit's foot and hold it out in front of me. Randall takes my hand and closes my fingers on top of it. He then takes my head in his hands, extends his neck, and plants a hard kiss on my forehead. A kiss that feels like a goodbye.

He whispers in my ear before he vanishes, "I think I've accomplished what I was supposed to accomplish. Thank you for taking care of Javier. I promise to look after Haley once I meet her."

TWENTY-EIGHT

Connected to her arms are numerous IVs pumping various medications into her body. I step further into her hospital room and see Haley lying under a white blanket, her head supported by a neck brace, while her back is propped against several pillows. Her eyelids are closed tight, colors of deep and light purple splattered underneath and at their corners.

She has stitched gashes covering her forehead, presumably from the handle of the gun. Her hair is shaved in what seems to be random spots around the sides and the back of her head. The beeps from the machines sound like Haley is doing well, but everyone in this room knows that is not the case.

Watching my mother cry is one of the hardest things. Knowing she doesn't have her husband—her partner—to cry with is what always gets me. Yes, he's sitting behind her, next to the window, knocking on the wheels of his chair. But, in reality, he's not capable of being that person for her in such important moments.

The trick Javier pulled with letting him listen to songs with the same message of what's going on in life has been working, but periodically the old Thomas Branson comes through. He's asked for food twice now, completely ignoring the fact that he, too, has to say goodbye to his baby girl.

For many, it's a different type of feeling to be able to share your emotions with your significant other, the person who is supposed to know everything about you, the person who is supposed to know exactly what to say and do to comfort you.

My mom doesn't have that with my father. Not anymore.

Even though sometimes she thinks I can be that person for her, I can only be so much. It's a dynamic that will always be, until the day it can't, and I've accepted that. She raised me to be the type of person who puts others first, and I'm proud to be there for her when she needs me.

Mom lifts her head from Haley's chest. "Hey, baby." Her face reads secure, but I know she puts on this façade so I feel better about this whole process. "Come say goodbye. I signed the papers, so they're going to turn the machines off soon. She hasn't made any improvements. They think it's the best decision, medically, of course."

I tighten my fist and feel the fur of the rabbit's foot peeking out in between my fingers. "Why don't you spend some more time with Haley? Don't worry about me."

There's a soft knock at the door before Dr. Mason makes his entrance, followed by three nurses. The crowd fills the room, but all of their faces are looking in different directions, seeming to avoid interrupting our last moments.

Judging by the message Randall gave me, I'm hoping Haley makes an appearance so we can say more appropriate farewells, but just in case and to appease my mother, I rest my hand on her shoulder and slide between her and Haley to give my big sister a kiss on the cheek and whisper in her ear that I'll miss her and think about her every single day from this moment forward. I apologize for not being the brother I should have been, even though deep down I know I shouldn't blame myself. And, finally, I tell her I love her and that I'll take care of Mom and Dad the best I can.

It's time.

Dr. Mason swallows hard and then announces his plan. He asks my mother if the family has all said what we needed. Mom nods, tears flooding her cheeks, not taking her eyes off Haley.

The nurses take their positions, turning off the equipment each is responsible for. Two female nurses are on standby, one holding a suction tube and bucket, while the other holds a towel. A male nurse cracks his knuckles, preparing for what appears to be the role of his lifetime—injecting my sister's body with palliative medicine in case the intracerebral hemorrhage in her brain tissue takes longer than ten minutes to damage the cells needed to bring in oxygen.

I might give off the idea I know what I'm talking about, but in all honesty, I have no clue. Hearing what Dr. Mason said about the palliative process went in one ear and then right out the other. Similarly, this is what happens to Thomas Branson when we ask him not to reach for something on the grocery store shelf as he's being pushed down the aisle in his wheelchair. I don't know how many smashed boxes of cereal and dented canned foods Haley and I had to pick up after him because he refused to listen.

Now, it's just me who has to pick things up.

Her vitals are crashing. The beeps from the machine

were turned off, but I can still see the numbers on the screen declining at a rapid pace, dropping faster and faster. Haley's body is shutting down quicker than we all anticipated.

They say life flashes before your eyes as you die, but they never talk about what happens when you watch a loved one's life fade away. With every waning moment, short, quick memories surface in my mind. I see the Christmas morning when we opened our shared telescope and spent all day arguing about who got to use it first. I smile when I see the day Haley and I threw a birthday party for Hamilton in the neighborhood dog park with random dogs we called his friends. Then, I see memories of the two of us sharing a bedroom after Dad's accident because it took two full months for us to renovate Haley's bedroom from the gym room Dad replaced it with when she originally went off to college.

The uproarious lament coming from my mother pulls me out of my reverie. The rest of the world stops as one of the female nurses flips the monitor off and the screen goes blank. My mother throws herself on Haley's body. She continues to cry, but this time it's different. It's not a wail or a sob. It's more like a hope that her baby girl is finally happy, that she's finally safe, and that she's not in any more pain.

A hand touches my shoulder. A nurse, probably, asking me to move aside. I take a step to the left and turn my neck to see who is behind me, and to my surprise, it's Haley. She's not wearing her hospital gown, but instead, she's wearing her favorite pair of blue scrubs with flashy white Dansko shoes. "Hey, Little Bro."

I don't speak but squeeze the rabbit's foot a little harder in the palm of my hand. I smile and nod over toward the door, hoping not to catch anyone else's attention. I open the hospital room door, step out, and close it. Haley stands outside the room, waiting for me as if she was never inside the room to begin with.

"Randall was right. You did want to say goodbye to me."

"Of course I did, ya turd!" Haley grins. "And it's not really a goodbye, now is it? I'll be with you every single day."

I try to swallow, but something in my throat catches. I let out a small choke, making my eyes water a little. Haley asks me why I'm crying, which triggers actual tears. "I'm so sorry I wasn't there for you when you needed me."

"Theo!" she shouts, slapping my arm. "I should be saying the same thing to you. I don't want you apologizing for the mess I got myself into. You do not apologize for how Jesse manipulated and controlled me. That's not your responsibility. You tried so hard, and I love you for that. I was just...I wasn't well."

"We could have gotten you the help you needed." I run my fingers through my hair.

"Kiddo, I didn't want your help. I didn't want Mom's help. Everything that led up to tonight happened because I felt like I didn't need anyone's help but Jesse's.

"Jesse had a really tight hold on me and made me feel so isolated from you all. He made me think he was the only one who could help. So, I fell for it. You've got to understand that." She slides her hands into her pockets and pushes up with her toes, playfully toggling between them and her heels. "Promise me something though?"

"Anything."

"Promise me you're going to live your life?" She smacks her lips together. "You know? Travel the world. Learn as many things as you can. Kiss lots of boys. Just live your life, Theo. I need you to do that. Not just for me, but for you."

I shake my head. "How am I supposed to do that now? With you gone?"

"You never needed me to do those things," she says.

"No, but we needed each other to help with Mom and Dad. We were supposed to take care of them together, and you just...*leave me?* How am I supposed to go on without you?"

"You have no idea how sorry I am for leaving you, but I guarantee you and Mom will figure it out. You two have always been the foundation of this family, and I'm so excited to watch you continue on. Kicking ass and taking names."

She seems so certain of what she's saying, like she knows what the future holds for me. I squeeze the rabbit's foot in my palm. She places her hands on mine as she notices the fur sticking out from the crevices of my closed fist.

"I'm scared, Hales."

"I know you are, Little Bro. I also know you're going to be just fine. You're going to fall in love, have a family, be the best fucking therapist there ever was, and sing and dance to many more new Reba McEntire songs."

"I would ask how you know all of this, but a little birdie already explained the whole ghost premonition thing to me."

She smiles and bows her head. "I will say, it is pretty cool."

"I love you, Haley." I reach out for one final hug around her neck. "I'm going to miss you so much."

She squeezes back, and before she disappears from my grasp, she says, "I love you more, and I promise I will always be right here with you, whenever you need me. It just might take me a minute because I'm about to hop on the afterlife train to Portugal... or Belize. I haven't decided yet. Just know

I'm always watching. Please go easy on yourself, Little Brother."

A weight drops from my arms, and I'm left standing in the middle of the hospital's hallway with nothing but calm and a subtle chill. Nurses walk past, rolling computers and medicine cabinets, holding blankets and pillows in between their arms, and attending to those patients who still need care.

A faint whisper catches my attention from behind. "Hey, Theo. How are you holding up?" Lianna's kind touch on my shoulder releases an immediate feeling of comfort. She knows how much Haley has meant to me, even through all of the conflict we've had over the years. She knows exactly what it's like to have the love of and for a sibling. She embraces me in a strong hold and tells me she's already emailed Dr. Ambrose and let her know I won't be in class for the next week.

"How did you know her...?"

"Honestly, I have no clue, boo. Her business card was in my wallet. I figured you'd put it there and would want me to let her know what's going on."

Randall.

Lianna continues, "She said she'd let the rest of your professors know and wanted me to tell you not to worry about the graduate assistantship and to focus on being with your family. She sounds like a really good professor."

"Thank you, Li." I give her a strong hug.

"Of course, darling." She kisses my cheek. "Oh, and by the way, that Javier man is so in love with you, T. He's been out in the waiting room being all adorable and supportive and shit."

The right side of my lip curls up in a soft smile, and I let out a heavy sigh. "I'm going to go in, check on my mom, dad, and aunt, and say goodbye to Haley one last time, and then I'll be out. Why don't you head home?"

"Hell to the no. I'll go keep Javi company out there. You come out when you're ready. I love you."

"Love you too, Lianna."

I STEP BACK inside the room. Mom and Aunt Kay are at the edge of Haley's bed watching my father. He sits in his wheelchair on the side of the bed, gently pushing back Haley's hair across her forehead and behind her ears. He whispers something to himself, but I can't make it out. In this rare moment, he seems to understand what we all do. The music he listened to with Javier must have helped him make sense of the fact that we all lost someone important to us tonight.

Important to him.

I will be sure to lock this memory in my mind for the future. I want to cherish the time I have left with my family and remind myself that I still have a father to care for no matter what mental state he's in. His display of affection over Haley's body proves to me that, even though he doesn't know how to show it sometimes, he loves his children and always will.

I know this moment won't last long. I know the heartbreak will set back in. This glimpse of fatherhood is what I wished for when my mother asked Haley and me if we wanted all extraordinary measures for him to take place eight years ago when he was lying in the same spot Haley was today.

Like Haley, I'll always regret being that child afraid to be fatherless, afraid to let our father go. We didn't know what life was going to look like for him, and we came to find out most of it wasn't fair to him either. It was the wrong decision to save him, and it's something our family has to live with forever.

But tonight...

Tonight is different.

Tonight we made the choice Haley would have made. We gave her the chance to travel the world, to be happy, to find an ultimate love within herself and whatever higher power she's given herself to. We allowed her to be free of pain, and I'm so happy to know she's in a better place.

I know this in my heart because of this silly rabbit's foot.

I guess I have Randall Stevens to thank for that.

TWENTY-NINE

The waiting room walls feature drab tan paint with maroon borders brimming with dust. Javier has sectioned off a corner of the room next to the triple caffeine drink vending machine and the basket full of Oreos, graham crackers, and chips. He has pulled together several chairs and has taken pillows from the adjacent couches in preparation for the night. If there were others in the room, I'm sure they'd be frustrated that he's hogging all of the amenities, but a big part of me is grateful he's being so considerate and taking care of my family and me during the most difficult night of our lives. I'll never forget what he's done for us tonight.

What he's done for me.

"Look at you, setting up a fort," I say, sitting in one of the empty chairs next to him.

"Hey." His cerulean-blue eyes flutter open before he sits himself upright from his slouching position. He rubs a couple small crust fragments from the corners of his eyes. "How long was I out? Is she...?"

"She's gone," I murmur, blinking to avoid another rush of tears. I was unaware of how that answer was going to sound out loud.

There's a sharp pain in my chest when I think of my big sister not being alive anymore. I know it's a thought I'm going to have to come to terms with in the future, and that it's something I'll have to reflect on forever, but tonight...tonight it's too heavy for me to say with credence. "The internal bleeding was too much, and she passed on quicker than anyone thought she would."

"Come here." Javier takes the back of my neck and pulls my head closer to his chest. "I'm so, so sorry."

I want to cry, but I can't find any energy to actually let it happen. His embrace feels good. I want to let out my emotions all over him because I know he can handle it. I'm just not sure I have any left to give at this moment. I let out my tears and my anguish when Randall showed me who he really was and what he felt he was sent to do here. I dried completely out when Haley and I said our final goodbyes. I am spent. Emotional, but hollowed out. It's a confusing feeling—one I hope Javier can make sense of.

He whispers at the top of my head, buried deep within my hair that probably smells like hospital and death. "It's okay, Theo. I'm right here. I'm not leaving you."

Hearing him say those words is all I need at this moment. It's all I want. The worst thing in my life just happened to me, and for once I have someone in my life who wants to take care of me.

I always thought being a caregiver was my identity. I lost the essence of my father so young, and the pain from that made me want to take care of him. I put him first before all of my personal needs, wants, and desires. In the way Haley was taken away from me tonight, I've learned that life is too short and too precious to give yourself to someone else so completely.

I'll always take care of my family. I want to be here for them for however long I'm able to. Caregiving is still a part of me that gives my life purpose. What's missing, though, is balance. The balance that Randall and Haley spoke of. The balance that Javier alluded to. The balance that I desperately need to figure out in order to take care of myself. Because if I'm not taking care of myself, then I'm definitely not giving the most genuine, healthiest version of myself to the people around me who matter most.

In this moment with Javier, I realize I've been given a gift from both Randall and Haley. They wanted me to open my heart to love, to accept and trust love from someone else, and, more importantly, to love myself just as much. To give myself the life I deserve. To simply *go easy on me.*

"My winter break is coming up," I say out loud without thinking.

"Okay?"

"We're having Haley cremated. It's what she would have wanted. And I'm thinking I'd like to take a trip somewhere nice to spread some of her ashes. Maybe Hawaii? Haley and I have never been."

"I think I can swing that." On the top of my head, I feel his lips curl into a smile and his cheeks rise. "I'll start looking at flights and hotels."

"I'd like that. And maybe on that trip we can say goodbye to someone else?"

"Yeah? And who is that?"

"Your Randall." I falter. "He meant a lot to you, and we

wouldn't have found each other if it weren't for him." I pause again, then recover. "Figuratively speaking, of course." I smile. "I think it's about time we send him off with a proper goodbye."

The sentiment catches him by surprise before he lets out a minimal utterance. "I'd like that."

I want to ask if he ever thinks about Randall, or if he's still in love with the ghost of his past, but I already know the answer.

Randall is unforgettable.

He's impossible not to love.

If fate were different, Javier could have accepted the magic of the rabbit's foot for himself. He could have listened to Randall's voice that day on the bench and believed in such a miracle. But the work Javier has done to process his grief over the years allowed him to move on and carry his love for Randall in a different way. I can't explain love, but I know the love Javier carries within him is infinite. And I'm lucky enough—thanks to Randall—to now be on the receiving end of that kind of love.

"Speaking of guys named Randall, have you heard from yours?" Javier takes my hand in his and walks alongside me in the hospital corridor. "I hope that's not inappropriate to ask? I just know how close you two were becoming."

"He actually did reach out, and we spoke."

"Oh?"

"Don't worry." I smile. "We decided to be friends. Me and him? It was impossible from the start, to say the least." A small smirk peeks out of the corner of my mouth. "I told him about you, and he was really happy for me. For us."

"That's...sweet." Javier pauses, looking down at the

object in my hand. "You gonna give him back that creepy rabbit's foot keychain?"

I flip the keychain between my fingers before eventually shoving it back into my pocket. "Nah, I think I'm going to hold on to it. Hope that's okay?"

"Of course, *cariño*."

The older I get, the earlier I seem to wake up. This is something I'm beginning to notice, especially when the man who sleeps next to me has to be up at the ass-crack of dawn to get to his eight o'clock music class he's lecturing at Colesville University.

Javier took the job at my alma mater two months after I graduated from my master's program. He and Dr. Ambrose hit it off when I took him as my guest to the graduate luncheon at the end of my final year. She introduced him to the dean of music education, and the rest was history. He loves his new job, and what makes it even better is that he is still able to sing for the children at the cancer center too. He sets up internships for some of his students with the hospital, giving the kids more voices and instruments to listen to.

Our morning routine is simple. Javier makes some noise in the kitchen while he prepares our lunches for the day, watches the morning shows at a low volume on the television, and sings at least one tune as he takes his morning shower. For me? I just sit in bed, trying to avoid Hamilton's sloppy sunrise kisses, and try not to listen to all of Javi's sounds while I toss and turn, cover my ears with any pillow I can grab, and groan at how much I don't want to start the day.

It's my own fault, really. I stay up way too late each and every night trying to catch up on all my TV on DVD shows I've collected over the years. After realizing my old DVD player still worked, I was able to finally finish all fifteen seasons of *Supernatural*. Javi still doesn't believe me when I tell him about the time I won that infamous Black Friday Smackdown against an old lady. Javi makes fun of me for choosing not to stream TV shows, but there is something special about opening up a DVD box set, pushing down on the plastic latch holding the DVD in the case, popping the DVD in the player and pressing *Play All*. I humorously remind him all the time that it's my life, so let me live it!

When I finally get myself out of bed, pull a pair of pajama pants over my legs, and slip on some house slippers, I step into the kitchen of the home we share. I sprinkle some dried superfood flakes over Hamilton's kibble and smell the fresh coffee Javier makes every morning, along with a sensational breakfast that changes day to day. It's a wonderful feeling to know that someone wants to take care of you.

Today's morning meal is some buttered toast, two strips of bacon, two sausage links, and two dippy eggs. Before me, Javier never ate his fried eggs with running yolk, but now he's obsessed and doesn't make them any other way. He looks to me for new experiences and to try new things, which is a nice reminder that I can still take care of someone else, but not burn myself out in the process.

We moved in together two years ago after we found out the neighbors living a few doors down from my mom and dad were moving and wanted to sell us their house for a far cheaper price than we could have passed up. Being three houses down from my mom and dad has its perks, especially since I still have the responsibility of taking care of my father a few evenings during the week while my mom works her night shift at the restaurant.

With my new job and some of the life insurance money my mom received after Haley passed away, we've been able to hire a professional caretaker for several evenings during the week. On the nights I'm there, my mom is usually home by ten o'clock, so I have about two hours to myself—and Hamilton—before I'm tired enough to go to bed when I get home.

With being the only one left to take care of Mom and Dad after losing Haley, the evening caregiving hours have not been ideal, but we've been able to make it work. Some evenings, I bring my dad over to my house so Javier and I can enjoy a dinner together, and on other evenings, Javier will come over to my parents' house with some popcorn and some snacks so we can watch a movie together.

Thomas Branson is the ultimate third wheel, which would be weird for other people, but with me and Javier, it actually turns out pretty well. With Javi being around, my dad's mood has been better. He doesn't anger as quickly as he used to, nor does he get as physically aggressive.

My dad loves to talk to Javier, especially about the food Javi makes him every couple of nights. Food and music conversations tend to be the only topics discussed in the Branson household when it comes to the two of them. I'm sure my father enjoys spending time with Javier more than he does with me, which, ironically, is fine with me. It's nice to know Javier has actually made a genuine relationship with the one person I thought was going to scare away every relationship I would ever have.

As for Sarah Branson, she's doing really well these days. Aunt Kay took her to a craft fair last October, where they met a group of local ladies their age. The ladies take turns hosting book clubs at their houses. Aunt Kay only goes for the wine and cheesecakes, but Mom has been enjoying the time she's getting to know her new friends. If a free Saturday evening once a month is all she requests from me so she can have an actual social life, then that's exactly what I'm going to give her. She deserves it, plus more, yet she'll never admit it.

My moving out was a challenge for her, to say the least. She's been able to manage, and I'm sure she's reveling in the alone time she's had. It took her a while to open up to the idea of the night-time caregiver we hired, but she knows it's for the best. She wants me to live my life the way I want to live it. The life she's given me. A life Haley wanted me to have. A life I've learned you only get to live once.

We've had conversations about what the future holds: Javier, kids, traveling, the direction my job is going to take me. All of it. She's been my number one supporter in starting over and cheering on the new life decisions I make. I just wish sometimes she would take her own guidance and find more meaning to her life outside of Thomas Branson.

She did have to get used to doing several things herself, though, things Haley and I used to do around the house in order to give her a break. I've noticed she has been setting more boundaries with me and asking me to do only *easy* tasks, like taking the basket of clothes upstairs from the laundry room but demanding I not fold them because none of those clothes are mine, so they aren't my responsibility, blah blah blah.

I fold them anyway.

I still gotta find little ways to take care of the one woman who deserves the world.

Lianna's last book about the world's obsession with *Schitt's Creek* did very well. So well, in fact, one of the show's producers contacted her and set up a meeting to discuss the research she did on viewership, psychology of television viewing, and the data and statistics that made the show a success. Lianna's currently in Ontario writing a behind-the-scenes tell-all about Dan Levy's newest comedy series. Her signed non-disclosure agreement enforces her secrecy, but I know whatever she's involved with, she'll excel in it, and I'm so proud of everything she's accomplished with her writing.

Still no serious boyfriend yet, that I know of, but she still texts that one Taiwanese guy for a good time, from what I hear.

When it comes to me, I'm doing the best I can. I've had my ups and downs since Haley's death, but overall, I'm learning a lot about who I am. Not only have I fallen madly in love with Javier, I've also fallen in love with myself and the life I've been given.

In my planner, my weeks look busy. Morning meetings, afternoon sessions, and times blocked out in the early evenings for the session notes. The nonprofit I work for is a community outpatient mental health clinic located in Balti-more. Dr. Ambrose coordinated an interview for me once I graduated and finished my GA position. We're still close. In fact, I still schedule supervision with her from time to time to go over my cases. The clients I see struggle with some of the most severe mental illnesses, but I feel like I've really hit the jackpot with the work I've been able to do. Some days are rough, but most days are rewarding.

I love my clients. I know therapists aren't supposed to say that, but it's true. I love what I do, and I love the impact I'm making in the lives of these individuals. The most ironic piece to all of this is that I believe Thomas Branson led me to discover this part of me. The humanistic, nurturing part. Therapy is what I was meant to do with my life, and I don't regret following my heart to do it.

When it comes to Thomas Branson, there are some days I think to myself that he isn't my father anymore, that he's gone. All that's left is this void of a man with little to no cognizance of how to act as a functioning adult in society. But then, there are other days, more frequent now, I realize that's not true.

Thomas Branson has done more for me than most fathers ever do for their children. He wasn't able to help me with my homework or even teach me how to change a tire, but his life's circumstances made me into who I am today, and I'm forever grateful. He taught me how to care and how to help others. Isn't that what every father is supposed to teach his son?

To this day, I still have the rabbit's foot. I even told Javier about my belief in what the keychain's magic can do, but he doesn't believe me. He respects my belief, but he's never been one to dwell on the past. I think that's what I love most about him.

Even holding on to the rabbit's foot—and hope, for that matter—I haven't seen either Randall or Haley. It's safe to assume they must have completed their unfinished business four years ago. Knowing they are happy, safe, and still loved and remembered by people in the world gives me a sense of peace. I carry that feeling with me every day, along with the tolerable rabbit's foot I keep in my briefcase.

Just in case, of course.

WANT MORE?

Subscribe to Bradley James' Reader's List and Newsletter over at www.authorbradleyjames.com

ACKNOWLEDGMENTS

Per google, *Caregiver Burnout* is a state of physical, emotional, and mental exhaustion resulting from the prolonged stress providing care for someone, often leading to feelings of being overwhelmed and depleted.

This book is deeply personal to me as I've been a caregiver for my father since I was fourteen years old and I've experienced some great losses in my life that may be mirrored in some capacity throughout this novel.

Growing up, I didn't have the most "normal" experiences of what teenagers and young adults would go through. The only days I could do anything with friends were Fridays and Saturdays. If I wanted to do extra-curricular activities, work, or pick college classes, it all had to revolve around my caretaking shifts at home.

My mother and my sister were the only two people that understood what I was going through and because of that, we grew closer—stronger, even. But sometimes, with leaning on only two people, loneliness creeps up quickly. Which is why I pushed myself to establish friendships that I knew would last long and would be reciprocal in the best ways.

Caregiving is really rough. On one hand, caregivers tend to self-sabotage and believe their situations are isolated and unique—which they usually are—but on the other hand, society forces caregivers to become silent survivors. Whether you believe it or not, there are not enough effective resources out there to show them they truly are not alone.

That's the reason I wrote this book. I was that caregiver that didn't want to let just anyone in because I didn't think they'd understand. I want this book to be something that gives hope to caregivers (young and wise) and to show that life is precious—for the person they're taking care of and for themselves.

With that, I need to thank some very important people:

Mom: My best friend. I know children aren't supposed to call their parents that, but we've been through everything together and I think we earned the right to break the mold on what people are "supposed" to do. You are the strongest person I know. In my life, I hope I turn out to be half the person you are and I hope I've made you proud.

Eddie: Thank you for loving me and taking care of me, especially on days where I didn't realize I needed it. I told you not to fall in love with me, but you did, and my life has been forever changed. Thank you for allowing me to write and share this part of myself with others. Lastly, thank you for helping me show Kennedy what love looks like. It's my greatest accomplishment and I'm so glad I get to do it with you.

Kennedy: You're a one-year-old, so unless Grandma is really pushing those flashcards on you, I don't think you'll be able to read this until you're at least five. But when you are able to read this, I want you to know how much you've changed my life. You've given my life a new meaning and I'm so proud to be able to call you my daughter.

Shaina, Chloe, and Lilly: You are three of the brightest

lights in this sometimes dark world. Thank you for always giving me something to believe in.

Britney, AudioShelf reignited my love for books, for reading, and got me through a very difficult time. You're my best friend and I'm so lucky to have you always in my corner.

Genna, Logan, Natalie, Jess, Jamie, and the rest of my crew, thank you. You have no idea how much I appreciate each and every one of you. Melody, thank you for all of your wisdom and teaching me how to take over the world—slowly, but surely.

Author friends: There are so many of you who I've connected with since raving about you and your books on AudioShelf. I have learned from all of you how to navigate this publishing world with grace, skill, strategy, and perseverance. There are a few I'd like to personally shout-out because they've given me more than just guidance and encouragement, but true friendship: Tati B. Alvarez, Brigid Kemmerer, Amanda Carol, Amalie Howard, Emily Carpenter, Hannah Mary McKinnon, Jodi Picoult, Kelly Coon, Kami Garcia, Sarah Blue, Audrey Goldberg Ruoff, Dylan Roche, Max Walker, Suzanne Young, Colin Brooks, and Vanessa Lillie.

Reba McEntire: You'll never see this, but I do want to thank you for giving me the soundtrack of my life. Whenever I'm feeling any intense emotion, whether it be glee or melancholy, you are always there to get me through it. We also share the same birthday and I've wished you Happy Birthday every year since I was ten. So, yeah, if you see this, Happy Birthday.

Readers: Thank you for choosing this book. Thank you for choosing me. I don't know any of you right now, but when I'm on tour or at a signing, I hope you come up and introduce yourself to me because I want to know you!

Last, but not least, my sister, Heather: I wish I had a magic rabbit's foot so I could thank you directly for everything you've given to me. I miss you so much. By the way, we named her after you.

ABOUT THE AUTHOR

Bradley James (he/him) is a Maryland-based writer who enjoys binge-watching television shows and cuddling up with his adorable Dachshund-Mix fur-baby, Benedict. Alongside writing, he has a degree in Mental Health Counseling and works within the field. When he's not writing, he's making wonderful memories with his husband and their beautiful daughter. *Go Easy on Me* is his debut novel.

Stay in contact on Social Media:
 TikTok: authorbradleyjames
 Threads: authorbradleyjames
 Instagram: authorbradleyjames